WHEN
CAPTAIN
FLINT
was still
A GOOD MAN

NICK DYBEK

corsair

Constable & Robinson Ltd
55–56 Russell Square
London WC1B 4HP
www.constablerobinson.com

First published in 2012 by Riverhead Books,
a member of Penguin Group (USA), New York

This paperback edition published in the UK by Corsair,
an imprint of Constable & Robinson Ltd, 2013

A copy of the British Library Cataloguing in
Publication data is available from the British Library

ISBN 978-1-47210-657-5 (paperback)
ISBN 978-1-47210-273-7 (ebook)

Printed and bound in the UK

1 3 5 7 9 10 8 6 4 2

For my mother

WHEN CAPTAIN FLINT
WAS STILL A GOOD MAN

By his own account he must have lived his life among some of the wickedest men that God ever allowed upon the sea.

—ROBERT LOUIS STEVENSON, *Treasure Island*

How sour sweet music is,
When time is broke, and no proportion kept!

—WILLIAM SHAKESPEARE, *Richard II*

WHEN MY SISTER WAS A BABY, MY MOTHER WOULD LIFT her from the high chair and sing, "Shake, shake, shake. Shake out the devil." We lived at 213 Seachase Lane, Loyalty Island, Washington. The living room was lit by brass fixtures that hung from the ceiling on four links of chain, low enough that—if I stretched—I could swing them with the tips of my fingers. Those evenings, my mother turned the dimmers up and held my sister to the window facing Greene Harbor, as if to press her through the glass. Years have passed, but I can still hear the melody. I can still see my mother holding Em stiffly, swaying at the waist. Beyond their half-reflected faces, I can still see the darkness broken by the soft lights in other windows, and by the lights on the trawlers below, swaying as if they too heard music.

One evening I asked my mother, "Did you sing that same song to me?"

"No, Cal." She fit Em in her swing.

I followed her into the kitchen. "Why not?"

This was the spring of 1987. My mother had come back from California that winter with hair dyed the color of hot iron. She no longer played her records, and she seldom sang anything else.

"I just heard it somewhere," she said. "It stuck to me. I guess sometimes that happens. Why?"

My sister had fallen back asleep. Wind blighted the window with rain. My mother waited for me to speak—to tell her I thought the song was a signal, her way of acknowledging what had occurred in our town and our home, to tell her things I couldn't have said at fourteen and can barely say now at twenty-eight. It was the closest I ever came to admitting my part in what happened. I've felt the silence ever since like an ache in my jaw.

CHAPTER 1

LOYALTY ISLAND WAS THE STINK OF HERRING, nickel paint, and kelp rotting on moorings and beaches. The smell of green pine needles browning across the ground. It was the rumble of outboards, wind, and ice machines, and the whine of hydraulic blocks. It was gray light that flooded and ebbed at dawn and dusk.

It was the habit of loneliness. We spent our time watching calendars, waiting for the chaos that came when the radios crackled and the phones rang and tires kicked dust in the parking lots around Greene Harbor. We searched the horizon for returning fishermen, who arrived shaggy and greasy, telling their stories but not their secrets.

It's only natural to think that the place you were born is unlike any other, but there were towns like ours across the entire peninsula, across the entire coast. Our libraries were stocked with books that were always checked in and movies that were always checked out. Our children played baseball in overgrown fields. Our high schoolers played hooky in greasy spoons and tried their parents' curse words on tongues scalded by sweet coffee. Our adults bought cars and washing machines on credit. We cried and consoled one another when faced with tragedy, of which we had more than our share.

Loyalty Island wasn't actually an island at all. The town sat on a nub of land jutting into the Strait of Juan de Fuca, a thin peninsula that turned ninety degrees like the neck and head of a giraffe. At our backs, a rain forest sprouted ferns and moss that glowed green against the bark. The highways were lined with leaning trees, dense enough to block the light, turning the roads into chutes you'd slide through as though over ice. Behind the forest, white mountains blinked in the mist.

The strait was a chameleon of gray, blue, green, and black water. You could spend days on a pier, or a hill, or, if you were lucky, as my family was, in your living room, thinking of nothing but naming the color. And beyond these plates of water and light the horizon was broken by islands, matted with dark trees. Beyond the islands the ocean pushed clouds across the sky. It rained all fall, winter, and spring. The sky rose and sank. The ocean dragged out and rushed in, but until the summer I turned fourteen, Loyalty Island never changed.

THAT SUMMER, the summer of 1986, gave no relief from the rain. My father returned home each night in squealing rubber boots. Usually I'd wait for his silhouette to appear against the leaded glass of the front door, but that night I was in the kitchen with my mother, under the buzzing oven fan.

"I'll be at the Gaunts' tomorrow," he said. "John may not survive another day."

"Come here," my mother said to me. She was stooped in front of the open oven, red heat on her face.

"He could die tonight," my father said, "but probably tomorrow."

I grabbed the dish of bubbling vegetables, but it slipped in the rag over my hand, and my mother had to steady the scalding glass with her bare palm. She snapped shut the oven door with her foot and plunged her arm under the tap. "That can't be right," she said.

"It's true."

"That's all you're going to say?" she asked.

"What more *can* I say?" My father had a scar above his lip from a long-ago dog bite; at times, he seemed to talk through the scar instead of his mouth. "Liver failure, kidney failure, I don't know. I could barely pay attention to what the doctor was saying." He dropped down on the red vinyl bench of our breakfast nook and rubbed the rain from his hair.

My father never knew how to tell us anything. It wasn't laziness or insensitivity. He didn't know because he didn't know us. He spent at least half of every year in Alaska and could only make up so much of the time away. In the summers he read to me each night before bed, mainly, I think, to impress my mother, to impress upon her how seriously he took her order that I not follow blindly in his footsteps. The year I turned eight he read *Treasure Island* to me front to back three times. I loved the young narrator, Jim Hawkins, but rooted for the doomed pirates. Blind Pew, trampled in the street. Black Dog, his fingers mangled like those of my father's friend Don Brooke. Israel Hands, struck down by the swinging tiller. And especially Captain Flint, dead and buried like his treasure. Captain Flint, whose shadow still fell years after he'd drunk himself to death in Savannah. I begged my father to tell me more.

"What more can I tell you?" he asked, laughing. "You'll have to ask Robert Louis Stevenson. He's dead? All right, let me think."

I waited under the covers as my father settled down in the blue beanbag on the floor and switched off the bedside lamp. I could smell the nightly cup of coffee on his breath. "Years ago," he began, "when Flint was still a good man . . ."

Every night for the rest of the summer my father told me a new story. Captain Flint defended villages from bandits in Haiti, freed slaves in Brazil, and befriended the yeti in Nepal.

My father left for Alaska as usual that fall, and all winter I thought about Captain Flint. How, I wondered, did the good Captain Flint change into the man who buried his treasure on Skeleton Island and murdered his crew to protect the secret, the man who left Allardyce to rot, his outstretched arms pointing the way? That spring when my father returned, this was nearly the first question I asked.

"It's just stories, Cal. You know that, right?" He was pacing from room to room, the way he always did when he returned from Alaska, as if he needed to relearn the house.

Did I know it was just stories?

I said I did.

"Well," he said as I followed him into the living room, "he probably just got greedy."

"For what?" I asked. "What did he want?"

My father's hands were as thick as strip steaks, and scarred, especially at the tips of his fingers. He had wide shoulders and short legs that seemed engineered for a rolling deck. Even at home, he stood with his legs apart, as if guarding his balance.

"That's not how it works," he said. "Greed doesn't mean you want just one thing. It means you want everything, that you don't know what you want. To want one thing, that's okay. We don't call that greed."

"What do you call it?" I asked.

I wish I could remember his answer. Why can't I? Who decides what we keep and what we lose? Who decided that I'd still be able to see the despair on my father's face the night he told us John Gaunt was dying? Normally he seemed like a perfectly balanced force of nature, crusted by salt, sopping from sea and drizzle, but that night he slumped out of his jacket, a tan corduroy with a shearling lining, and draped it on the table. He laid down his cheek.

"It's like you don't realize it when it's been staring at you for years," he said. "John owns everything. When Richard gets here he'll get it all."

My mother's mouth twitched. Her green eyes were ridged with fine white lines, like waves about to break. My father used to say that he married her so he'd never be away from the sea. Bad poetry, but he meant it.

"Didn't you just say John was dying? Did you really just come in here saying that?" She stared at him, then shut her eyes as if she couldn't bear what she saw.

"I don't feel good about that either," he said.

She'd returned to the faucet and had to shout over the water. "How long have you known? Why haven't you said anything?" She started to say something else, but I couldn't make it out. Eventually she turned off the faucet and wiped her eyes with the dishcloth.

My father looked up, his cheek still pasted to his jacket. There was an iceberg of paint on his wrist. He smelled like turpentine. "He just collapsed yesterday, but no one knew how bad it was until tonight. I feel awful. You should know that." He sat up and the heels of his boots squealed across the orange tiles as he stretched his legs. My mother knelt at his feet, her burned hand wrapped in a dishcloth. Slowly, with her free hand, she pulled off his boots. I'd never seen her do this before.

"We're going to John's tomorrow too," my mother said. "Cal and I."

My father said nothing. He hadn't learned how to tell her no.

The water for the spaghetti was boiling off in sheets of steam. She dropped his boots by the kitchen door. "Please drain those noodles, Cal," she said. Then she started to cry. My father looked at her a moment, then laid his head back down on his jacket, pressing his lower lip against a metal button.

JOHN GAUNT was president of Loyalty Fishing, the only man in town with any real wealth. He owned the one-hundred-fifty-foot crab boat my father captained, the *Laurentide*, and the boat my father's friend Sam North captained, the *Cordilleran*, and every other boat in Loyalty's fleet. He owned the cold-storage plant. He owned the reeking cannery and the crab pots stored up in Dutch Harbor and the gill nets in Greene Harbor. He owned the trolling poles, the jigs, and the six-and-a-half-inch spoons. He owned the lorans, the radios, the radars, and the Fathometers racked in the pilothouses. He owned the teakettles and the coffeemakers and the chipped mugs and the pine cabinets in each galley and the tiny brass hooks where the coffee mugs dangled. He owned the slips in Greene Harbor where his trawlers docked, and all the other slips, for that matter. And a share of all the fish that came to port: king crab, opilio crab, tanner crab, salmon, halibut, cod, haddock.

He'd owned these things since the day he was born. The fishing company and, supposedly, the town itself were founded by John's great-grandfather, Raleigh, and passed down through three generations of Gaunts.

For us, the Gaunts' story was as fundamental and elusive as Greek myth. Supposedly, Raleigh was the unwanted son of a Seattle prostitute, who, one moonless night, placed her baby in a bassinet and dropped him into Elliott Bay. The tide carried Raleigh across the Sound and into the Pacific before pushing him back onto the northern shore of the Olympic Peninsula. Another version painted Raleigh as an English balloonist, a gentleman adventurer, who attempted to cross the Pacific alone. Within a few hundred miles of Vancouver, his balloon ran out of hot air and settled on our rocky shore.

Don Brooke, one of John's other skippers, told his own version of the story every September. He was a miserable, dwarfish man. It's not that he was short, although he was—what I mean is he was *small*. He avoided eye contact with everyone, especially children. His idea of a joke was to pretend to choke you, and he always squeezed too hard. One day a year, though, he was my favorite person in the world.

In Loyalty Island, we didn't die in war. We died in the currents of the Bering Sea. Just before the season began in September, we celebrated our Memorial Day, mourning in a moment of silence before the salad. After dinner John Gaunt would clink his wedding band on his glass and wash his soft voice over the table. "To another year," he'd say, raising the glass. "Which is all we ask for."

The adults lit cigarettes. They pulled the napkins from their laps and planted them on the table like flags, wiping their mouths with the backs of their wrists. This was Don's cue to lumber to the head of the table and tell the story of Raleigh Gaunt in a cutthroat drawl, the voice of Billy Bones. Resting a knee on a chair to support his ailing hip, he cast his gaze at the children's table, glaring at each of us in turn.

"Raleigh Gaunt," he'd say, holding up a fist as if the very name were cause for celebration. "What do we know about Raleigh Gaunt? He was a mate on a whaling ship out of San Francisco. We know that. And we know that instead of heading to the South Seas, the ship turned north for humpbacks in Juan de Fuca, where they ran into weather. There were twenty-six men on board at dusk. By morning, half of them had paid Davey Jones." Here he would pause, shutting one puffy eye, scanning the other over each child like the tip of a cutlass. "How many men did that make?"

"Thirteen," we shouted.

He pretended to count the men out on his fingers, one by one. The index finger on his right hand had been ground down by a bait feeder and at the number thirteen he wiggled the nub ominously and grinned.

"And what does tradition say about thirteen hands?"

"The plank," we shouted.

He'd stop again to let the next line sink in, but it didn't, not for years.

"Tradition, we know, is history's muscle. Tradition said thirteen

11

hands was unlucky. Thirteen hands was a last supper. The captain rounded them up in the morning. 'I'm sorry, mates. We'll have to draw lots.' But Raleigh Gaunt stopped him."

Here, Don turned to John Gaunt. "What did Raleigh say?"

John always ran his hand through his beard, as if actually considering the question. "Why not me?"

"Why not me?" And Don rattled his knuckles against the table as if to demonstrate the body's fragility, to remind us what Raleigh was giving up. "Brave words."

The sun, Don said, was low in the east but bright as the remaining crew lined the gunnels. The pulleys squealed as the whaleboat descended two stories to the ocean. In the glare Raleigh couldn't make out the crew's faces, but he could still smell the pine soap they'd used to wash the deck after the storm, and, as I sat in my chair at the kids' table, I could almost smell it too. I could almost taste the hardtack they'd given Raleigh as a final meal, and I could almost hear the wind pummel the flags and fill the mainsail as the ship came about, leaving him to oblivion.

"But why not Raleigh?" Don asked. "Someone had to give all this up. Raleigh was just the one brave enough to do it. Within the hour, the ship looked like a fingerprint on the horizon. But within a week, he'd founded us."

We clapped and cheered. Raleigh's story was our own; it meant something about who we were. And who was that? The descendants, in spirit anyway, of a man of unaccountable bravery, who calmly took his seat in the aft of a whaleboat because tradition demanded as much. A man who piloted an open boat alone across the north Pacific, who touched down on the tip of the continent, exhausted, lips blistered, and forged new traditions from old. At that moment, it felt like there was no fate in the world as extraordinary as my own.

This feeling stayed with me even after I left Loyalty Island. Sometimes on Sundays in September, I'll spend an entire afternoon peeling potatoes, simmering fish stock, sautéing floured halibut, re-creating the Memorial Day feasts of my childhood. As I cook, I can't help but imagine sitting down to the meal with my father and the rest of the men on their way to the Bering Sea. But instead, I invite friends, some of whom have never even seen the ocean.

Don's story was probably bullshit. More likely, Raleigh came west from nowhere for gold and, when that didn't pan, cast his lot with fish, moving far enough up the coast to have free reign over a stock of lingcod, salmon, and a few stubborn gray whales. In thirty years the lingcod were gone, and in forty years the salmon were mostly gone, but by then it didn't matter. Diesel engines and cold-storage plants allowed the Gaunts to push farther and farther into the ocean, north and west, generation by generation.

Unlike the mill towns that collapsed or turned to hollow tourist traps, Loyalty Island remained more or less the same for a hundred years. We had the Gaunts to thank for that. Bigger boats, better gear, all bought on credit, all bought ahead of the curve, allowed us to follow the fisheries up the coast as we diversified and killed. When the Alaskan crab fishery exploded in the seventies, John was better prepared than almost anyone in the Pacific fleet. His newly commissioned armada of five crab boats, two of them a hundred and fifty feet long and capable of carrying a hundred and twenty crab pots each, put Loyalty fishermen at the head of million-dollar hauls.

Because of the Gaunts the fishermen kept their work, and, consequently, the teachers and the electricians kept theirs. Bob Rusk continued to pull pints of Olympia at Eric's Quilt (named for the blanket that warmed Bob back to life after he was fished from the Bering Sea). Mrs. Zhou continued to press the button at the dry cleaner's, whirring her carousel of plastic garment bags to life. Will Percy continued his awkward chats with the patrons at the single-screen Orpheum Theatre, its lobby always smelling of his pipe smoke. Mrs. Gramercy, whose face was half frozen from Bell's palsy, continued her rounds, wiping the dust from spine to spine to spine in the stacks of the public library.

JOHN GAUNT died on the sort of northwestern morning when it seems the sun has burned out in the night, leaving nothing but falling ash. While I was in the shower, my mother came into the bathroom without knocking. Through the foggy plastic of the curtain I watched as she fixed her hair at the mirror. If she said anything, it was lost in the hiss of hot water. When I returned to my room I saw my gray suit laid out on the bed. Downstairs she handed me my overcoat, black and too heavy for the weather.

Before my father swept her up to Loyalty Island, she'd been a schoolteacher in Santa Cruz, California. It was difficult to imagine. For one thing, she was far more beautiful than any teacher I'd ever had. That morning she wore a full-length charcoal dress. An amber pendant shaped like an arrowhead burned on a string around her neck. She was five months pregnant, and I hadn't seen her in anything but floral maternity dresses in weeks. The stark figure in front of me was startling.

Once, years before, the phone rang while we were eating lunch. My mother held the receiver to her ear for a long time, saying nothing, pulling at her ponytail. After she hung up, she sat in the breakfast nook and put her palms to the yellow table. "Andromeda," she said. *Andromeda* was that month's code word. The first of every month my father was away we'd choose a new name from Edith Hamilton's *Mythology*. One month *Hermes*, the next *Hades*. When we had something important to discuss we said the word and planted our hands, palms down, fingers splayed, until we both agreed it was all right to move.

"The *Laurentide* dropped off the radio yesterday," she said. "They'll keep searching. Do you understand?"

"Yes."

"They haven't found any floating debris, and that's a good sign. Do you understand?"

"Yes."

As she said the next words she looked me straight in the eyes, as if she'd practiced. "The chances still aren't good. Do you understand?" She put her arm around me and brushed back my hair, speaking softly into my ear. "Are you all right?" she asked.

"Yes," I said, and I was. I would have been hysterical if not for the endurance of her gaze and the steadiness of her voice, both of which I was sure came from a certainty that my father was alive, that he would return from Alaska as usual. And he did. A day later they found the *Laurentide*, electronics shorted and radio dead, but otherwise fine.

That night at dinner my mother set a third place at the table, the way she often had when I was very young and my father was away. "You know the only way to really celebrate?" she asked. "You have to cook and dance at the same time." She poured a glass of whiskey and sent me down to her basement studio to pick out a record. There were hundreds to choose from, lined up on shelves that rose well above my head. She rarely allowed me in there alone, and I took the job seriously. I chose something called *Quartet for the End of Time* because it sounded like an adventure story.

"Hmm," she said. "Well, we'll give it our best try." When the music began—ghost-story violins and discordant piano chords— she started to twist her hips.

"I'll get something else," I said.

"I think this is perfect," she said.

She swirled out her long skirt. The kitchen smelled of simmering tomatoes. She drank more whiskey and spun, knocking a spoon onto the floor. She turned off the overhead fixture, leaving only the light above the stove, like a spotlight over the wrong part of the stage.

"Come on," she said. "There's no such thing as dancing alone. Not really." She took my hand, and we spun a few waltzlike turns.

"That's not right," I said. "It doesn't fit."

"True. You lead."

The piano sounded like pounding hooves. A clarinet whined and trilled. I tried to move to the music, and my mother watched me with a wide smile. She began mirroring me, dancing in a herky-jerky swivel, her hands raised above her head, until we were both laughing too hard to keep it up.

But later during dinner she stopped laughing, and I could see she was no longer happy. I was used to this sort of switch. In the past she'd applied for jobs but refused to go to the interviews. She'd cooked entire dinners only to throw them away. Maybe she found some strength in this, some freedom in the ability to change her mind, to rebel at any moment, if only against herself.

"You see how dangerous this all is," she said. "You see what could happen to you."

Of course I saw, but the news of my father's survival again put to rest the notion that anyone important to me could ever die.

"Everything worth doing is dangerous," I said, parroting my father. My mother nodded, got up from her seat, poured herself more whiskey before saying, "It's not your fault. But I can't tell you how stupid that is, what you just said. If you want to do something with your life at least be able to explain why. Don't just use somebody else's ideas. I know that's what most people do, but you shouldn't. It wouldn't be fair."

"Fair to who?" I asked.

"To me," she said.

When it came to my father, when it came to my future, there was no compromise. She was nearly always that solid. But on the day John Gaunt died she paced the living room, rubbing the pink corners of her eyes. Her cheeks were spotted and swollen, her eye makeup already starting to run. As I tied my dress shoes she coughed into a crumpled tissue. As I headed for the door she pulled me to her and pressed her forehead to my shoulder.

"I need your help today," she said softly. "When we get to John's I'll probably need your help." I was too surprised to ask with what.

JOHN HAD BEEN off the boats for as long as I could remember. He no longer even looked like a fisherman. He was sixty-five years old, maybe, and tall, with delicate bones. In my first memories of John, his beard had already faded to white but still maintained a tinge of orange like dawn on fog. He walked with a limp and a polished cane.

In the off-season, when he and the rest of the captains came to dinner at our house, John always arrived first, announced by two raps of his cane on our front door. *Thwack thwack.*

On those evenings, as my mother cooked, the entire kitchen seemed to shriek: the sizzling oil in the sauté pan, the click of lighting burners, the blue flames blooming under the pots. She'd stand over the stove, inspecting soup and vegetables through clouds of steam. She'd swivel from cutting board to sink, her heels clicking on the orange tiles.

I grew to recognize the staccato of John's knock as the cue for my mother to smooth her hair and steal one last look at the living room. When she opened the front door the pressure seemed to drain from the house.

Once the other captains, Don Brooke and Sam North, arrived, the six of us would sit down at the table draped in cream linen and tug napkins from plastic rings. My mother never asked anyone's opinion of her cooking, but when John complimented her she would twist her lips just a little, as if to smile would give something away.

Table talk was all business. John, Sam, Don, and my father bickered about fuel costs, about which processor they could count on for a screw job and which they could trust. I pushed my chair back, ground my elbows into the place mats just as they did, attempting to catalogue it all. I thought that if I could remember everything, a week would come when Don, Sam, or even my father would make a mistake, just a small one, and I'd be there to correct it. But inevitably my mind would drift back to the fish on my plate or to the jazz on the stereo.

It wasn't until talk turned to where to send the boats that I could concentrate. The Inside Passage. Cape Decision. Veta Bay. Alaska. These places sounded no less fantastic, and no more real, than Skeleton Island, Atlantis, or the City of Apes. At the sound of the names, I could feel my brain stretch. I could imagine white seas and silences. Trickles of light and bolts of cold wind. Boats plowing through waves under flocks of birds, black as keyholes in the sky.

THOUGH WE'D KICKED UP dust in the Gaunts' driveway, though we'd hurried through the dark living room and up the stairs, my mother stopped us outside the open door to John's bedroom. There were voices.

"There's no reason to decide anything now—your father, for Christ's sake, we just don't know yet." The first voice was Sam North's.

"Does it look like my father will be sitting up in bed anytime soon? Not to me." The second voice was muddy and cruel. I knew immediately it belonged to John's only son, Richard. I hadn't seen him in at least a year. He'd been away. That's what they always said about Richard. He was away. No one ever said where.

"Then you'll be making the decisions. The timing is obviously fucked. We're at king season in a month. We'll handle everything, but we just need to know that we'll be going," Sam said.

"Or I could come with you," Richard said.

"You could if you want."

"It would only cost a couple patches of frostbite on my face, right?"

Sam laughed. "At the *most*."

"Then again, I might not want to look like a horror movie."

"Richard, you have to know what this meant to your father."

"What it *means* to John," Don Brooke said. "Not what it meant. He can hear us. I don't want him to think—"

"He's not thinking anything," Richard said.

They were talking about what would happen to the company once John died. I knew that Richard was slated to get everything, even though he had never set foot on a fishing boat. I knew that my father and Sam and Don's disdain for Richard was rivaled only by his hatred for them. But I also knew that nothing would ever change.

Every fall the boats left for Dutch Harbor. Every spring they returned. And every summer the sun stayed out late for parties around the grills in Cousins Park. On weekends, fireworks lit the sky over Greene Harbor, and a band played on the small stage near the boardwalk. But by August, Safeway had stocked up on frozen food and powdered milk. The men who had spent the summer sleeping late or watching baseball returned to work, to paint and mend the boats and gear. The rest of us could only watch the summer dwindle, weeks to days to hours.

Every man had his own way of leaving. Justin Howard, a deckhand on Sam's boat, drove all the way to Ashland, to see a play at the Shakespeare festival because he was in love with one of the actresses. Andrew Ramzi stayed up all night watching movies so that he'd have something to replay in his mind during the shifts on deck. Others, many others, drank themselves off their stools at Eric's Quilt.

My father shaved off his beard. Every September: the click of scissors as he trimmed; the swish of the old-fashioned brush as he slowly painted his face; then the scrape of the razor, the shaving cream peeled away. Until he had a new face, a face that seemed less kind somehow, maybe because I knew what it meant. That night he'd hug me against a smooth cheek smelling of Bay Rum and in the morning he would be gone, leaving only the trimmings in the sink—almost red against the white of the bowl, though the hair on his head was brown.

Those of us left behind dug in. Through the fall, through the winter, it seemed we lived on the border of a real life lived elsewhere. It seemed that the absence was ours somehow, not theirs, that we were the ones who were gone. Is it any surprise that so many of us would have given anything to be part of that life, no matter how little it suited us, no matter how little of it we understood?

"Go in," my mother said.

There was the feeling of a previous century to the room: the four-poster bed, empty and crisply made, the deep red drapes tied with twine and falling across dark floorboards. The books that lined the walls wore blouses of dust. The air smelled like dirty fingernails. In the far corner three men stood with their backs to us.

"Henry," my mother whispered, "we're here."

My father turned and took a single step toward us, breaking the circle and revealing John in a hospital bed surrounded by green-black monitors. My mother shut her eyes.

"These are yours, Henry?" Richard said. He sat, elbows on knees, in a chair next to the hospital bed. He wore a black striped shirt, unbuttoned at the collar, where a shock of dark hair showed. The ends of his black bangs hovered just above his eyes. His nose sloped to the right, giving the impression that his face was trying to sneak away from his skull.

"Do you want them to leave?" my father asked.

"I don't really care." Richard rose from the chair. "They have as much right to whatever this is as any of you." He crossed the room and threw himself on the four-poster bed. "I mean, it's a time for family. But who's to say where the family ends, right?"

"Just say what you want, Richard," my father said.

"Do what *you* want," Richard said. "I can't think now." He propped himself on one elbow and offered a thin smile. "Henry, do you think that Chinese woman who runs the laundry might want to visit my father on his deathbed? She always seemed to like him."

"Richard, we can all leave," Sam said, "but I don't think it's good for your father to hear that kind of thing."

"You're right. I'm hysterical or something."

"That's understood," Sam said.

"Of course it is," Richard said quietly. When he looked up again his gaze found me. "That's quite a suit. You graduating from junior high today?"

I looked down at the creases in my gray slacks. Don Brooke's flannel shirt was rolled up at the sleeves. My father's work boots were rimmed with gray mud. I felt ashamed and then furious, but not at Richard. I stared at my mother, but she only bit her lip and shook her head, seeming more angry than sad.

My father ignored me too. He hadn't looked at me or my mother since his first glance when we'd arrived. He'd taken Richard's seat next to the bed and leaned back with his chin up, as if someone were pulling him by the hair. My mother and I stood alone, barely inside the doorway, until Sam North came over and squeezed my bicep.

"You holding up, Iron Man?" He always called me Iron Man, as in Cal Ripken, Jr.

"Tell me what's happening," my mother said.

Sam was exceptionally tall. He had to stoop to put his arm around my mother's shoulder.

"Everything's happening and nothing's working," he said. "Now it's his blood pressure. They have him on some drug to keep it up, but it wants to drop."

"Is he, I don't know, can he even hear us?"

"That one's on blood pressure." Sam pointed to the bedside and its armory of chirping screens. "We've been standing around all morning telling old stories. Sometimes, when we hit a good one, we can actually see the blood pressure rise. We've got that, not much else."

"What kind of stories?" my mother asked.

Sam turned to me with a smile that smelled like whiskey. "I've got a job for you, Iron Man. Jamie's outside somewhere. Find him for me, would you?"

"What kind of stories, Sam?" my mother asked again. "Do you think I've never heard your dirty stories before?"

Sam's mouth went tight. "Donna," he said, "I don't know what you've heard."

WHEN MY FATHER finally rose from the chair beside John's hospital bed my mother reached for his hand. He turned his shoulder toward the door. He didn't look back as he walked out. No surprise. When my parents were unhappy they usually looked in the opposite direction, sometimes for weeks at a time. I can think of only a few occasions when they actually fought. Once, when I was six or seven, shouting drew me to the living room. My mother kicked a lamp over, knocking loose the shade. Light exploded in the room and threw my father's shadow onto the ceiling. He did nothing but stoop to pick up the lamp and carefully readjust the shade.

"I'm sorry about that," my mother said as my father patted dust from the pleats. "It's just that he could do a lot of things. There's a lot else out there besides what you do. Maybe you don't know that."

"Really? You think I don't know that?" my father said. "That's the last thing I want for him."

Afterward I blamed my mother. Not for what she'd said but for what my father had said. Just as I blamed her as my father passed by in John's bedroom, ignoring us. Once he'd gone into the hall she turned to me.

"When my grandfather was dying," she said, "I went over, even though I was scared, and kissed him on the forehead."

"I'm not scared," I said. "And he's not my grandfather."

She clucked her tongue, her most devastating expression of disappointment. Why couldn't my mother see that we should have already left? Our very presence was breaking a code, a spell.

As I walked toward the hospital bed I listened for the creak of floorboards under my feet, some sign that I was moving, but the Oriental rug muffled everything. The sheet was crumpled across John's stomach. My first thought was that I'd fix it, pull it up to his chin. The hairs of his beard were dirty around his gray lips, tubes snaked every which way, and I couldn't trace any of their lines to the bleeping monitors. It all looked so fragile; I feared an extra breath would crash the whole thing.

I pressed two fingers to John's hand. His skin was cold, and as I slid my fingers between his index and thumb, it seemed to grow colder. I looked at the blood pressure gauge, half expecting the numbers to fall in protest. I wanted to leave the room, but I felt eyes—Sam's, Don's, Richard's—trained on me.

I'd never noticed how long John's fingers were. And I remembered something my mother had told me about him, how when he was in college he'd studied classical guitar. No one I knew had ever seen John with a guitar, and I was suddenly curious about whether this story was true.

I stood beside the bed for what felt like a century, my hand in John's. I was almost glad to be wearing the suit, to think of the sober image I made: carefully combed hair, backlit by weak sun. I imagined the men staring, admiring my composure. But when I turned to face the room the men hung in the corners, their heads bent, talking in low voices. Only my mother was watching.

OUTSIDE, I found Jamie North on a hill that sloped into forest. We weren't far from the water, and ocean storms had stripped the highest black branches and scattered them on the hillside. Jamie held a long branch, bent and wedged under his shoe.

"Cal," he said. "What the hell?"

Jamie—my mandatory friend at weddings, dinner parties, and the occasional funeral—was almost exactly my age. He was always saying things that sounded good but didn't seem to mean much. When we were nine he'd stayed at my house for a month while his father was in Alaska and his mother was recovering from some kind of illness. During that time he'd spoken to me mostly in a gibberish he swore was French.

"What the hell what?" I asked.

"I don't know." He smiled. "What the hell are you doing here?"

"Same as you, I guess. My mom brought me."

"Not me," he said. I didn't like the way he smiled. He stuck his tongue straight out of his mouth like a clown. "Did she dress you too?"

"What do you mean, 'not me'?"

"My mother's at home. My dad dragged me, said if I didn't come today I'd forget it forever."

"Regret it?"

Jamie picked up another branch, wedged it beneath his foot, and leaned. *Crack.* "Yeah, maybe that's what he meant."

"My dad wouldn't even look at me," I said before I could stop myself.

"I guess he's had enough bad news," he said.

"Fuck you," I said.

"Come on," Jamie said, digging in the pockets of his corduroys. "I was hoping you'd be here. I got a baseball and five cigarettes. What do you want to do?"

"Can I see that ball?" I asked. As soon as he put it in my hand I hurled it into the trees.

If I was caught fighting in John's backyard while he was dying inside I'd never be forgiven, but I was glad Jamie had given me a reason to feel angry. I expected him to shove me, but instead he put his arm around my shoulder and began to laugh.

"Sorry. I forgot you've retired from baseball. Really sorry," he said. I have to admit that what I liked least about Jamie was that he knew I was a liar.

Two summers before, Sam North had caught a virus that wreaked havoc in his inner ear. He'd faint out of nowhere or topple from fits of vertigo. Eventually the worst of the illness passed, but he couldn't shake it altogether. He couldn't go back on the boats, anyway. Landlocked, he sulked for weeks. Sam had played some semipro ball as a young man, and so he vowed to make Jamie into a first-rate ballplayer—a pitcher, a shortstop. I was asked to help.

Every evening that summer Sam drove Jamie and me out to the ball field behind the high school. In the dying light we shagged towering flies, racing back and forth across the outfield, gloves raised, catching with two hands until the sprinklers coughed to life. We took grounders, the plink of the aluminum bat keeping time like a hi-hat, Sam shouting, "Get in front of it, butt down, butt down."

But this was only the warm-up to marathon sessions of a game

Sam invented called Off-the-Wall. He'd chalk a rough square on the brick face of the school as the strike zone. Sam was all-time pitcher, and it was up to Jamie and me to knock the hard rubber ball into zones marked as outs, singles, doubles, and triples. The home-run zone was so far away that we never got within fifty feet of it.

By late June, Jamie had begun to wander into the stands, meandering through aluminum bleachers that reflected rays of evening sun. When Sam called for him to return to the field, Jamie called back, "Your voice really echoes in these metal seats. Say something else."

Sam reached into his canvas sack of baseballs and continued to hit to me.

By July, Sam's attention had floated to me entirely. He'd become a fountain of praise, especially when Jamie was in earshot. "I've never seen someone your age throw so accurately from the outfield," he'd say. "Your arm's good—not a cannon, but good. But the accuracy. It's something special." Or, "With your build, the power is gonna come. Pretty soon those line drives you're hitting are going to turn into gappers."

These were pathetic compliments, but by the end of the summer I felt invincible. As I fell asleep, I'd relive the feeling of hitting line drives just the way Sam had taught me: Spray the field. I'd track imaginary ground balls as they skipped across red dirt. I'd feel my knees bending, preparing for last-moment adjustments, because anything can change a ball's path—a pebble, a breeze.

Baseball is a game of rituals, and soon I had mine. I'd wedge a handful of sunflower seeds in my cheek and spit out exactly three shells before each at bat. But what I loved most about those evenings out on the field was that I could say whatever I wanted. And it wasn't even me talking, it was this phantom, this *ballplayer* that Sam and I were inventing. One night in August, I yelled, "I don't think you're throwing me your best stuff."

"Because I'm not," he said.

"Then show it to me."

"What good'd that do? I'm still building you up. Teardown's next summer."

"One pitch," I said.

Sam dropped his arms to his sides, squared his shoulders, and, with a swing of his hips, brought his mitt to rest for half a beat against his potbelly. In the moments that followed, there was a nearly hypnotic grace to Sam's body that I never saw again. He kicked his leg to his waist, his right arm rising as if the two limbs were on the same lever. As his palm circled above his shoulder he revealed, for an instant, the white rubber ball gleaming in the dusk like snow. That was the last I saw of the ball until it struck the wall behind me and shot back up the middle of the field. I didn't even think about swinging. I might as well have been swinging at a thunderbolt.

Sam's grace left him abruptly. He set his foot down wrong and stumbled onto one knee. The ball bounced past.

"Did you hit that?" he asked, blinking. There was a look of such admiration on his face that I didn't dare tell the truth.

"Christ, you hit that?"

"Not really," I said. "That had double play written all over it."

He turned and stared at the ball, which lay maybe twenty feet away in a patch of unmowed grass. "Jamie, did you see that?"

Jamie rose from his place in the bleachers and waved. "Can you hear that echo?" he shouted back.

"Cal, that's pretty incredible." Sam shook his head. "That's really something."

After that, Sam was convinced I'd be a star—the next Teddy Ballgame, Mr. Cub, Yankee Clipper. It was embarrassing how he'd go on about it. He cited scouting reports on the game's best hitters and offered to take me across the Sound so I could work in some "legitimate" batting cages—an offer I always refused. Anyway, by the end of the summer Sam had recovered enough to return to Alaska, and my career as a ballplayer was over.

JAMIE AND I STUMBLED down the slope, picking our way through young trees, until all but the gabled roof of the Gaunt house disappeared behind the crest of the hill. Jamie produced a crushed soft-pack of Newports, green-and-white-striped. It said "Kings" in green letters across the top. He shook out two cigarettes and handed me one, bent in the middle like a finger. I held it carefully. He spun the flint on a lavender Bic. I held out my hand.

"You might want to put that in your mouth first," Jamie said. "Breathe in, now." The ground was mud under a blanket of bronze needles. I leaned against a tree, nibbling at the cigarette.

"If you don't stop that I'm gonna start laughing," he said. "There's no firing squad. Relax. You're smoking like a girl."

"What the hell are you talking about?"

"You're holding the cigarette between your first two fingers and taking it out of your mouth with the same fingers." He demonstrated, girlishly brushing back his hair. "That, Cal, is how a woman smokes. A man starts the way you do, but when you take the smoke out of your mouth, pinch it with your thumb and index finger. Like so. There you go."

"How do you know all this?"

"Remember *In a Lonely Place* in English last month? Ms. Sullberg let me stay after school to watch it again, since it's sort of what I want to do. Something in movies, maybe samurai movies."

"Really?" I asked. It wasn't often that anyone my age claimed a future as anything other than a fisherman.

We finished the Newports without saying much more. Afterward I lay down on the slope.

"What do you think is going on in there?" Jamie asked.

"In John's bedroom? An old man is dying," I said.

"Nice answer, tough guy. You couldn't care less, right?"

"I'd care less if you were dying." I turned my head toward Jamie, the larch needles digging pleasantly into my cheek. "Can I have another of those?" I smoked lying on my back, imagining that I was in a hotel room, on a business trip, my head propped on white pillows, my dark-socked feet crossed at the ankles, a glass ashtray balanced on my chest. "I like John, but he's how old?" I said. "I mean it's natural when you get to a certain age to die, isn't it?"

"Just because it's natural doesn't mean it's not sad," Jamie said. "You could at least be sad for your mom and dad."

"My dad, who knows?" I said. "My mom seems pretty broken up, though."

Maybe John didn't study classical guitar in college, but he did return to Loyalty Island with a love of music, a love my mother shared. When my father was at sea John still appeared at our door at least once a week. He and my mother retreated to her studio in the basement to listen to records. She invited John there but never my father, even though he'd built the studio for her.

My mother, Donna Parson, moved to Loyalty Island the year I was born. That summer my father, Henry Bollings, caught the ferry to Seattle and a flight to San Jose. He rented a moving van and drove it to her doorstep on High Street in Santa Cruz. This was no small feat. My father was the son and grandson of fishermen. He hated airports and expressways the way some people hate doctors.

It became a family story, his trip to Santa Cruz. He used to tell it in the summers on car trips to Sand Point Beach, but I doubt he tells it anymore. When families dissolve so do their stories, and now I have to reimagine most of it.

He'd planned on arriving in the freshly ironed white dress shirt he'd bought for the rehearsal dinner. But he'd begun sweating on the plane. No matter how much he fiddled with the plastic vent above him he kept sweating. And he kept sweating as he crossed the jetway; as he waited, chewing a straw, at the carousel; as he sat in the back of a cab; as he waited at the small U-Haul storefront. By the time he hit Highway 17, his new collar sagged below his Adam's apple, soaked through to the cardboard tabs. Ahead, the road twisted up the mountain like snarled line.

He should have expected this. He was, after all, coming to move every possession his wife-to-be owned. He just hadn't thought that anything having to do with my mother could be strenuous. From the photographs of her back then, it isn't difficult to see why, her slender waist and neck, her gauzy hair. He'd imagined lifting hatboxes and garment bags. He'd imagined lifting her easily up to Washington, lifting all her belongings as if they were as light as she was.

When he arrived at her bungalow on High Street, he found none of the things he'd imagined. She had no hatboxes or garment bags, and the furniture had been sold or given away. What she had kept, what she had asked him to fly and drive all the way to Santa Cruz for, was her records. Boxes and boxes of records, and they were heavy.

They walked to a supermarket on Mission where my father bought two rolls of masking tape and twelve Negra Modelos. Later, as they sat on the dusty floor sipping the beer, my father packed every single record, crumpling newspapers to stuff up the space, wrapping the masking tape in bandagelike strips, crisscrossing the boxes corner to corner.

They weren't yet married, but she was already pregnant, and it must have been difficult for them to find the right words to say to each other that first day. Certainly it was in the years that followed. I can almost hear their voices, his soft, hers sharp.

"So, play me some of this," he says.

"What kind of music do you like?" she asks. "I guess I don't even know."

"Me? I like everything."

"That's what I thought," she says. "When you say you like everything that really means you like nothing."

Tape screeches around a box. He's wrapped them many times over because he enjoys sitting there with her. "I don't think so. It means I like everything."

"I'm tempted to prove you wrong," she says, but she picks Otis Redding, *Live in Europe*, and lets the whole album play as she sits with her knees pulled to her chest, her head on his shoulder.

They spent the next week weaving their way up California. They stopped to eat peaches on the roadside. Asked tourists from Iowa to photograph them smiling over cliffs on Highway 1. Held hands among the burned-out husks of sequoias. Drove with a gospel station on the radio and the sky spread in patches of white and blue like a chessboard.

But when they arrived in Loyalty Island my mother had no job, no friends, and it was almost fall. My father pulled up the shade on the picture window, throwing sun on the bare walls, revealing the bay below. The living room was empty but for a few pieces of furniture, three generations old. "I have to get back to work soon," he said. "But this is us now." And my mother turned to him with tears in her eyes and said, "It's very nice."

The first week my mother didn't unpack a single box. But the next week my father returned home to chaos. He could hear the music before he even turned off the car. A trumpet, honking like a sea lion. A saxophone, pitched like a steaming kettle, bawling trills over a clatter of drums. He wouldn't have known or cared at the time, but the record was Coltrane's *Live in Seattle*.

Inside he found my mother in the middle of the floor, one leg outstretched, the other knee supporting her chin. The sofa was layered with slip jackets and paper sleeves. His carefully packed boxes had been ripped open, and bits of tape hung from the flaps.

My father began work on the studio the next spring. He thought of her old house in Santa Cruz, its floor-to-ceiling bookshelves. As a man who spent months at a time crowded with others on a steel ship, he understood the necessity for private and familiar space, and, more than anything else, he wanted his town, his home, his life to become familiar to my mother, to become hers.

The studio was half built already. My father had inherited the house from his own father, who, years before, had erected a wall dividing the basement. He'd meant to build a darkroom, but got only as far as installing an iron double-basin sink in the corner. My father cleared out the old junk—his rusted childhood Schwinn, netting and buoys, cans of paint, an old Christmas-tree stand, piles of *National Geographics*. He swept up the dirt and tore out the spiderwebs. He laid down a bright orange carpet and built shelves into the walls out of white pine, reinforced by bolts to manage the weight of the records. He built a window seat, though there was no window, and ordered a mohair cushion from Vancouver. He bought sheets of corkboard to line the walls and trim the ceiling. He refused to let my mother downstairs until he was done, as if he were Michelangelo guarding his ceiling.

When he finally finished he waited until she'd taken the car ferry to Seattle to go shopping and see a movie in Spanish. He lifted her boxes yet again, nineteen in all, and placed the records on the white shelves in alphabetical order. He was meticulous by nature, but he also knew he'd dragged his wife out of her life and into his. The records were the grammar she used to express that change. If she'd come all this way for him, it was only fair that he learn to speak her language. But my mother never became less of a mystery to my father. And the place he'd brought her to, the place that became my home, always remained a mystery to her.

Once—I was nine probably—Mrs. Gramercy, the librarian, stopped by. She said she knew my mother had been a teacher, perhaps she would be interested in helping with a book club, something to make the season pass? From the way my mother scrambled in the kitchen for iced tea and stale cookies, I knew she was touched Mrs. Gramercy had thought of her.

My mother and I designed the flyer together: bright green paper, a book sprouting wings, lifting, it seemed, off the page. My father came home while we were laying it out on the kitchen table.

"Who's Edith Wharton?" he asked.

"I barely know myself," she said. "It was Mrs. Gramercy's idea."

But that wasn't true. I'd heard my mother insisting to Mrs. Gramercy that *The Age of Innocence* would be the perfect choice. Just that morning she'd told me about the first time she'd read the book, in the back of her parents' Dodge, on a road trip through Arizona.

"Well," he said. "I guess you'll find out."

That night the three of us walked the streets, hanging flyers on telephone poles and in storefront windows and on the bulletin board near Greene Harbor after my mother tore down last season's employment ads. But on the night of the meeting I found my mother on the couch in the living room, watching an old James Bond movie.

"I can't go," she said before I could ask. "I've already called Mrs. Gramercy. I said I wasn't feeling well. If you happen to see her don't tell her the truth, all right?" She put her feet up on the coffee table. She was wearing a pin-striped skirt and dark nylons. "I already feel disappointed," she said. "I don't know why."

She didn't look at me, didn't seem to expect an answer. I heard her in the kitchen sometime after that, and then I heard her steps on the basement stairs, music coming from her studio. By then the studio had become her refuge—from my father and from everything in Loyalty Island, including me.

Sometimes I'd sneak downstairs with my blanket and pillow, and lie on the floor, my ear pressed to the heating vent in the living room where the music seeped out. I'd listen to her listening to her music. In the winter, when my father was away, I could stay all night if I wanted. When the furnace kicked on I'd feel the heat from the vent on my cheek and I'd watch the strings of swaying dust. Why do we want to be closest to people at their most private times?

"Your mom is sad," Jamie said to me as he smoked his second cigarette. "I bet she is."

"Yeah, she is. Didn't I just say so?"

"You know, I never believed what people said about them."

"About who?"

"About John and your mother. I never believed it."

"John's her only friend," I said.

I lay back in the needles, feeling sick to my stomach. Once I'd said it, it seemed true enough. John probably was her only friend. I finished the last of the cigarette, closed my eyes, and opened them sometime later when I heard my mother's voice.

"Foul, foul? Who's shouting that?" Jamie asked.

"That's Cal, Cal," I said.

I ran up the slope toward the house. My mother stood on the crest of the hill. The wind had picked up, and her hair was blowing loose from its ponytail. As soon as I was close enough, she seized my arm and began to swat the pine needles from my jacket and pants. "He's dying, right now," she said. "Right now." She pulled me toward the house. "The doctor just came. They've decided to take him off of the blood pressure medicine. God, I don't know how long these things take. Your father told me to get you." She said this last phrase as if to emphasize that she wouldn't have left John's side otherwise.

We raced through the front hall and up the stairs to the

second-floor landing, where, again, she asked me to stop. She smoothed her hair and drew in a long breath. We walked the rest of the way down the hall. The door to John's bedroom was closed. My mother knocked once, softly. She waited a few seconds and knocked again, louder. There was no response. She tried the knob but it wouldn't turn.

"What's wrong?" I asked.

She bit her bottom lip and wiped her eyes. "You reek of smoke," she said. "How can I take you in there like that?"

We waited in the hall until John Gaunt was dead and the men filed out.

CHAPTER 2

I N PORT ANGELES, A STONE WOMAN CLUTCHES A CHILD against her thigh and looks to the sea, stone hand bridged over her eyes. In Seattle, a copper man hoists a rockfish on his gaff, but his line has flown around his head, nearly strangling him. Loyalty Island's Fisherman's Memorial, erected by—who else?—John Gaunt, stands on a strip of boardwalk a quarter mile east of Greene Harbor.

A man in a slicker and hat crouches in tangles of rope. His body faces the bay, but his face is turned up and to the left, mouth sealed, eyes wide. He braces with his right leg and holds out his left arm at the same angle as his face, as if warding off an evil spirit. You can almost see the green wave looming above him, buzzing with force. He's a dead man.

I don't know how it was in Port Angeles or Seattle, but in Loyalty

Island we stared through our memorial. The statue told us only what we wanted to forget. So it was strange to find Richard Gaunt squinting hard at it in unusually bright September light.

I hadn't seen him since John's funeral. That day, the supermarket and the dry cleaner's, the movie theater, the schools and the skies had closed. Fog sank through the trees and onto the cemetery paths. As I followed the procession of pallbearers—Richard, my father, and the rest—I lost sight of their black shoulders and white hands for minutes at a time. I walked beside my mother, paced by her swollen ankles. I would have run ahead, but every time I broke stride she clutched for my hand, pressing it against a scrap of damp tissue.

Since then home had become unbearable. I was used to my parents living like strangers on an airplane, squeezing politely past each other in tight spaces. But since John had died it seemed their patience with each other had finally run out. At dinner my father drummed his fingers on the table and looked around the kitchen as if he had just discovered what an interesting room it was. My mother regarded her fork and spoon with a cold glare. One night she said, "Well, it's not all bad, is it? If the boats don't go out we'll have all year to do this."

My father looked at her, too exhausted, maybe, to summon any anger. "I'm working on solving that problem for you. Pretty hard, actually."

"I'm sorry," my mother said. "That wasn't fair."

But mostly in the days following John's funeral my mother wasn't interested in being fair. She spent hours on the phone with Meg, her best friend in Santa Cruz, and when I came near she put her hand over the mouthpiece and waited, looking at me the way she sometimes looked at my father, as if I'd given her a reason to be angry, even though I hadn't said a word, even though I'd done nothing but step into the room. She spent her evenings in the basement studio, the door shut. At night, through the vent in the living room, I listened for her music, Springsteen's *Nebraska*, Dylan's *Blood on the Tracks*, Miles Davis's *Porgy and Bess*, but I was really waiting for the silences between the records, for some sign of her, a cough, a sob.

I'd needed a place to go and someone to talk to, but I would have turned the other way if I'd thought Richard would acknowledge me. He sat on a green bench under circling gulls. He wore a black military-style overcoat buttoned to his chin, as if in protest of the warm weather. "Hey, man," he said.

"What are you doing?" I asked.

"Can't you tell? I'm staring out into the infinite, the deep, the hidden and secretive, something like that."

Since John's funeral he'd been on everyone's lips. My father had been home every day, printing coffee rings on the kitchen counter, rattling the phone. Every few minutes, it seemed, I heard the name: Richard, Richard, Richard. If my father spoke to me—a rarity—it was Richard. If Sam North was on the phone it was Fucking Richard. And if Don Brooke was at the door it was Faggoty Fucking Richard.

I guess there was something feminine about him—his willowy posture, the way he held his hands as if he were about to play the piano. No one ever explained why he didn't work the salmon boats during high school summers, or why, when he graduated, he went to Seattle for college instead of to Alaska for crab. People wondered what John was thinking, what he was planning to do with the company when he died, but he never said. And once Richard left Loyalty Island it was easy enough—for me anyway—to pretend that he was gone for good, at least until he inevitably reappeared, a sudden, dark shape, strolling the boardwalk with his father.

Once I glimpsed him driving through the halo of a streetlight, hanging from the side of a convertible, laughing, dragging a sparking shovel along the street. And once he came to our house for dinner with his father and the other skippers. He drank most of the wine and went outside to smoke every ten minutes even though everyone else was smoking at the table. At one point he turned to me and said, "You understand a word these guys are saying? You want me to take you for a drive?"

The rest was rumor. It was said that John had tried to force him onto the boats and that Richard had broken his own father's nose trying to resist. It was said that one summer night at Eric's Quilt Richard got drunk and pleaded with his old friends not to go to Alaska, crying as he did it. It was said that he was a homosexual, that he was part Indian, part Mexican, part Japanese, that he wasn't John's son at all. That he'd been waiting for John to die and continued to show his face in Loyalty Island only to make sure he remained in John's will. It was said that he'd been approached by the Japanese months before John even got sick, that they wanted John's licenses and boats and gear. That he'd been seen on the boardwalk at dawn, wearing a kimono and pouring tea.

On that day in September, Richard was not yet thirty. He had the high cheekbones of the actors in the foreign films my mother watched, and when he smiled his skin seemed to bunch over the bones. Luckily, he hardly ever smiled. I can still see that face. Sometimes, even now, when a man passes me on the street or boards my bus, I'm sure it's Richard. And for the split second before I realize it isn't him, I feel inexplicably happy.

"Hey. Hey, don't go," he said. He reached into the inner pocket of his coat, removing a cigarette tin with a winking girl on the lid. "I have a question. Ever been to Alaska, Cal?"

"No," I said. I'd begun to walk away, and he must have known the question would stop me. "Not yet, I mean. My father's warming a job for me when I finish high school."

This was a lie. We'd never discussed it, and even the passing references my father once made to my future on the *Laurentide* had tapered off. Already I'd begun to realize that I'd probably never see Alaska, not on a fishing boat anyway.

"When I was in high school," Richard said, "just after high school, I guess, I begged my father to let me on the boats. Here, sit down, Cal."

I shook my head and held my ground.

Richard shrugged and paused just long enough to smirk; he couldn't care less what I did, what anybody did. "I absolutely begged him. He said no way, not ever. So, I've been hearing about this place all my life, and I still don't have a clue what it is. Do you?"

I could have described the Alaska of my fantasies: clouds that baked from white to red-orange, morning to evening. The sea a gray mouth, waves poking like tongues. "I guess not," I said.

"All of my friends went, you know. My dad gave them all jobs. Jim Osborne, Dan Fosse, Bobby Rollins. Me, though? I got a fraternity pin. My freshman year of college I drove all the way up here on the day the boats were coming back. I had this Audi convertible, and I waited in the parking lot over there for like five hours."

He switched the cigarette to his right hand and rubbed his scalp, as if coaxing the memory. "I saw them all come in. Still wearing their slicker pants, filthy, unshaven. They looked like hell, like if hell was made of slime instead of fire. You know, that's what I remember thinking. And I just drove away. Went to the movies or something. Couldn't even say hi, welcome home, fuck you."

Richard swung his gaze at me, but I couldn't tell if he expected me to speak. I couldn't see him as anything other than the brat who'd hocked yellow phlegm at me from a moving car as I walked to third grade, and I wondered why he was telling me all this.

"Dan Fosse died the next year," he continued. "Drowned just off some place called Coronation Island. Supposedly calm day, not a roll or a cloud. No one heard a splash, no one even knew how long he'd been gone. After Dan died, I mean, after I'd finally heard that Dan died—I was back at college, and no one thought to tell me for about a month—I kept trying to picture it. But I couldn't get past the name of the place. Coronation Island. All I saw was a hump of sand with evergreens growing like spikes on a crown, right? What does that say about me, Cal?"

"Is that why you're here?" I asked.

"Is what why I'm where? Go on, try to string together a sentence."

"No one looks at that statue."

"Wanna know who designed this piece of shit that no one looks at? Right here. Me."

"You designed a statue?"

"After Dan died, my father set me up with this Swede from Eureka. If you want to be technical, he designed the fucking thing. But I told him what I wanted. I said make the poor prick look like he doesn't have a chance in hell."

Richard pulverized the cigarette between his fingers before flicking it away. He leaned back on the bench, tilting up his face, sweat beading on his forehead.

"This sun has some balls shining like that, right?" he said. "Do you talk anymore? I could have sworn you used to talk."

He undid the first few buttons of his coat, revealing a silky shirt, bright red; there were huge black buttons on the collar and pinwheel-shaped flowers across the chest. He must have seen me staring. "I wasn't thinking when I got dressed," he said. "My father died a few days ago, and I choose *this* shirt. Sometimes I wonder about myself. It's almost funny, isn't it?"

It wasn't funny at all. On any normal day in early September, Don Brooke, Sam North, my father, and fifty other fishermen would have been painting and mending in salt-stained flannels a quarter mile down the boardwalk. Instead they were sitting at home, waiting for some word from Richard. I thought of the public deference they had shown him, their private conversations. They were scared of him now that he owned everything and had no idea what to do with it. Watching Richard sweat under his heavy coat, I realized I knew something they didn't. He was scared of them too.

I sat down on a corner of the bench. "Are you sending the boats to Alaska, Richard?"

He took another cigarette, holding the tin open long enough that I thought he was offering. He snapped it shut as soon as I moved my hand. "I haven't decided."

"You could go."

"You think so?"

"There's nothing stopping you."

"No," Richard said. A scowl passed over his face like a cloud across the sun. "No, there's nothing stopping me. Except the fact that I haven't quite lost my mind yet. I sure as hell couldn't skipper. What *would* I do?"

"You went to college, didn't you?"

"I studied psychology. Could I go aboard as the ship's analyst? What do you think Don Brooke would do if I asked him to tell me about his mother? Pop out an eyeball? Or just duct-tape me to the mast for fun?"

"No one could touch you," I said.

"Out there?" He rebuttoned his coat and, grabbing a handful of the collar, cinched it around his throat. "They could do anything they wanted to me out there."

RICHARD DISAPPEARED the next day. He left no instructions and no clues as to what he planned to do with the company. King season began in less than a month. Were the boats going out? Would they ever go again now that John was dead? The violet puffs under my father's eyes told me not to ask.

He returned to work and came home smelling of nickel paint, the last coat before the boats left. He spent the evenings slumped in his chair, a bamboo-framed tiki with green jungle-print cushions. He winced when the phone rang, as if each jangle dropped like a link of chain. One night I answered to snowstorm static, to a man's voice saying, "Bollings? Fucking Bollings? Bollings?" Those were the sounds of Alaska. My father snatched the receiver and slammed it to his ear.

"How many other ways can I say it? No." As always, he spoke softly and slowly, as if his tongue could barely lift each word. "I don't care what you've heard. Have we been there every last one of these ten years? That's what I thought too." He dropped the phone into the cradle and offered me a low-watt smile. "Game?" he asked.

My father returned home from Alaska each year in either a frenzy or a depression. It took him weeks to sleep through the night, to sit still for an entire meal. But these were the easy readjustments. He must have felt that he came home to a new son every spring.

I gained inches and lost teeth. One year I loved radio cars, the next Robert Louis Stevenson, and my father never caught up. Sometimes I wondered why he came home at all.

One night, when I was eight or nine, I found him sitting alone under the yellow fixture in the breakfast nook. He'd been back for less than a week. He patted the bench next to him when he saw me in the doorway. The overhead fluorescents were off, and the table lamp showed just enough light to reveal the gray threads in his hair. There was a map of the Bering Sea spread out across the table, held flat by two empty beer steins.

"Come here," he said. "I'll show you where I've been."

He pointed to Bowers Ridge and the Pribilof Islands, talking fast, sipping from a blue-flowered mug of black coffee. "We were here, and here, and here," he said, spreading his thick fingers over the map. Abruptly he picked up one of the steins and let the map roll shut. He leaned back against the bench and blew out a sigh. "It's hard," he said. It seemed like a perfectly simple truth to me, but he continued. "Because when you're out there, all you can think about is back here, and when you're back here, all you can think about is out there."

It was the most he'd ever said to me about what he did. What was out there? I knew that until I saw for myself we would never understand each other. In the meantime, we clung to what common ground we could find.

So my father pulled the taped and retaped Connect Four box down from the top shelf of the hall closet. We set up, as always, at the kitchen table, the plastic grid in the center, our checkers stacked before us. As we played he rubbed his beard or towed out the hair at his temples.

"You've heard me on the phone," he said. The sharpness in his voice surprised me. "You're worried?"

"I don't know. Not really."

"Why's that?" He cocked one eye, aligning it with a hole in the board.

I was only being honest. It felt as though I'd watched the last week and a half through the red plastic viewfinder I'd once had as a toy. Hold it to your eyes to see a red sun setting over GIs howling into walkie-talkies. Pull the lever and another slide clicks into place. A purple gridiron, a football frozen in a perfect Hail Mary parabola. This choice, to simply click away the image, was the power childhood still allowed.

"Know who doesn't worry?" he asked. "The same people who don't pay their taxes. Fools, fucking assholes."

He'd never sworn like that, not at me anyway, and I felt the words prickle my neck. My father wasn't like most people. He wanted nothing other than exactly what he had: a family, a livelihood. For one who didn't know him well, me for example, it was easy to take his gentleness for weakness. I only realized later that it was what made him so dangerous.

We continued to play, wordlessly. Dinnertime passed and my mother failed to emerge from the basement. The kitchen windows turned the deep green of a chalkboard. The evening rain began, beading against the glass of the back door like sweat. I won game eight and, as victor, pulled the lever, spilling the checkers back onto the table. As we sorted through reds and blacks my father said, "We might not always have the luxuries we do now, that's all I'm saying. We can't just float around and wait for money to fall like mensa."

"Manna," I said. I wouldn't have corrected him, but I could see him cracking, getting angry. I'd always suspected that there was another side to my father that he left in Alaska each year, a part of him we never saw. "Mensa's the club for geniuses."

His eyes narrowed through the board, his mouth narrowed under his beard. "Which you're clearly in." He still didn't raise his voice.

"All right," I said. "I know."

"What do you know?" He leaned back against the kitchen booth, snapping his heels on the floor, and it was as though a beam had been broken, this trance I had finally pushed us from. "How are you going to learn anything when you know it already? You think I'm trying to scare you? I'm not. We're in a lot of goddamn trouble. I mean you and me and your mother. But we're not the only ones. There's exactly one industry here, Cal. Any idea what it is?"

"Fish," I said.

"Fish? Yeah, fucking fish. But we're talking about millions of dollars. The boats alone, Jesus. All of that's Richard's now. All that could be gone. And it's not just the boats, or the gear, or the cold storage. It's the licenses, and those are Richard's too. You can't just go up to Alaska and toss in a crab pot. Sixty thousand dollars just to get one. *If* you could get one, and you can't. All of that, according to certain lawyers I've had the pleasure of speaking to, is Richard's, and all of that is going to be sold."

"To who?"

"Japs, probably. They'll pay what we couldn't pay in a million years."

My father wasn't telling me this because he wanted me to know. He couldn't talk about anything else, couldn't think about anything else. He didn't expect me to really hear, or understand. But I thought I did understand. He'd said *we*. "What can we do about it?" I asked.

"Convince Richard not to sell it all off, which is proving difficult since we couldn't get him to say more than five words to us and now we don't know where the hell he is."

I thought of Richard's words on the boardwalk and was stung by the chance I'd missed. I hadn't even mentioned the encounter to my father, and I didn't dare tell him a week too late. So I said nothing, and my father steamed on. Normally he spoke in tight phrases, self-contained as packets of salt. But now he was practically foaming at the mouth.

"I'm telling you this," he said, "because, basically, the guy that owns it all now is just like you, except much worse. Hasn't breathed a breath that didn't come easily, and he still thinks he knows everything. So when I hear you say 'I know, I know,' I want to reach across this table and strangle you."

He clamped his hand to my shoulder, scattering his pile of black checkers. I tried to twist away, but he held me firmly in place for a moment before he drew back. I shrank against the booth, still feeling the vise of his fingers.

We blinked at each other.

"Sorry," he said. "Are you all right? Sorry."

I thought I'd been waiting, even hoping, for such a moment for a long time. I managed to keep from crying, but I couldn't answer him.

A FEW DAYS LATER I woke to find every window and door wide open. My mother stood in the kitchen, hacking a broom at the crevices under the counters. Her hair was tied back in a green scarf.

"This house has gone to hell," she said, but her eyes were clear. "I guess this is what happens when I spend a week ignoring it."

"It's been two weeks," I said.

"I know," she said. "You must be wondering what's wrong with me. I've been sad, that's the simple way to put it. And I'm angry."

"At who?"

"I don't know who. It's like I'm in a submarine, like I can feel myself moving, but I can't see it. Does that make any sense?"

"I don't know."

"I don't know either. It would help if you forgave me, though. It might help me feel like the living again. What do you say?"

"I guess I say, okay."

"Good," she said. "Because we have a lot to do."

"What do you mean?"

"Your father didn't tell you? He volunteered us to host Memorial Day."

I rubbed my eyes, frustrated. I'd tried to take my father's advice, tried to worry, but again something had changed, and I'd missed it.

"The boats are going?" I asked.

She shrugged. "Isn't that what Memorial Day dinner usually means?" She pulled me in with one arm, and when she spoke again her voice was lighter. "Anyway," she said, "suddenly we're hosting dinner for fifty people. That's plenty for us to think about."

She put *Presenting the Fabulous Ronettes* on the record player, and we set to work with Fantastik and sponges. She bent over the sink, her round belly—noticeably larger now—pressing the counter as she scrubbed the basin white. She lifted one foot at a time as I mopped around her, as I slid from bucket to corner to corner, smiling, because, with the music on and my mother humming to it, the windows open and the sunlight pouring in, it was easy to pretend she was happy. And it was easy to picture us in Santa Cruz.

Even now, imagining my mother happy means imagining her in Santa Cruz. We spent at least a week there each June, at Meg's bungalow just off Pacific Avenue. Meg sold homemade soap at farmers' markets, and the house always smelled of palm oil and lye. There were Oriental rugs in every room, stacked one on top of another sometimes; as a child I imagined I could peel back the layers of the house like an onion.

Some nights it was just the three of us, playing Trivial Pursuit, my mother sneaking drags from Meg's cigarettes. But other nights Meg's friends—my mother's old friends—would blast through the door. "Dee Dee," they'd shout. "Hey, Dee Dee." It was the name Meg called her too.

The connection these people shared with my mother was deeply mysterious to me. There was a man named Gary with a tattoo of Sigmund Freud on his forearm. A man named Fritz who let his pet ferret run through the house. A bald woman named Darlene who claimed to know the Rolling Stones, and a woman named Casey who recorded everything with a clicking Super 8 camera.

For hours they'd talk about people they knew and people they'd read about or seen in movies; it was never clear exactly which was which. And every so often someone would get up on a table and read a poem, or a guitar would be urged into someone's hands, and the others would raise their glasses and cheer. At a certain point, as if by a secret agreement, the lights would come down, the record up. When the dancing began the floor creaked and buckled.

Though I was left mostly on my own those nights, my mother always made a point to find me every so often, no matter how out of breath she was from dancing, no matter how red her mouth was from wine. She'd put her hands on my shoulders. "Are you having a good time?" she would ask over the music.

I always told her I was, and often this was the truth. For the most part those people were kind to me. They were curious about me. Even when I was very young they talked to me in a way my father's friends never did, like an adult—Meg especially. One night—I must have been twelve—Meg had had too much to drink, and the two of us were alone on the porch, and she began to tell me how my mother and father met. "It's not that he wasn't handsome," she said. "And she actually liked what he did for a living. She had these ideas she got from her father—he was a socialist, I guess you know that— very romantic, but she didn't really have any idea what she was saying yes to. She just didn't know what it would mean for *her*. I'm sorry, I shouldn't be saying this. It's just that I miss her, you know?"

I did. Those nights, as I watched my mother dancing, laughing, drinking, I missed her too. She was herself, but not herself. There was a lightness to her movements, an unguarded quality to her expressions I'd rarely seen. I wondered why she couldn't be that person in Loyalty Island. And even now I wonder whether she might have been happy if she'd come to Loyalty Island under other circumstances, if she'd only *chosen* her life there.

Hadn't she chosen it, though? Meg told me that night on the porch in Santa Cruz that my mother had chosen to visit Seattle. She'd chosen to let the soft-spoken man with the curious scar above his lip buy her a gin and tonic at a bar in Ballard. And she'd chosen to stay and have another with him, telling Meg she'd find her own way home. Afterward she'd chosen to spend the night in his mildewed motel room on Aurora Avenue. The next morning, as she buttoned her coat at the door, he'd raised his head from the pillow and shyly asked for her phone number in California, and she'd chosen to give it to him. And when he'd called the next week, she'd chosen to skip a friend's party so they could keep talking. And when, at the end of the conversation, he said, "I know it's crazy, but, if you'll let me, I'd like to come visit you," she'd chosen to say yes. Most important, two months later, when she'd learned she was pregnant, she'd chosen to tell him. So, the problem wasn't that she hadn't chosen; the problem was that she'd had no idea what she was choosing. The problem was that choice was a cruel illusion.

For so much of my childhood it was just the two of us, and I have to give my mother credit. She tried. She arranged scavenger hunts on my birthdays, took me to cello lessons in Port Angeles. When I quit after six months she didn't protest, even though she was clearly disappointed. In the winters we stayed up late watching videos, and she bought red-striped cardboard containers for the popcorn, and melted butter on the stove. She really tried. But then, as if all of her strength had been used up, she would disappear into the studio for half a day, for an entire night.

Eventually even the studio was not enough. One day when I was ten I came home from school expecting to find her waiting. You could reach our yard without being seen from the street if you walked through Henderson Park and the scrap of forest that bordered it, and I liked to pretend that I had reason to hide, that I was a spy or a criminal. But when I found the house empty, I left and tried coming in through the front door. It was the only thing I could think to do.

She came in an hour later, her arms hung with shopping bags. "I'm sorry," she said. "I'm sorry. You should have seen me almost crash on the way from Port Angeles. I was driving like a maniac."

Her cheeks were red, and I could smell the wind from the ferry in her clothes when she hugged me.

"I wanted to make veal tonight," she said. "They don't have it at the Safeway here, so I drove to Port Angeles. I thought I'd be home in time. Did you get something to eat?"

"I just wondered where you were," I said.

"I know. But look, you survived! I trust you by yourself, don't worry. You did fine."

She'd begun to unpack the shopping bags: Books and videotapes. Small birds wrapped in butcher paper. Bottles of wine with Italian labels. Clearly she'd been to Seattle. She had to have left the minute I'd gone to school.

After that I noticed other lies, in part because she didn't try to hide them. Once I heard a public-address announcer blaring over the line when she'd supposedly called from Belinda's downtown. Another time I found a stub for the Vancouver Island ferry on the dash of the Chevette.

At first it felt almost like a game. The lies seemed harmless enough, and I read them like a code I might crack. I came to accept that my mother needed a secret, that she needed someone to know she had a secret. Only much later did I learn to see the trips to Santa Cruz, and the nights she spent locked in the studio, and the white lies she told as what they were—rehearsals for an escape.

Was that what John Gaunt was to her? My father liked to tell the story of his trip to Santa Cruz, of building the studio, of filling the shelves, record by record. But my mother must have met

John sometime that first summer too, and no one ever told that story.

Sometimes when John visited I'd answer the door because my mother was changing her clothes or setting flowers. Sometimes he'd ask me about school or share news of Alaska. Sometimes he'd arrive with a bottle of wine. Once he came with an empty mason jar. "What's that for?" I asked. "For my teeth," he said. "I might have to take them out at any moment." I didn't know how to answer, and he must have seen me blush. "I'm joking." He laughed. But before he could say more, my mother swept into the room smelling like perfume and led him down to the basement.

When she emerged from the basement in September of 1986, she placed that same mason jar on the windowsill above the sink. John Gaunt was dead. The glass was foggy and lime-stained, but I could still make out pennies inside, brightening from green at the bottom to bronze at the top.

"Should I wash that?" I asked her.

"No. Smell." She held the jar under my nose.

"Smell the pennies?" I asked.

She petted her ponytail like a cat and gazed out the kitchen window. It seemed that if I ran my sponge along her arm I could wipe the sadness away like dust from the windowsill. "This place still looks terrible," she said.

"We have more to do," I said.

"Or we could just burn it down." When I didn't respond she smiled and stepped to the sink. "I'm joking, of course." She refilled the bucket for the mop, then lifted it by the handle and dumped it along the floor, as if she were bailing a boat. I watched the arc of soapy water smack the tiles. "No fires here," my mother said. Then she sat down at the kitchen table. "But I don't think that helped." She laughed.

"Not really," I said.

"You know, I haven't cried this much, maybe in my whole life. I've tried to stop, and I really just can't." Her eye makeup had run, not down her cheeks, but to the sides; she looked like pictures I'd seen of ancient Egyptians.

"What is it?" I asked.

"My sleeping's just off. I should have known all I needed was housework to tire me out."

"Do you want to watch a movie?"

"I'd love to do that," she said, and smiled.

As the floor dried we watched *Sansho the Bailiff*. My father had special-ordered her nearly every Mizoguchi film from New York. She asked me to watch the movies with her all the time. Usually I felt that anything on earth was more interesting than the slow pans across gray landscapes, but that afternoon I did my best to pay attention. I knew she'd like it if, afterward, I had something to say.

Midway through the film, the heroine, knowing she'll be tortured and branded by the master of the slave camp, runs to the woods. Framed by branches and reflecting sun, the pond she finds looks more like a surface that could crack a skull. Yet she descends easily, never flinching at the chill. Ankles, knees, waist, breasts, throat. The water hardly ripples as she sinks.

THE GAUNTS' HOUSE was built for banquets; our house was built for picnics. We could fit a cramped eight around the dining room table, another five in the nook in the kitchen. That left us with thirty or so to plate on card tables packed into the living room. My mother insisted everyone take their shoes off, and by seven o'clock work boots and pumps were piled in the front hall like bones in a lair.

I served deviled eggs on cafeteria trays as headlights flashed past the windows and branches flinched in the wind. Husbands and wives padded through our living room in their socks, whispering greetings, ashing into their hands. They shuffled from foot to foot, room to room, trailing blue plumes of smoke. They slid through doorways, tapping shoulders, mumbling apologies.

There had never been a Memorial Day dinner, let alone a fishing season, without the Gaunts. The air in the living room had grown thick with the familiar smells of smoke and sweat, it was still the wrong living room. Though our guests had known one another since childhood, they were as polite and timid as strangers, finding reason after reason to break conversation—a drink, the long wait for the bathroom. They sipped punch from paper cups beaded with condensation and fogged the windows with their breath. Outside, the rain trampled the roof and the windows, the black asphalt on the roads, the docks, the stone beaches; and the waves beyond the beaches trampled one another.

I dropped the empty trays into the kitchen sink and retreated up the back stairs, my hands smelling like shoes, planning to hide out in my bedroom until dinner. I flicked on the light to find Richard Gaunt on my bed. He wore a black suit with a yellow paisley tie. A brown suitcase, with a Donald Duck sticker in one corner, sat on the floor between his legs.

"You can't just come in here," he said.

"This is my room," I said.

"Your room? Sure you want to admit that?" Richard gazed at my bookshelves. "You're going to want to change a few things before you invite any girls up here. Are those Legos? You think anyone has ever been laid in the same room as Legos?"

I scanned the room, as if through Richard's eyes. A Mariners pennant, gaping shark's jaws, a print of van Gogh's room I'd gotten from my mother. My fleet of fire engine–red Lego ships—schooner, sloop, aircraft carrier—rested at anchor on the top shelf, complete with eye-patched, peg-legged sailors. Worst of all was the giant stuffed tiger at the foot of my red steel-pipe bed, whose wide-eyed, wide-mouthed face expressed my feelings perfectly.

"How did you get up here?" I asked.

He rose to his feet, a bit unsteady. "I wasn't sure about the etiquette. Are uninvited guests supposed to use the back or front door?"

"Neither, I guess."

"I went with the back door. There wasn't anyone in the kitchen, and I thought that was a bad sign. Good parties always have people in the kitchen, don't they? I thought I'd come up here, wait until things started to heat up."

"No one knows you're here?"

"Everyone's invited, right? I must be included in *everyone*, right? Once I got the message from your father saying he was planning on sending the boats out, I had to come."

"But what are you doing *in here*?" I asked.

"That's a fair question." His voice dropped to a whisper. "Maybe I'm hiding."

"Hiding from what?"

"You think I'm hiding? I'm not hiding, Cal."

"I didn't say you were hiding."

He paced the room, pinching his lower lip. He picked up my Lego schooner and cradled it. "My father," he said, "was the king of these parties, the absolute king. I mean, I noticed that when I was seven, how people would just look at him when he walked in, like they wanted to give him a gift basket of firstborns. Like, 'John, you have something hanging on the corner of your mouth. Here, use my first-born to wipe it off. Don't worry, he's still got a nice soft head.' Fuck, what am I talking about?"

Richard held the Lego schooner like a baby in the crook of an arm. The plastic mast poked his chest.

"Do you want to come downstairs?" I asked.

"No," he said. "Absolutely no, just give me a minute to think."

He put the ship back, setting it down exactly where it had been on the top shelf, and sat on my bed, elbows on his knees.

"That guy, my father, I mean, knew everything there was to know about each and every one of those people down there. But did he share any of that with me? Just give me a minute, okay? I mean, I know it's your room, I can clearly see that, I just need a minute alone."

I was more than happy to give Richard the room. I shut the door and went looking for my father.

DOWNSTAIRS, the card tables, borrowed for the occasion and sheathed in white paper, were crammed with fishermen and their wives. Everyone was drinking beer and slurping oysters. Dinner had begun. I took an empty chair next to Jamie at a card table in the living room, the kids' table.

"Have you seen my dad?" I asked.

Before he could answer, the clink of forks and knives on bottles began to pass from table to table, signaling a speech. By the time the message reached us on the cold edge of the galaxy, the speaker's voice was nearing a shout. At first I wasn't listening. I needed to find my father, needed to warn him about Richard. It took me a moment to realize that the speaker *was* my father.

"That's not how we remember these dinners, is it?" he said, his voice booming, lacking its normal dog-bitten hush. "I don't know what to say, except things change, don't they? We've been lucky, all of us have been extremely lucky, lucky to work with John, and lucky that because of his work and all of our work we can still do what we do. And we will still do what we do. This season, I mean."

From the front room I could hear murmurs of approval, and I tried to get a view around the corner, into the dining room. I caught a glimpse of Don Brooke running the tooth side of a black plastic comb against his lips like a harmonica. But I couldn't see the head of the table.

"For what we have," my father said, "I'd lay my life down in a second. I almost have. A couple of times. And I still expect to lay down at least a couple of fingers before I quit this. Why not, right? I usually don't take more than three fingers of whiskey anyway."

Everyone laughed. I didn't understand the joke, but the joke probably had nothing to do with it. Someone in the dining room yelled, "Better take off a couple more of Don's fingers, then. Might save his life." More laughter. Don grinned and yelled back, "Come on, we'd have to chop your whole hand off to keep you sober, Borky." A few others whistled, and a few others clapped. And suddenly it seemed that my father had relieved the fear of the last few weeks, the fear that Loyalty Island would shrivel and die. The boats were going out. This season there would be the spindles of king and tanner crab legs to crush and can. There would be work and money to pay mortgages and debts.

But among the smatterings of applause came another voice, timid by comparison. "Excuse me. I'd like to say a word or two. I hope that's all right. I hope no one minds."

"Richard," Jamie said in my ear. He stood up. "Richard's here." I followed Jamie through the clusters of tables to the edge of the dining room. The faces I passed seemed to contort, adjusting to Richard's presence, his weight.

"I feel . . ." He paused, his mouth open. "Very, very conflicted. I just don't know what to thank Henry for first. I'm obligated to thank my host. But I also know that it was my responsibility to host this party, and since I was in New York I couldn't. So I have to thank him for that too.

"As you may or may not know, my father recently passed away. And I haven't been much of an heir. Henry—and I shouldn't give just Henry credit here, because I know everybody pitched in—has really helped me, graciously. I didn't even have to ask."

My father, still standing at the head of the table, kept his feet in their usual wide-set stance. The rest of the men and women sat motionless—elbows on the backs of chairs, necks craned. Delia Dole, Thurman Dole's wife, had frozen with her water glass at her lips. The wide doorway between the living and dining rooms was filled with faces, the chairs in the living room deserted except for Tom and Linda Riley's eight-year-old, Kip, who remained at the kids' table, mesmerized by the paper napkin he was tearing into strips.

"So," Richard said, "I think the best thing is simply to say one thank-you for all of it and hope Henry will understand." He extended his hand with ringmaster bravado. My father looked at the hand as though it were something dead, but shook it anyway.

"And to everyone else," Richard said, turning back to the room, "I'd like to wish you the best of luck this season. I'll pray for your safe return." He grabbed a beer from the table, Betty North's, as far as I could tell, and raised it for a toast. "To us." He gulped half and coughed.

The men at the table stomped their feet like an orchestra celebrating its conductor. And, standing at the head of the table in his dark suit, Richard began to look less like the bad-tempered brat we'd known, and more like a benevolent pastor. Suddenly it seemed foolish to have thought he would turn his back on everyone and everything he had ever known.

As the table rumbled, silverware danced and flashed back the light from the chandeliers. I saw my mother standing in the kitchen doorway, clapping. Sam North rose and put his hand out to Richard, who took it and pumped. Jamie clapped. I clapped. Don Brooke stuck his pinkies in his mouth to whistle, but no sound came.

Eventually Richard took a seat and, as if on cue, Don stood, raised one crooked finger and bellowed, "Raleigh Gaunt. What do we know about Raleigh Gaunt?"

All the rituals: laughing, chanting, swearing. But I did it all by rote. As Don recounted Raleigh's heroic deeds, I saw Richard's smile fade into his stormy face. He'd pushed his chair back and propped his feet on the suitcase. His lips twitched around cigarettes. By the time Raleigh volunteered for the short straw, Richard was slumped with his hand over his eyes, as if he were afraid to find out how the story ended.

Once Don returned to his seat, Richard rose and led the room in another round of applause. "Thank you, Don. That story never fails to make me feel something." He paused. "Nausea mostly."

This didn't seem far from the truth. The greenish tint of his pale skin gave him the appearance of a seasick ghost. He wiped his mouth with the back of his hand, his Adam's apple working against the skin on his throat. He swayed forward, steadying himself on the back of a chair, the table stretching before him—a wasteland of mismatched forks and spoons, of oyster shells stuffed with lemon rinds, of overflowing ashtrays.

"What do you need that patron saint for?" he asked. "What do you think that says about you?"

"It's a story, Richard," Sam North said. He spoke in the same even voice he'd used to offer advice on my inside-out baseball swing.

My father's lips were pressed together so tightly they'd vanished. I looked for my mother in the doorway, but she'd vanished too.

"Well, I don't like this one," Richard said.

Sam untucked his napkin from his shirt collar and laid it on the table. His hands looked nearly twice the size of Richard's. "Okay," he said softly. "I guess it's up to you now."

Don opened his mouth and bit down again on the plastic comb.

"Let me ask you, Sam. How do we know any of this?" Richard said. "I mean, how do you know that Raleigh was such a hero, bravely taking his seat in the aft, blah, blah, blah?"

"That's just the way it's remembered."

"But memory, you would agree, is fallible. Imperfect, that is."

"I guess it is," Sam said. His gaze floated from Richard to Don to my father. One signal and I think he would have put those big hands around Richard's throat.

"You can't *just* trust memory, Sam. Let me give you an example. I got this message from my friend Henry Bollings when I was in New York. Do you remember what you said in that message, Henry?"

My father didn't answer. He sat, elbows on the table, hands clasped in front of his mouth. If I hadn't known better, I'd have thought he was praying.

"You said, 'Richard, we'll be sending out the boats unless I hear otherwise,' isn't that right? So I thought I needed to get to this party as soon as I could. Christ, if anyone knows what goes on at these parties it should be me, right? But when I thought back on it, I remembered these dinners as potlucks, when obviously they weren't."

"Richard, what's your point?" Sam asked.

"My point is: What's a man if he can't contribute? Dead weight, right? So I thought, well, I've been having some very interesting conversations with some nice Asian gentlemen recently."

Don Brooke was wrapping his napkin around his fist like a boxer taping up for a fight. Betty North sat with her legs crossed, picking at a hole in her nylons. I'd expected to see O-shaped mouths, cheeks drained of color, but not a single face registered surprise. In a sense, from the day John died, it had seemed inevitable that Richard would be standing at the head of this table, flint-eyed, raving.

"My father always said all you needed to be a good deckhand was the ability to do five things at once, right, Sam? That the only measure that mattered was *contribution*. So I went down to Chinatown before I left New York and grabbed everything I could carry. Really, money was no object. If you have it, spend it on the people you care for, right?"

He wrestled the suitcase with the Donald Duck sticker from the floor and held it to his chest. Something leaked from the hinge, dripping along the crease of his slacks.

"It's a fucking cornucopia over there. Crickets, fish eyes, pig cheeks with teeth, calf spleen, oh, and I got some calf heart too. The sea horses were expensive, so I only got a couple of those, but plenty of *uni*, that is, urchin roe. And bulls' balls, which I hear are *magnifique*."

He was talking fast. The weight of the suitcase strained his arms.

"And I did all this because I have bad news. I'm sorry, but those boats aren't going anywhere. They're just not. They're going to stay right here until Fuji and Kim-Chi come to sail them away."

He unfastened the clasps and the case sprang open. A waterfall of broken glass, briny liquid, and a mass of color poured onto the table—the orange of pea-size fish eggs, the deep red-brown of inner organs, the metallic green of cricket backs, the silver of wings.

The mess spread across the table, carrying a smell that stung the nostrils—salt and rot and garlic and soy—sending chips and splinters in every direction. The crashing glass fought its way into a war of other noises—the scrape of chair legs as everyone shot back from the table, and a collective groan, not of disgust, but of resignation.

CHAPTER 3

Y EARS LATER, I WAS DRINKING AT A BAR IN CHICAGO called the Bowman when an older woman, a nurse, wandered in. She'd just come off a graveyard shift, and she looked exhausted, like she'd survived the worst night of her life. She took a seat next to me at the bar and got drunk fast. Her name was Martha or Marta. "Goodbye Pork Pie Hat" was playing on the jukebox, and she said the song reminded her of northern Michigan, where she'd grown up—the train tracks that ran behind her parents' house, the ice storms, the wheat field where they'd released the family dog after he bit a neighbor. I have to admit I found her endearing, the way her eyes teared up, the way she fell into nostalgia after just a few bars of music.

"What was it like," she asked me, "what was it like where you grew up?"

"I hardly remember," I said. "It's been so long."

What I didn't say was that in Chicago sometimes the smell of the sewer would blow up through the grates in the sidewalk, or the wind would kick up as though spell-cast, snapping banners, swinging traffic lights, and I would find myself back home. The details of that past were just too strong—they refused to untangle from the present. The sour reek of the sewer was the smell of Greene Harbor. The sting of wind was the cold howling through the Strait of Juan de Fuca. The grinning drunks at the Bowman were the men who lined the bar at Eric's Quilt. The music leaking from the jukebox was my mother's music, and the nurse crying softly to it was my mother.

THE NIGHT AFTER RICHARD destroyed Loyalty Island, I couldn't sleep. I got out of bed to see if my mother was in her studio. I'd done this so many times I knew exactly where along the maroon runner to step. It was a minefield, and though I knew it was more than a little childish, I walked an imaginary path that weaved through fallen vines. One hand gliding along the banister, I snuck past the bathroom, under the searchlight moon shining through the hall window, under the hanging spider fern, back into shadows, to the top of the stairs.

I had a method for the stairs too, but I froze a step past the bathroom when I smelled cigarettes. Neither of my parents smoked. I flattened myself against the wall and slid to the floor, nearly slipping as the runner bunched underneath my feet. I knew who was downstairs even before I heard the voices.

"I guess it *is* that complicated, 'cause I still don't understand a fucking word." Don's voice. "Hank, I'm sorry you've had to spend all your time with these lawyers, but don't talk like one, all right?"

"Basically, Richard is John's heir for everything," I heard my father say. "Just like we always knew. If he says don't fish, then we don't."

"And if he wants to sell off all the goddamn fucking everything that we've nearly killed ourselves over?"

"That too."

"How could someone as smart as John have blinders on with this?" Don said. "He must have been the only person who didn't see this coming all the way from Asia."

They burst into laughter. "Maybe that's the wrong way to say it." Sam North now. "I guess he wasn't expecting to die so fast. Anyway, everyone's an idiot when it comes to their children, Don. If you had any, you'd know that."

"That's right," my father said. "Every parent is the fool of the world. We can't blame John, really."

"Who are you, Jack London?"

"Don, you're the fool of Canadian Club," my father said.

"In that case, I'll have one more," Don said.

"Maybe you should switch to sake," Sam said.

More laughter. I inched closer to the banister.

"Maybe if this all does go, I'll head to Japan. Why not? I could get a couple of porcupines."

"They're called concubines," Sam said.

"No, it's perfect, though," my father said. "Didn't we used to call you needle dick anyway?"

"I know what they're called," Don said. "I was joking. But I have to go somewhere, don't I? What else can we do?"

There was no answer. I heard a lighter flick, and someone—Sam, I thought—sighed. I heard a bottle being uncorked, dishes clinking. I could picture the three of them, elbows on the dining room table, smoke weaving through the chandelier. They were sitting in the exact same place where, just a day before, Richard had told them that the only work they'd ever known was no longer theirs.

I don't want to romanticize their work because I've never done it. But *they* romanticized it because they suffered for it. They stumbled from their bunks, having slept two hours in seventy, onto decks sheathed in ice, onto twenty-foot seas. They winched up enormous crab pots dripping foam, dredged from the bottom of the coldest ocean. How could each man explain to himself a lifetime of red eyes and frostbitten ears, of knees in salt water, elbows in chopped herring? It had to be part of some larger destiny; the fight to stay awake and alive had to be turned, somehow, from drudgery to heroism.

To venture from the wheelhouse, on the rare clear day when the sea lay as still as glass, the live wells plugged with red king crab that would sell for $1.50 a pound—already negotiated with the cannery—was, to them, as good as it would ever get. To pilot a steel ship that slid over fathoms of ocean churning secretly below was art. Out there you had the freedom to do anything. Out there, who could tell you otherwise?

But their freedom came with risk and was shaped by consequence. Don Brooke lost his index finger at the knuckle. My father shattered his ankle on the second day of tanner season and had to grimace through two weeks of constant work. But it was Sam North who'd suffered the most. My father told me one night the true reason Sam had temporarily quit fishing. If I ever breathed a word of it to Jamie or anyone else, he said, I'd be red-assed and out on the street.

Normally John Gaunt's boats were worked exclusively by men from Loyalty Island, but that year one of the crew learned of a family emergency just before they shipped out of Dutch Harbor, and was obliged to fly home. They filled his slot with a kid named Ramo who'd arrived in Dutch Harbor with a duffel bag and half a diploma from USC. By the time they'd motored out fifty miles, Ramo was green with nausea. Seasickness was permissible, even an omen of good luck. But Ramo refused to work through it. Apparently it wasn't even the rollers that dropped his stomach; it was the smell of the bait herring.

The crew a man short, Sam left the wheelhouse to take shifts on deck. With one of the eight-hundred-pound crab pots—a steel frame the size of a double bed, covered in nylon mesh—in the launch, Sam crawled in to bait it with the same herring that had driven Ramo into fits of nausea. But his fingers were numb from the cold, and, at forty-five, he was no longer built for baiting. He lagged an extra ten seconds, more than enough time to invite calamity.

A rogue wave—a real monster—washed the deck, knocking everyone off their feet and sending the crab pot over the rail, Sam along with it. The pot was weighted to sink five hundred feet to the bottom of the Bering Sea, and as the door shut behind him, Sam realized that he would be coming along.

How many times have I seen this in nightmares? Liquid ice flooding Sam's boots, sleeves, and nostrils. His fingers curling around the mesh of the pot. The pressure after only two fathoms beginning to rattle in his ears, the vertigo of black water and weightlessness. He tries to pull his hands away but his fingers are claws in the net; the electricity in his blood and brain is already slowing, freezing.

The pot races downward, wrapped in violent foam. Sam's hands still won't release, and he writhes against the mesh. He feels the shallowness of the pot, the narrowness. In the black rush of water the pot feels, of course, like a coffin. He's deep enough now to have been buried four times over. The pressure is in his sinuses, his inner ear, and his temples; it seems to curl up his fingernails and earlobes. Somehow, amazingly, he resists the temptation to scream and to breathe. He imagines he can smell the herring as its slotted plastic jar floats beside him like a streamer on the back of a bicycle. The herring that will be a siren call to armies of king crab, three feet wide, scuttling across the bottom of the sea, pincers raised and swinging like lanterns. Sam pictures himself dead, after a two-day soak. The pull of the hydraulic winch, the pot rising, breaking the surface, banging against the *Cordilleran*'s steel hull. He is unceremoniously dumped onto the deck, his body swollen by seawater, half devoured to white bone.

His feet stab the dark, and, miraculously, the pot breaks open at the bottom—or the top? His fingers finally release; he pulls back his arms. He slides from the pot into open water and is tempted to breathe it like air. He wants to kick his legs, but is afraid they might only take him deeper. He spins, trying to locate himself in the gauze of bubbles, and spies the buoy line, nearly phosphorescent in the darkness. With the line to orient him, he can see the pot rushing away like a train.

He's down fifty, maybe sixty feet. He follows the buoy line up, hand over hand, starving for breath as his ears pop again and again. He bursts from the water and has just time enough to draw a three-quarter breath before a breaker hurls him back down. When he comes up a second time, the ship is nowhere to be seen. He doesn't expect to live, but is grateful that he won't die caged on the ocean floor. He gropes for the buoy, brings it to his chest with both arms.

He wakes below deck, wrapped in blankets, shaking and vomiting. He can hardly feel his body but figures the crew would not be gazing at him with such openmouthed amazement if he were dead.

When Sam returned home, he told my father and only my father that he couldn't face the Bering Sea again. And perhaps he did suffer from vertigo afterward, but it was the vertigo of those moments twisting in the dark of the crab pot, locked in a terror he would never be able to describe or forget.

I was about to slink back to my room when I heard Sam speak. "There are still two things we can do."

My father spoke then. "We can try to convince Richard to go out with us. I still think if he just got a taste of it he'd feel different."

"That's not going to do any good," Sam said. "Let's go over it again. For Don's benefit."

"If you want to do something for me, shut up," Don said.

"What does the will say?" Sam asked.

"Everything goes to Richard. How many more times do I have to say that?"

"And if Richard is somehow unable to assume ownership?"

"Then the estate, including the company, goes into probate court. Meanwhile the company goes to a trust, to be run by the trustees for Richard's benefit until he can take ownership. I guess I've read the thing enough times to memorize it."

"Never thought you'd memorize someone else's will?" Sam asked.

"Better than my own," my father said. More laughter.

"And what if Richard never takes ownership?"

"I don't know. They'd have to find an heir, and far as I know there's no close family, so it could take years to sort that out in court."

"And during all that time we keep fishing."

"Yes."

"Who are the trustees?"

"*You* sound like the lawyer. A few people. The three of us, for example. The lawyer. But what's the difference? All Richard has to do is show up and sign his name and none of it matters anymore."

"But he hasn't yet," Sam said.

I could see the light from the dining room sloping up the staircase, but little else. I felt like Jim Hawkins in *Treasure Island*, hidden in the apple barrel, listening to John Silver and the rest of the pirates plan mutiny. Except I'd known the pirates my entire life, and I had no one to report the news to. I was a spy for myself only. I closed my eyes so I could hear everything.

"Sam," Don said, "you better slow down. We'll find work. Ours aren't the only boats in Alaska."

"If you think you're just going to show up in Dutch Harbor and have someone hand over the keys to the wheelhouse, best of luck." Sam spoke with a blade in his voice. "And what did you just say, Don? You said 'our boats.' Those are our boats, not some prick's. You want more reasons? What did John always teach us about safety? Even if some of our guys do find work up there, fifty-fifty chance it will be with some cokehead. How many of our guys might die over the next five years? The next ten?"

"Step back," Don said.

I strained to hear my father. I imagined he must have been talking too quietly for his voice to carry up the stairs.

"It would be easy," Sam said.

"It?" Don asked.

"People die out there all the time. They never find them."

I held my breath. Finally I heard my father's voice. "We need to talk to Richard. I think he'll get it eventually. He has to."

"Not everyone needs it like us, Hank," Sam said. "In fact, most people don't."

"Hey, none of us *need* to stick it to your wife, but we do it anyway," my father said.

"I appreciate that," Sam said. "Christ, have any more of that Glenlivet? This whole thing hurts, doesn't it?"

"The bottle's upstairs," my father said. "I had to hide it from Don at the party so he could get through his story. Only guy I've ever met who gets whiskey dick *and* whiskey tongue."

Using their laughter as cover, I streaked back to my room.

THE NEXT MORNING my doorknob squeaked and my footsteps thumped, the blue notes of an empty house. Around noon the phone rang. My mother was in Seattle, shopping. There was a Malle film playing at the university. She'd catch the last Edmonds ferry, she said. I kept her talking. What's the movie about? Who stars? Same director who did the one with the blonde walking in the rain? I was buying time, trying to decide if I should tell her what I'd heard the night before. Through the line, the bustle of Pike Place overpowered her curt answers, but at least I knew she was telling the truth about where she was.

"I would have come with you," I said.

"I know," she said. "I just needed a little time by myself."

"Why?" I asked. "Why do you need so much time by yourself?"

There was a crash, maybe someone dumping ice. I knew the pay phone. There was a bakery and a lunch counter a few steps away, a vegetable stand just beyond that. They had the best apples, my mother said.

"That's a question I don't think I can answer."

"Try," I said.

"Well. This morning I woke up thinking about that green screen next to John's bed. I kept thinking about how his blood pressure fell little by little until he was dead."

"Did you even see that?" I asked.

"I went to get you out in the yard, remember? And the door was locked when we got back. So, no, I didn't see it."

"Is that my fault?"

"No. No, of course not." She took a loud breath. "See, I told you

I can't explain it. Anyway, I'm late. I'll tell you about the movie after I see it."

My father was gone all day too. He didn't call. I went to bed that night without speaking to another soul. But I planned to listen.

In the old days, when John, Sam, and Don came to our house for dinner, I always knew there was something under the surface of their talk that I wasn't allowed to hear, something that emerged after my mother had sent me to bed. I felt like I'd finally caught some of it the night before, but what I'd caught was terrifying.

I set my clock radio for 1:12 a.m. Why I chose this particular time, I don't know, but I felt a strange satisfaction when the glowing green numbers hit. I turned the volume on the clock radio up all the way. I put earphones on and slept on my back, still as a vampire. I awoke to a brass section playing James Brown on the oldies station.

I crept through the hall to the top of the stairs. From the living room I could hear my father's voice swinging behind a screen of noise. The same James Brown song played, then faded, as if someone had turned down the volume.

"If you see another way, then tell me," he said. "I'll listen. I promise I will."

I dropped to all fours, my left hand slipping on the fallen brown leaves of our spider fern. I hadn't heard my mother come home. Had she missed the Edmonds ferry?

The volume spiked again. Not James Brown now, but the Platters'

"Smoke Gets in Your Eyes." The singer's voice seemed to shred the tinny speakers before the volume plummeted.

"Help me," my father said. "I need help."

Something crashed to the ground. A chair? From where I lay on the landing I could see only the top third of the room, the brass curtain rods, the highest bookshelf. I noticed a blue hardback I'd always thought was called *Exotic Washrooms*. From my angle on the landing I saw that the title was actually *Exotic Mushrooms*. Below, in the dining room, my father was talking loudly, but the radio was up again. The music was maddening, distorting every syllable. Midway through the bridge the song snapped off, leaving only dry, clear voices.

"I'll smash that fucking thing, I promise. Who is 'him'? Who are you talking about?"

"John," my mother said. "You shouldn't be asking me about Richard, you should be asking me about John. You've heard what people used to say. Isn't that why you're telling me this?"

The muscles in my back tightened. I looked at the blue book spine and read: *Exotic Mushrooms, Exotic Mushrooms, Exotic Mushrooms*.

"Are you crazy? I'm thinking about *that* now?" my father said. "Rumors don't bother me. I know too much about you."

"What do you know? What do you think you know?"

"Let's leave it."

"I'd love to hear what you know about me," she said. "I've been wondering for years."

"That you're moral, I guess."

"Would you like to know how moral I am? I used to daydream about the chances that you wouldn't come home one spring. There's your permission if you need it."

The blood felt thick behind my eyes. The volume on the radio spiked again, but cut out before I could tell what was playing. I heard another crash, metal skidding across tile. For a while no one said anything. I heard a door open, the broom scraping the kitchen floor. When they spoke again they both sounded exhausted.

"Did you really?" my father asked.

She didn't answer.

"Okay," I heard him say then, "okay, okay, okay," almost like a chant. His boots tapped the tiles, and I could picture him pacing back and forth, saying okay, okay, okay, patting his pockets to make sure he had everything he needed before he left for work.

"I'm sorry," she said. "I shouldn't have said that. It's just that I'm afraid of everything and I feel like I can barely lift my arms."

"There's something wrong with you."

"Everyone knows that. You should've paid more attention."

"I have. Paying attention and talking about it aren't the same thing. But now we have to talk about it."

Without warning, my mother stepped from the dining room into the living room. She stood at the foot of the stairs, her red hair in a bun, her dress the color of lead, belly heavy, feet bare. She saw me immediately but said nothing, just raised her hand, palm down, and flicked her wrist. *Get out of here.* I couldn't read her expression. Her eyes were slits. Her face had the warm rawness of winter

Sundays I remembered from early childhood, when we'd both slept late and awoken to a deserted and smoke-colored day.

THERE WAS NO PRAYER of sleep. I listened, ear to keyhole, ear to the slit beneath my door. Not a sound, but I didn't give up for an hour. Still, I couldn't bring myself to open the door. At two, I got back into bed and closed my eyes and, as I'd done often that year when I couldn't sleep, pretended to ride the rocket.

I'd read a book about *Voyager* and in my mind I followed the satellite's route. I'd read that *Voyager* was sent to space with a golden record aboard, bearing greetings in fifty-five languages, many of them dead. I'd hear those recordings in my mind as the rocket plunged through cold darkness—alien, unknowable, but no longer wordless. "Hello, hello," I'd say in Quechua, the language of the Incan Empire. But *Voyager* was pathetically slow. I'd shoot past cue ball–smooth Io and the lonely crust of Triton in seconds, not decades. Beyond Pluto the sky opened like a garden. I'd recognize the Horsehead Nebula, the Crab Nebula, and the Cat's Eye Nebula from photographs I'd seen in my mother's books, colors that grew from the darkness as if on stems.

I returned to these images, I think, because they brought back one of my earliest memories. Night on Black's Beach. My father wrapped me in his coat during a red tide. We sat on dry kelp, watching the plankton shine, their bioluminescence smearing a bright sea onto the dark one. We shared a cup of hot chocolate as the cold light crested and fell.

But that night another memory of Black's Beach bled in. My father and I were skipping stones. He had just hit a seven, and I was trying to keep pace. I took a running start. My stone only skipped once or twice, but my momentum spun me a quarter turn so that I was staring up the beach. About fifty feet ahead, two naked legs poked from the valley between a drift log and a gray boulder. I knew instinctively that the man was dead.

My father grabbed me by the arm and told me not to move. He jogged down the beach and, when he reached the man, put one of his own legs up on the wood and bent down as if to speak. When he returned, he squeezed my shoulder. "Don't worry," he said. "It's nobody we know."

Around three, I heard footsteps in the hall. The door opened and my mother stood in a wedge of yellow light.

"Cal," she said. "You're not sleeping."

"What were you talking about?" I asked.

She stepped past the blue windows and stopped a few feet from my bed. There was sweat on her forehead, and she seemed out of breath.

"You know your father wouldn't actually hurt anyone. Don't worry about what we said."

She stepped closer and sat down, her hands around her belly.

"What do you mean? Who would he hurt?"

She'd never come into my room in the middle of the night. She'd never sat there in the darkness, and there was something unnatural about it, something staged.

"But what you do isn't the only important thing," she said. "What you think, what even seems possible, those things are important too. I'm not saying I'm better than him."

"I don't know what you're talking about," I said.

She looked out the window and frowned, though it was dark and there was nothing to see. "I'm going to Santa Cruz. Do you want to come?"

She looked at me as if I could give her an answer. What could I possibly say: Yes? No? Those words didn't mean what they'd meant before.

"We'll stay with Meg. It could be fun."

"For how long?"

"We'll figure that out."

"I'd go to school?"

"We'll figure that out too. We'll figure everything out."

"Have you thought about this at all?"

"It's all I've thought about."

"Have you thought about what I would do?"

Her skin was red and raw, her expression as blank as the marquee of an abandoned theater. In that moment, all I wanted from her was distance. I'd heard my father in the kitchen. He hadn't mentioned hurting anyone. He'd been trying to tell her something about Richard, about the future we were all supposed to share, and she had been unwilling to listen. He was the one who needed help. Not her. And I needed help, not her.

"I don't want to go," I said. "But I think you should go think about him dying wherever you feel most comfortable."

"Cal."

"I heard what you said."

Maybe I spoke too loudly, or maybe, in the half-light of the room, my face said something more than my words, because she leaned away, then shot up from the bed as if electricity were running through the blanket.

"People say things they don't mean," she said. "Maybe you are too."

But I had meant what I'd said. And I didn't say anything else.

AT SEVEN I was within my rights to open the door. It was morning. Still, I listened at the keyhole for a full minute before walking a hall of land mines. The light in the living room window belonged more to dusk than dawn. The harbor roiled in the distance under clouds like knots in the sky.

In the dining room a green bottle of Glenlivet stood empty on the table. I examined the bottle, a tiny chip on the rim, the label curled at one corner. The cap was turned up, the cork pointing like a hitch-hiker's thumb.

The basement door was closed. Oil stains marked the space in our driveway where the Chevette was usually parked. The kitchen was spotless. The house roared like an empty shell.

I pulled *Exotic Mushrooms* from the shelf. My father had promised to take me to collect, but we'd never gotten around to it. I decided I'd study the English and Latin names of as many of the mushrooms as I could, but I got only as far as *Amanita ocreata, The Destroying Angel.* The cap was centimeters wide, the stalk salt-white.

I flipped back to the beginning of the book—was in the process of flipping the glossy paper—when my father appeared at the head of the stairs. He took one heavy step, then another, his hand fumbling for the banister. He wore yesterday's shirt buttoned to a V at the collar. But what had happened to yesterday's pants? His pale legs were naked up to his boxer shorts.

He missed a step, crashed down two more, his hip creaking the railing. His eyes were closed, his lips parted like a wall-mounted fish. He wore white ankle socks. There was a hole in the left sock's heel, and only a stirrup of cloth held it to his foot.

He was headed for his tiki chair, and in my mind I saw him collapse into it and scrape the sleep from his face. I saw myself—*Exotic Mushrooms* on my lap, my elbows on the book—saying, "Dad, what the hell has been happening? I've tried to figure it out like you said, but now I just want you to tell me." I saw him look at me somberly, respecting the gravity of my question, appreciating the moment I'd chosen. His mind was still foggy, and at such an early hour everything seemed simple enough to explain. He had to give me a little credit. "All right," he said. "Here's the thing."

But none of that happened. My father bent over the chair and pulled up the seat cushion. He pulled out his dick, exhaled, and began to piss on the chair. He put his hands on his hips and arched his back. Eventually he wiped his hands on the tail of his shirt and dropped the cushion back into place. I might have tried to stop him, had I been able to move.

I WOKE HOURS LATER when my father flung open my bedroom door, rippling a wake across the bookshelf. He took a step into the room, but only one, as if he'd forgotten why he'd come. His shirt was the same, but he'd found pants somewhere, and boots. He'd shaved his beard.

"You're awake. Good." But he didn't look pleased. "Good. It's almost three." He played with the wristband of one fingerless glove. He put a hand to the back of his neck.

"You and I are leaving today," he said.

"You don't know how to say anything," I said, rubbing my eyes, trying to snap my mind back from sleep.

My father's stare was like a steel bar. He shifted his weight to his back foot. He took off one of the gloves, and for a second I thought he might slap me across the face. "Thanks for letting me know. I'll look into it when I get back from Alaska."

I shot up in bed. "Since when?"

"We're leaving today. All the boats."

"Richard?"

"He's coming with us," my father said. I studied his face. It was a vault.

"How did you change his mind?" I scissored in the sheets, trying to leap up. He raised one hand, still gloved. The tips of his fingers were red as tongues.

"That's a fine question, but I have a lot to tell you and no time." He took a step toward the bed. "Don't you have a chair?"

"Just the beanbag."

He sank into the blue lump on the floor where, years before, he'd chronicled the life of Captain Flint. "It happened too fast," he said, "so you'll have to pack fast."

"I'm going with you?"

"No. You're going to the Norths'. You're going to stay there until I get back. I can't leave you here alone."

I felt my eyes burn, my neck start to sweat. "What about Mom?"

"She's on her way to Santa Cruz," he said.

"Without saying good-bye?"

"Didn't she?" He seemed to consider this for a moment before focusing his gaze back on me. "Listen, I'm sure you've noticed she hasn't been all that well. You've noticed that, haven't you?"

"Yes."

He looked at me hard. "Do you want me to tell you what she said?" I didn't answer, but he went on. "She said she can't stand to be in this place anymore, not even if I'm gone. Is that how you feel too?"

"No."

"Good." He smiled, but his smile was sad. "We decided together. We decided that she shouldn't be here alone, with the baby coming. She wanted to go right away. She really didn't tell you?"

Yes, she had asked me to go, and, yes, I'd told her I wouldn't. But the conversation already seemed like a dream. I'd been sure I'd wake the next morning to find her sitting at the kitchen table, that I'd hear her music from the basement at least. Without meaning to, I jumped out of bed, took a couple of steps across the room and froze. "She wouldn't have been alone," I said.

"Grab some pants," my father said.

I was in tighty-whiteys, a plum-size rip in the left side below the elastic. As I scooped my jeans from the floor and fed them my legs, my father looked at me with a puzzled expression. Not displeased or angry exactly, but confused, almost amused. It was an expression that never failed to fill me with cold shame. How can I be more like you if you don't help me? I wanted to ask this question but never did, because sometimes he did try to help me, and that was even worse.

Three years before, the boats had come back heavy. The season was highline. There would be a summer with money for everyone. You could feel the vibrations of this everywhere, in the pitch of voices in line at Belinda's Deli, in the popcorn at the Orpheum Theatre, in the starch in Mrs. Zhou's laundry. Money, as my father used to say, is only energy, energy that—in this case—began as worms and mollusks on the floor of the Bering Sea. Energy that passed to the bellies of king crabs, to the bellies of steel ships, to the bellies of steel banks.

My father brought home a VCR for my mother, a luxury in those days, along with an armload of the movies she loved by Kurosawa, Antonioni, and Bresson.

"Anything for me?" I asked.

"Get in the car," he said. "You'll need this when we get to the *Laurentide*." He handed me a fillet knife in a black plastic sheath.

We parked in front of the *Laurentide*'s slip and climbed the steel ladder. The deck had just been washed down; fresh water beaded the rails. My father breathed in with his nose and slapped his thighs.

"I'll be back in a minute," he said, grinning, "so no ideas about joyriding, okay?" He went below deck, returning a few minutes later with an enormous king salmon slung over his shoulder. Before I could say anything, he swung the fish by its tail and whacked me in the arm. I slipped on the deck and went down hard. "That's my present?" I asked, but my disappointment was faked. We were both laughing.

We set the salmon on the worktable in the stern. My father took a white handkerchief from his back pocket, folded it in half, and tied it around my forehead. "We don't want sweat in your eyes. Now, the scalpel, Doctor."

He unsheathed the fillet knife and presented it to me on the flats of his hands. I'd seen him do this a hundred times. I rolled up my sleeves and took the knife as two brown pelicans flapped onto the rail, tucking long beaks against their breasts.

"Gills first, right?" I asked.

"Yeah, now careful. I can't take you home with a finger like Don's."

I dug the blade into the salmon's head, just behind the gills, sliced vertically, and then drew the knife toward the mouth. The flesh was as cold as the water it had come from, but the knife glided. Above me, gulls screamed. The gills, on the inside, looked like maroon clay. I tossed the scraps overboard without looking, the way I'd seen my father do it. I could hear wings beating, a chorus of shrieks and splashes. I flipped the salmon and attacked the other side.

"That's it, Doctor," my father said. "Belly-dance him, now."

I looked up at a swirl of feathers. More birds had descended around the table. They swooped and dove, coming close enough that I could feel a rush of air.

"What are you waiting for?" my father said. "Not too deep. Don't slit the stomach or these birds will go crazy."

Bits of scale clung beneath my fingernails. My hands felt covered in sticky snow. I wiped a palm on my doctor's bandana and pointed the tip of the fillet knife just below the gills.

"Stay on the beam," my father said. "Steady hands. Watch the stomach, now."

I knew the trick was to go just deep enough to flay the flesh without messing the organs. But as I sliced, I imagined the gulls alighting on my shoulder, felt their feathers under my nose and their beaks in my ears. The knife clung to a scale and I pushed smoothly through, not sawing, just the way I'd seen him do it. But too deep. I was carving through the stomach. I knew it, but I couldn't stop. I looked up at the swirling white birds, and when I looked down again my hands were covered with black needlefish. The needlefish poured from the stomach, hundreds of them, over the cleaning table and onto my pants and shoes.

I dropped the knife and stumbled three or four steps back, brushing at the needlefish as if they were sparks. I think I managed not to cry out. The gulls descended, shrieking, stabbing the fish, puffing their wings. They tore at the deck, all white feathers and black eyes. Then they fell silent, mouths too full to shriek, and the deck churned as if under white clouds.

My father shooed three gulls with his boot and stooped for his knife. "All right, wash up before you get in the car. I'll finish this off."

"Let me help you," I said.

Three years later, standing in my bedroom, I said it again. I meant to demand that he explain the night before, that he explain how my mother could have left like that. I meant to accuse him of a crime, but different words came. "Let me help you. Let me go with you."

As he smiled, the skin around his eyes crinkled like cellophane. There was a square flesh-tone bandage on the side of his neck that I hadn't noticed before.

"I don't think so," he said. "Richard on board's too much already. Anyway, I'm almost sure you have school this year."

"Did you really change Richard's mind?"

"No," he said. His mouth shrank as his eyes carved mine. "I didn't have to. He never wanted to sell. I took your mother's advice, and I drove Richard around this morning, to the Orpheum and Zhou's and Belinda's, and explained that it was up to him to keep them alive. He finally understood that."

"But why? Why now?"

As an answer, he gently cuffed the back of my neck and rubbed it with his rough thumb.

MY ARMY-GREEN DUFFEL, too stuffed to lift, thumped each step down to the living room. *Exotic Mushrooms* was back in its place on the top shelf. The tiki chair was nowhere to be seen. My father walked in from the kitchen, gulping water from a frosted Coca-Cola glass. The dirt under his nails looked like ten black moons.

"I need your keys," he said.

"What for?" I asked.

"I need to leave an extra set with Marty at the office, in case."

"In case of what?" I asked.

"You know what."

I dug my house key from my pocket. It was terrible luck even to allude to not coming home, no matter the circumstances.

"Anyway, you won't need to come back," my father said. "Looks like you packed the whole house." He slung the bag over his shoulder with an exaggerated groan, and we headed outside. It was raining, so we stood under the eaves with our backs to the wall.

"Jamie's mom is coming to pick you up," he said.

"You don't need to wait."

"Betty will be here any minute."

Too much had happened. I couldn't keep any one thought in place. I could have asked a hundred questions, but, though the silence was unbearable, talking about anything important seemed pointless. There wasn't enough time.

"I was reading your mushroom book," I said. "Ever know anyone who died from eating *Amanita*?"

"No." He scratched the bandage on his neck. Then, as if doing his best to be a good sport, "But I've known people who've died for dumber reasons."

The tips of our shoes were shaded with rain. The Norths' blue

Skylark pulled into the driveway, wipers blinking. My father dumped my bag into the backseat, clutched me briefly with one arm, then dumped me into the front.

"The road's slippery, Cal," Betty said. "Seat belt, please."

Metal tongue. Plastic snap. When I looked up again our front door was closed and shrinking behind a screen of rain.

JAMIE'S ROOM was unusually neat and spare—a blond wood table for a desk, a bunk bed, a gleaming hardwood floor—but every inch of wall was covered in movie posters. Some I recognized— *Jaws, Blade Runner, The French Connection*—but most featured wild-eyed swordsmen with black hair and white robes. Betty had told me not to bother knocking. I lived here now; I should act like it. Those words weren't as comforting as she probably hoped.

Jamie was bent over his desk, but he turned when he heard my duffel thud against the floor.

"Meissenier, chelat te'jeneten cormer."

"What?"

"That's the new language I've been working on. It sounds like French, right?"

"What did you actually just say?"

"Hmmm, well, I haven't gotten that far."

He popped up from his desk and grabbed my duffel, sliding it across the hardwood, halfway under the bed. I felt a sudden, scalding hatred for him, though I must have at least had a dim sense that he had nothing to do with my problems.

"I'm just messing around," he said, "but I should—actually we should—make a language. It could be like a project while you're my guest."

I'd never punched anyone, not really. I imagined my fist sailing like an arrow to a bull's-eye. I imagined standing splay-legged over an unconscious ball of Jamie on the floor. Instead, I landed only a glancing blow on Jamie's shoulder. He spun away, his face more surprised than hurt. I lunged shoulder first, catching him from the side, just below his armpit. We tumbled toward the bed. He ducked to avoid the top bunk and his feet slid out from under him. My cheek smacked the floor and seemed to stick there like batter to a griddle. I didn't recognize what my arms or legs were doing and could barely tell them from Jamie's. I felt him pull away, rise to his feet. I caught him by the knee and beat it with my fist. He took another step— tried to—and crashed to the ground. I took one more halfhearted shot before collapsing onto my back.

"*J'emaine tulouse confitette.*" Jamie sat up, panting.

"What?" I said.

"I think I asked why you did that."

But I couldn't even explain why to myself.

I LAY IN BED that night, as I did every night for the next few months, staring into the eyes of Sigourney Weaver dressed as Zuul from *Ghostbusters*. But in the darkness I saw Richard Gaunt's face as he emptied the suitcase onto our dining room table. For all the frenzy of the broken glass his face was still. It was the face of a man killing his sick dog. How could Richard have planned a performance like that if he'd intended to go back on it? I tried to picture him on the *Laurentide*, heading north to Dutch Harbor.

Jamie's father had *seemed* to suggest killing Richard. But even so, my father had said he'd talk to Richard again, he'd convince him. And now it seemed that this was exactly what he had done. Maybe Richard had just changed his mind. Why not? Did I know enough about him to say that he couldn't have? I knew more about my own father. I knew he wasn't a murderer.

But did my mother know that? "He would never hurt anyone," she'd said.

I thought of her, standing in my doorway the night before, sitting on the edge of my bed. She had to have known my father was leaving the next morning. She'd known, and she'd gone anyway. Had I driven her away? I'd meant to be cruel. I wished I could take back the words I'd said to her in the half-light, and yet now that she'd left, I meant them more than ever.

I stretched my legs over the sheets. They were soft, worn thin. I could almost feel Jamie's old sleep under my back. The blanket was made of mothy wool, too warm for the weather. New sheets, new blanket. New space. Everything was new.

Every minute or so a spot of light darted onto the far wall. I heard pages turning in the bunk below.

"*Penthouse* or *Playboy*?" I asked.

"I'm usually strictly *Hustler*. But lately I've been more into *Film Comment*," Jamie said.

"Right at home," I said.

"How's that?"

"My mother subscribes to *Film Comment*. What are you reading it for?"

"Sometimes they have stuff about samurai movies. Will at the Orpheum told me about it. Actually he said I should read it when I got older, but I didn't want to wait. That's funny. I didn't think any-one else on the peninsula had a subscription."

"It's like you and I were switched at birth or something."

"Okay, asshole." I heard Jamie turn the next page, the next and the next. "Where is she anyway?" he asked. "Your mother?"

"Santa Cruz? I don't really know."

"You don't know? That's beastly."

"Who are you, fucking Roald Dahl down there? I'm sure your mother will be in here to breast-feed you any minute."

"I doubt it," Jamie said quietly. "She's out."

"Out where?"

"She's probably in her room. But when Daj leaves she gets this way."

"Daj?"

"My dad. When he leaves for the season she just sort of goes out. You'll see soon enough, I guess."

It was true that few people in the world seemed as scattered as Betty North. She had willowy, freckled arms that fell toward her waist like extensions of her dark blond hair. Her eyes were like windshields on a bright day. My father had often encouraged my mother to strike up a friendship with Betty. They had a lot in common, he said. Beauty, sons the same age, smelly and insensitive fishermen for husbands. "Get together and complain about us," my father said.

"I spend enough time alone," my mother answered.

"Be fair."

"Try making eye contact with her sometime," my mother said. "It's about as easy as catching the gaze of a lighthouse. It's like she's phasing in and out of the room."

"Is that hard?" I asked Jamie from the top bunk. "About your mother?"

"I don't really have anything to compare it to."

"Did you ever talk to your dad about it?"

"Are you serious?"

"Well, anyway," I said, "thanks for the bed."

"It wasn't up to me," he said.

"It was a sad fucking surprise for me too."

Jamie clicked off the flashlight and lowered his voice. "A surprise, yeah. I didn't think Richard would ever go to Dutch Harbor. Did you?"

Of course. Jamie was wondering the same things I was. But let him wonder. I didn't need his help, and he wouldn't get mine.

"You've never changed your mind about anything?" I asked.

"Not after dumping a shopping cart's worth of pickled pig organs and bugs onto a dining room table. There was also that thing about selling everything. Did you catch that part?"

I sat up, nearly bumping my head on the ceiling. "No, I hadn't thought about it. In fact, where am I? This doesn't seem like my room. I don't have all of these gay posters. How did I get here?"

"Sarcasm is the refuge of the weak," he said. "John Knowles."

"Jamie North is a whiny little bitch. Everybody." He didn't respond, so I went on. "I'd bet you anything that all Richard wanted was for people to beg him, for our dads to beg him. That's the kind of guy he is. How could he actually sell everything? It's been in his family for like a hundred years."

As I spoke the words I began to believe they were true.

MY MOTHER CALLED TWICE the next day, a Friday. The first time I pretended to be sleeping, but the second time Betty cornered me in the kitchen and handed me the phone. She'd made break-fast that morning, and the room still smelled of bacon smoke. The walls were cluttered with framed photographs—family portraits, Christmas-morning candids of Jamie as a toddler, yellowing shots of dead relatives—pair after pair of investigating eyes.

Without putting the phone to my ear I pressed the receiver back into the cradle. I turned to Betty, half expecting her to slap me—maybe I deserved to be slapped. Her smile was sympathetic, but her eyes were tired. She lit a cigarette with a match, shook it out, and kept shaking it after the flame had died. I thought of her among the crowds in Greene Harbor in September, waving until long after the boats had disappeared in the distance. Whistling, with two fingers in her mouth, a shrill, sad sound.

"Why did you do that?" she asked.

"I can't talk to her," I said.

Betty nodded, as if she understood. "Maybe she'd do the talking."

"Will you tell her?" I asked. "Will you tell her I can't speak to her?"

Betty had freckles under her eyes that made her look younger than she must have been. I wondered if she had taken all the photos. A series of landscapes hung in the living room—storms and mountains and fields—but there weren't any of Alaska.

"Oh, honey," she said. "Your mother would never forgive me."

The phone rang again.

"I can't forgive her," I said.

"Hear what she says before you decide."

"I'll try," I said. "Could I do it alone?"

As soon as the kitchen door swung shut I picked up the phone and hung it up again. After another moment I took the phone off the hook and went out the back door. The streets downtown were deserted, as they always were in early September. Still I kept walking, all the way to Greene Harbor.

Sleepy birds lined the pier. The big ships were gone. I could almost see the impression they'd left on the water.

WE STARTED SCHOOL that Monday. On Wednesday we came home to find Betty standing at the kitchen counter, drinking white grape juice from the carton.

"I've asked you not to do that," Jamie said.

She glided to him and put the back of her hand to his cheek. "I've just had some bad news from Don Brooke," she said. "Richard Gaunt went overboard in the Inside Passage. They've called off the search."

I wasn't upset or surprised. I only wished my own mother had been there to tell me the news.

CHAPTER 4

B Y THE MIDDLE OF SEPTEMBER THE SUN SEEMED to rise and set three times each day. After two weeks of faked indifference, I crawled onto Jamie's dresser and out the bedroom window. I'd seen him do it ten times by then, an easy and fluid feat. But my knees couldn't find space on the sill. I scraped my back on the window sash, and tumbled, shoulder first, into darkness.

"That didn't hurt too much, did it?" Jamie asked. He sat on the flat roof, his back to the house, his legs stretched over the tar and gravel, like a hobo who'd just jumped freight. I picked a piece of gravel from my palm and flicked it at him.

"Oh God, my eye." He burst out laughing.

"Are you done smoking?" I asked.

"Are you saying you want to join me for some fine tobacco product?"

"Can I?"

The morning had been damp, but the afternoon had sizzled. The tar was still warm. The flat roof lay like an apron over the darkness. Jamie tossed me a pack of Winstons. A match hissed, lighting the freckles around his nose.

"Thanks," I said. It was more words than we'd spoken since Richard was lost at sea.

That day, the news had raced across our town's roads and wires. Men in rectangles of yellow light announced the death to dark bars. Women outside storefronts downtown exchanged sighs of grief—or was it relief, this time? The Norths' phone rattled for hours.

As I walked along the boardwalk that afternoon I passed two police officers, Garrett Lindstrom and another whose last name was Heiner. Both men had once worked for my father. They stood, straddling their bicycles, draped in blue ponchos slick with rain.

"I mean, what was he expecting?" Heiner asked. "I thought he was smarter than that. Not, you know, capable, but smarter than that at least."

"Cal," Lindstrom said, grinning when he saw me. "You already heard about Richard, I guess?"

But on Monday nobody mentioned Richard at school. I listened for his name at Belinda's and didn't hear it once. It felt as if he'd been erased. No surprise, really. What is there to say about a fire once it's out?

His death was, for everyone in Loyalty Island, a remarkably fortunate tragedy. As much as Richard was hated, he was also a Gaunt. There had never been a Loyalty Island, Washington, without the Gaunts. Now there was. There simply was no way to express what that felt like to the guy on the next stool, or to the woman behind you in line at Safeway, or to the kid next to you in the bathroom, sneaking a cigarette at lunchtime.

There was only one person in town—that I knew of, at least—who still wanted to talk about Richard, and, unfortunately, I shared a room with him. The morning after we heard the news, Jamie stood silently in the bathroom doorway while I brushed my teeth.

"What," I asked. "What? What?"

He took a breath. "*What* is right. Don't you think—?"

I spit toothpaste on his foot and shut the door.

In those next two weeks AR—After Richard—Jamie never said what he was thinking, but I could see his suspicions twitching at the corners of his mouth. I was sure he had some theory—he always did. On the way to school, I walked two steps ahead. I ate the dinners Betty prepared alone, upstairs. As Jamie had predicted, she didn't seem to care.

I couldn't decide what Richard's death on the boat proved. The details coming in were still sketchy. The season didn't stop when a man went overboard, even if the man was Richard Gaunt. For a while I told myself that I would know soon enough, that if I could be there when my father returned, if I could find his eyes just as he stepped off the boat, I would catch him off guard and everything would be clear. After a day or two I had to give up that fantasy.

The problem was that my father had never been so alive in my mind as he was once I began to suspect him of murder. I could see each wrinkle around his eyes, the sapling-shaped scar twisting between his upper lip and left nostril. I saw his first full day on the Bering Sea, his first view of the waves that cracked against the boat like chunks of slate. I smelled the green mud the crew rubbed on the back of his slicker—for luck, they said. And I saw him waving away Don and Sam's cigarette smoke with the back of his hand, so that he could lean in close enough to whisper terrible, murderous things.

My mother was a different story. I'd expected her to call again, but she hadn't. By the second week I no longer checked the answering machine when I came home from school. Instead, I replayed our last conversation. Sometimes I regretted what I'd said. Sometimes I thought that if I'd acted differently during those brief minutes in my dark bedroom, then everything would be different. My mother would still be in Loyalty Island. Richard Gaunt would still be alive. Sometimes I thought that nothing I'd done had mattered at all.

One night I dreamed I was walking the dim hallways of a hospital. Pools of water slid from the cracks under doors. I opened one of the doors and found my mother in bed, her stomach the size of a tortoise. John Gaunt stood next to her, dressed as a surgeon, clutching her hand with long white fingers. "Cal," he said, "you're quite the explorer. Fearless!" Then he plucked out his teeth and placed them on my mother's head like a tiara.

I woke up wanting to talk to her. It would have been easy enough to find Meg's number. But when I tried to imagine our conversation I heard only the strum of a guitar, smelled the lye in Meg's threadbare rugs. So I talked to her in my mind. Again and again I returned to what she'd said that last night in my room. "Your father wouldn't hurt anyone." And I returned to my father's words the morning he'd left. "She hasn't been all that well. You've noticed that, haven't you?"

What had I seen? It was the question I asked myself nearly every day that September. At the same time, though, the answers seemed distant and only slightly real. It was as if I'd stepped into another life, a life I felt sympathy and concern for, but a life that was not mine to change.

One day after school I passed a lawn where a sprinkler jetted in circles, pointless on the Olympic Peninsula in September. I took a quick step to avoid the spray swinging toward the sidewalk, and my binder slipped from my hand. As I bent down to pick up my World History homework I was nearly leveled by a thought. *Where is she?* And suddenly I had trouble breathing. I sat on the strip of lawn dividing the street from the sidewalk for probably half an hour as the sprinkler clicked like a toy train.

Later that night I found Jamie on the roof. The cherry of his cigarette glowed. In the darkness it seemed as far away as the blinking light on a jet's wing. I heard his tennis shoes scrape across the gravel and felt a twitch of breeze.

"Okay, tell me," I said. "What about Richard, what do you think?"

"I don't really understand what you mean," Jamie said. "He's dead, I guess I know that."

The shadow thrown by the side of the house blacked out his face. There was no slyness in his voice.

"That's it?" I asked.

"What's wrong?"

"I thought that you had some idea," I said. "Why the hell have you wanted to talk to me if you don't have an idea? What else is there to talk about?" My voice cracked, and I could say no more. I heard Jamie stand up.

Two hemlocks grew from the ground below to eye level. Jamie reached out and grabbed a handful of flat needles, grinding them between his finger and thumb. He sat back down beside me.

"I love how these smell." He offered me the pulp of needles. My nose was running. I hoped it was too dark to see my face. He flicked away the hemlock and lit two cigarettes, handing one to me.

"We're not on a date," I said.

"You don't have anyone else to talk to," he said.

Jamie North. I wasn't impressed by his intelligence, though it was apparent. I wasn't impressed by his pretensions either, but I was jealous of him. When *his* father took us out to play baseball I chewed sunflower seeds and hit line drives. I had to. But Jamie could just wander off into the bleachers, listening for echoes. His problem was he couldn't see that the rest of us weren't so lucky.

Jamie's first crush was a girl named Andrea who moved to

Loyalty Island the summer before sixth grade. At twelve she was already beautiful, in the way a woman is beautiful, not a girl. She would have been everybody's crush, except for one thing. Her right leg was longer than her left by a couple of inches. She did her best to hide it with skirts that dragged on the floor, but once you saw the slight unsteadiness of her walk, the thick sole of her left shoe, it was impossible to unsee.

In Loyalty Island we were used to four-fingered hands and paraplegics, but, for most of us, Andrea's imperfection was suspicious because it made so little sense. Jamie wasn't like most of us. He followed her everywhere. They ate lunch together, alone on the stage in the gymnasium. They dissected the same frog in Biology and wrote a one-act play about Neanderthals that ended with Andrea knocking Jamie unconscious and dragging him back to her cave. On Halloween they both went as vampires, and Jamie got to dab fake blood on her lips before the school carnival. "I could have kissed her," he told me later, "I'm pretty sure I could have kissed her."

Then that January, a kid in our class named Kinjo called Andrea "Odds" during Geography. Kinjo was a bully, and we all knew that an insult from him was as good as a compliment. Still, in the middle of class, Jamie leaped to his feet. He yelled, not just at Kinjo, but at all of us, saying we were stupid to judge her. Andrea is different, he said, is that such a problem? He spoke as if he'd written the speech out in his mind; he probably had. Our teacher, Mrs. Waltz, stood at the head of the room, beaming.

But Andrea's features shriveled; her mouth wired shut. If Jamie had just paused to look at her he would have seen the tears under her quivering eyelids, her chin smashed into her shoulder. But he kept on until finally Andrea whispered, "Shut up, Jamie." Then louder, "Just shut up, please shut up, please, please shut up. Shut up. Shut up."

The next day Jamie ate alone in the cafeteria and dropped his eyes when Andrea walked past. He seemed to accept that she wouldn't forgive him, but he clearly didn't understand what he'd done wrong, that his defense had humiliated her more than Kinjo's insult ever could. At the time, I was sure that he would never understand. I certainly never would have guessed that, two years later, Jamie would feel like the only person in the world I could talk to, the only person I could trust.

We sat on the roof's edge, legs dangling into darkness. I could smell the hemlock on my fingers, a smell that reminded me of winter. Wind told the branches to tremble.

"I'd ask you about what's happening with your folks," Jamie said, "but you don't want to talk about it. If you did, though."

"If I did," I said, "sure."

"I'm not messing with you," he said. "You were right. The other night I was going to say I thought our dads might have something to do with what happened."

"But now you don't?"

"Now I think we both just grew up hearing a lot of stories."

We crawled back through the window and into bed without turning on the light. Jamie was right. Even as I had crept through the hallway on Seachase or listened at the crack beneath my door,

I'd been thinking about Jim Hawkins in *Treasure Island*—trying to live out a story that was no more real than any Robert Louis Stevenson wrote. I felt relieved, but also oddly disappointed. And I realized this disappointment at the thought that my father was not a murderer was all the proof I needed. I'd nearly fallen asleep when Jamie spoke again.

"One thing, though," he said. "Do you remember who my mother said told her about Richard?"

"Don Brooke," I said.

"Yeah. Why isn't he on a boat in Alaska right now?"

MY BICYCLE TIRES CHURNED UP gravel at the foot of the driveway. I'd been back to the house on Seachase only once before, swiping my bike from the garage, pedaling away and puffing quick breaths across the handlebars. This was in the first week after Richard died, when my father's shadow swayed above me every time I'd stepped into the sun. "You won't need to come back," he'd said. But now almost a month had passed, and my father's words no longer held the same power. Still, I leaned my bike on a bench in Henderson Park and wove through the woods to the backyard.

I rummaged under the gas grill for the key, and let myself in by the back door, quickly and quietly. My father wouldn't be home for months, but I expected to hear his boots at the door any moment. His tiki chair was behind the house, the cushions spongy with rain, the wood white with mold.

I'd spent every night of the last two weeks on Jamie's roof, smoking his cigarettes and talking about the girls we knew who were developing breasts, and the guys we knew who were lying about getting hand jobs, and the places in the world we someday hoped to see. We argued about *Star Wars*, and I listened to Jamie describe the samurai movies on the posters he'd sent away for, *Harakiri*, *The Sword of Doom*, *Yojimbo*; and the movies he'd read about in magazines, *Strangers on a Train*, *Night and the City*, *The Third Man*.

"Have you actually seen any of those movies?" I asked.

"Where would I have seen them?" he asked, impatiently. He explained that it didn't matter, and maybe it didn't.

Years later, when I finally saw *The Third Man* at a student theater in Ann Arbor, Michigan, all I could think of was sitting on the roof with Jamie, talking about what a fuckhead Kinjo was, how if he died tomorrow no one would care. Sitting in the darkness, so many miles and years away from Loyalty Island, I wondered if Jamie ever got around to seeing *The Third Man*. And I felt incredibly sad because I knew that if I called to ask him he wouldn't even recognize my voice.

One of the films that Jamie brought up time and time again that fall was Kurosawa's *Throne of Blood*. I knew it was sitting in a cardboard box next to our VCR, along with about twenty other Japanese movies whose names I couldn't pronounce. I'd been a jerk since I'd arrived at the Norths'—in fact, being a jerk had been my intention. Now I hoped to make it right by taking the VCR and all of the tapes I could carry back to Jamie. I figured my mother owed me that much.

Inside, I took off my shoes automatically. I expected the sullen odor of trapped air, of basement boxes and yellowed packing tape. Returning home after a week or more away, I'd always noticed the smell first. Is this the way my life smells, I'd think, or is this the smell of my life's absence? Now the house smelled rainy, as if the windows had been left open. But the windows were closed, and the carpet had a soft, lonely bounce. The kitchen cabinets were closed, the books shelved. Still, instinctively, I looked for signs of life. Was a sponge stuck in the drain of the kitchen sink when I left? Was there a coffee ring on the Formica table? A black smudge on the phone number taped next to the telephone?

When I was still too young to know better, I'd told my father that I missed him when he was away. He'd picked me up and put me on his lap. "You know," he said, "if you ever need to reach me, it's possible. It's not easy, but it's possible." He tore a strip from an envelope and wrote out the number of the Pacific Cannery in Dutch Harbor. "They can get me on the radio," he said. "It might take a while but I'll get to you." We pasted it next to the phone in the kitchen, and, even as the tape yellowed and the blue ink faded, the number remained as a reminder that gone didn't mean gone, it just meant somewhere else.

But as I surveyed these empty rooms, it occurred to me that the people who would return to Loyalty Island in weeks or months wouldn't be the same people who had left in early September. The man who'd sat at the nook in the kitchen drinking coffee was gone. The woman who'd stood at the stove dropping noodles into boiling water, fanning away the steam, was gone.

I stuck *Throne of Blood* and as many other movies as I could fit into my backpack. I wrestled with the wires of the VCR, trying not to forget what plugged into what. I crawled behind the TV stand to get a better look and, there, I froze. I crouched, still, for a full minute, trying to keep my breath down, waiting for the illusion to pass.

But it was no illusion. I heard music. I crawled to the vent. The metal was warm against my ear. The heat was on, rumbling under the soft chords of Duke Ellington's "Lotus Blossom," a song I'd heard my mother play a thousand times.

CHAPTER 5

GRAY CLOUDS FLOATED AND BUNCHED IN THE sky, shaking off rain like dogs. The days grew faint as they shortened. The bay turned a dim green, and no matter how long I looked, it stared back with the same bored expression. Was it winter already? I couldn't say.

I'd been stealing time at the house on Seachase most afternoons. I slipped away after school, snuck out of the Norths' when Jamie was staring at the TV and Betty was lost in a crossword puzzle. I returned, blowing on my hands, rubbing my calves as though I'd been out biking.

It wasn't that I didn't expect Jamie to understand. I didn't want to have to explain what I was doing because I couldn't explain it. Those afternoons alone in my parents' house felt foggy and mysterious, exactly what I needed.

Anyway, Jamie had his new VCR and an armload of grainy, subtitled videos to keep him busy. "Do you have any idea how hard it is to find some of these?" he said as he rooted through my backpack.

"Don't jerk off to them while I'm around," I said.

"Seriously, thank you." His face hid nothing, ever. I would have felt proud, had I been able to think about anything other than home.

The first afternoon I'd run from the house after only a few bars of "Lotus Blossom." That night I lay in bed hearing fingers settling into minor piano chords. I returned the next day, still half expecting to find I'd invented everything. But I heard music as soon as I stepped into the living room. Synthesizer runs from Brian Eno's *Another Green World* crept through the heating vent like vines. After Eno, she played *Saxophone Colossus* and, after that, an R&B record I didn't recognize, then Robert Johnson. I could hear—I thought I could hear—the needle prickling as she replayed "Kind Hearted Woman."

I didn't understand what was happening, but, at first anyway, I barely cared. It was enough to feel the floor rumble as the furnace kicked on, to feel the heat drying the cuffs of my jeans. I could have gone down to the basement, could have knocked on the door, but I feared that if I upset the dream it would dissolve before me, or I before it.

It didn't occur to me that my mother would hear the ceiling creaking above her, the back door closing, the sink running. I couldn't allow myself these sensible concerns. Her departure made so little sense, and her presence now, though mysterious, felt strangely familiar, strangely comfortable.

I searched the house for evidence. The refrigerator was bare except for a crusted bottle of French's mustard and half a jar of olives. The blue-and-orange-checked quilt on my parents' bed was neatly turned down. I tore a corner of paper from my notebook and left it at the foot. It was still there the next day, untouched, the only sign I ever left of my own presence. I walked the neighborhood, looking for the Chevette. I checked the grime in the rims of the toilet bowls. I scrutinized damp impressions in the living room carpet, forgetting my own footprints.

But it was all for show. I didn't call Meg's number, which was scribbled on a scrap of paper stuck beneath the number of the Pacific Cannery. I didn't go down to the basement, didn't approach the mint-green door of the studio, because I felt better with my shoulder to the wall in the living room, listening at the vent, than I had since John Gaunt had died.

I let myself pretend that the records she played were coded signals, and I was surprised by how much I understood. Though I didn't recognize every record, I recognized enough. I'd never realized how much of her music had stuck with me over those winter months she and I had spent alone in the house. One afternoon she played Bud Powell's *The Invisible Cage*. I remembered the day she'd bought it at a store in Pioneer Square. "I've been looking for this one," she'd said. "Bud was already half dead, but still . . ." Another day she played a record called *Firebirds* by a saxophonist named Prince Lasha that she'd had since I was a little kid. I remembered looking at the sleeve and asking if he was really a prince. She'd smiled and pretended to read the liner notes. "I'm not sure," she said. "It doesn't say here." Another day she played Neil Young's *After the Gold Rush*, and I remembered her teaching me the words to "Tell Me Why" as we made dinner. I'd find myself trying to guess what record would come next.

I thought of my mother in the blue flannel robe she'd worn when I was a child with the gold lion's head on the lapel. I thought of her pacing the narrow room, sidestepping slipcovers. I thought of her arm stuck elbow deep in a yellow box of cereal, her hand cupped under the tap of the double-basin sink. I thought of her lying on the bench seat, her feet pressed to the wall. I thought of her eyelids fluttering, startled by a knock on the basement door. "Cal?" she said. "Just a little time. There's nothing to worry about. Just a little more time."

All I had to do was knock.

At school I'd sit at my desk feeling the mint-green wood against my knuckles, hearing the hollow *tap-tap-tap*. Day after day—the Zombies' "Tell Her No" on repeat, Erik Satie, *Spirits Rejoice*, more Robert Johnson, *Brilliant Corners*—I couldn't do it.

The next week I woke up in the middle of the night choking down a scream. I crawled off the bunk bed and out the window. The sky was clear enough to see a thousand stars, and still it rained. Wet gravel stuck to my feet. In my dream the door had been opened by my mother, her spectral green eyes sunk in, walking on her toes with the herky-jerky motion of time-lapse photography, smelling of worms and grass.

"Haven't you gotten my messages?" she asked.

I saw myself nodding.

"What do they say?"

"You've been murdered," I said.

She leaped through the ceiling, her hair flying above her, and I ran up the steps in time to see her pass through the living room, into the attic, and out into the sky.

THOUGH I BARELY NOTICED, the tides continued to spit drift-wood onto the stones of Black's Beach, and new issues of *The Loyalty Ledger* piled unread in orange cellophane on porches, and time continued to pass. By the first week of October reports were coming back from Alaska.

My father always said you could tell what kind of season you'd have before the first pot surfaced. If the hydraulic block whined and creaked you knew you'd just made serious money. As a matter of tradition, he would stop work on deck at that moment and let his crew line the rail, waiting to cheer or curse.

That year, apparently, the block whined, creaked, shuddered, and coughed. There wasn't even energy to waste on celebration. They plugged their 200,000-pound hold in days. And not just on the *Laurentide*, but on the *Cordilleran*, and on nearly every other boat in the Bering fleet.

Every captain brags that he's learned to think like the crab, but the crab usually prove him wrong. That year the crab decided to boycott Kodiak Bay en masse. The fishermen there clanged empty pots onto the rails, cussing one another, their captains, and their kids. But, in the Bering Sea, where the Loyalty boats fished, the kings seemed to swell from the ocean floor, crab like no one had ever seen.

The disparity had left the processors in Kodiak chain-smoking and chewing toothpicks. This was the beautiful part. The same motherfuckers who in years past had kept boats waiting all night to unload while the catch died in the live wells, who'd shrugged their shoulders and spit when you complained about the money they'd just cost you, were on their knees. They were putting in calls to the Bering fleet, begging them to bring their catch to Kodiak, offering more per pound than they ever had before.

My father phoned one night from one of these Kodiak processors, speaking in the rapturous, exhausted voice of Alaska. There was a blizzard of static every time he paused for breath. As soon as I picked up the phone we began the old routine.

"How's the quality?" I asked, as if I were standing in the kitchen on Seachase, as if I were buying time before I had to hand the phone back to my mother.

"Unbelievable. Really un-fucking-real. Almost no old-molts or nothing like that."

"And the weather hasn't been too bad?"

"No, it's been miserable, but when the fishing is like this you feel like you're made of steel. I feel like the Green Lantern, or what's his name?"

"Superman," I said.

"Superman," he said. "Of course. Superman! What did I say? I need to catch a few hours."

"You should," I said, then broke the routine. "I heard about Richard." Static hissed back for a few beats.

"Everybody has, I imagine," my father said.

How many miles of wire had those words just traveled, only to tell me nothing? I let the white noise answer, hoping he'd say more.

"Yeah, it's a tragedy. But it happens. You've always known that. So did he."

"That's it?" I asked.

"No, that isn't it. It's been a disaster. Insurance companies, about ten different lawyers. So many questions to answer. It's lucky for us that Don decided to stay home this year with his hip. He's mostly been dealing with all of it, poor guy. Lawyers really scare him. Anyway, the whole thing's terrible, but, you know, we don't talk about it, right? There's lots of good news to talk about. I've never seen anything like these crab. They must be making some kind of love down there. Really. I wish you could see it like this. Someday you'll have to."

"All right," I said. "I'd like to."

If I needed money for anything, he said, just ask Betty, and he would square it later. How was school? He told me to think about where we should go for vacation next year, to think big. I let him hang up a minute later without mentioning my mother.

MY MOTHER USED TO SAY that finding a superstitious fisherman is as easy as finding an unreliable musician. Everyone in Loyalty Island was a fisherman, if not by profession, then by temperament, and it was becoming apparent, as the good news spread, that there would be life after the Gaunts. Was it purely coincidence that the best fishing in years had come just after they'd died out? Was it possible that instead of pushing us forward all these years they had really been holding us back?

For a few days my nightmares kept me from the house. I killed some afternoons with Jamie at the movies, at the library. We smoked dried banana peels in coffee filters, and bought Mini-Thins at Safeway. We took dizzy strolls on the boardwalk in the rain. One afternoon Jamie and I passed two older women sitting on the bench next to the Fisherman's Memorial, the same bench where I'd seen Richard the summer before. They wore raincoats over floral dresses, and rubber boots. The older one held the leash of a tugging white dog. She turned to her friend and said, "And just to think what that bastard would have cost us."

A few days later, as Jamie and I waited for the lights to go down at the Orpheum, I heard voices behind me, a son, younger than me, and a father, older than mine. "Did you hear the last thing Richard said to John before he died?" the kid asked. "Don't worry, Dad, I won't forget to feed the fish." The father shushed him, but chuckled through the previews. A few more seasons like this one, and I wondered if the Gaunts would even rate a punch line. Tragedy ages into comedy and dies when the jokes are no longer funny.

WHEN I RETURNED to the house I could hear Bob Dylan singing, "They say I shot a man named Gray," from the kitchen. And I heard something else. In the living room the floor trembled on the backbeat. Someone was pounding on the wall or the ceiling. *Thwack thwack.* I listened. "Idiot Wind" bled into "You're Gonna Make Me Lonesome When You Go." *Thwack thwack,* just behind the beat. Hot air coughed from the vents. The heat was way up, I realized.

I stripped down to my T-shirt, but didn't dare open a window. The walls seemed to shimmer, the floor to slope. The pounding continued. *Thwack thwack thwack*, disregarding the song now, rolling as though from a snare or an automatic weapon. The music and heat seemed to merge into one tangible thing that I climbed like rungs of a ladder. A layer of hot dust danced with every *thwack thwack*. I'd seen the sand bounce from the tympani at the Seattle Symphony that way, when I'd gone years before with my mother.

My mother. The music. The heat. Sound spewed from the vent like St. Helens ash. The house became an opium den, a fluking whale, a downpour over church domes, an air raid. *Thwack thwack.* Outside it was already dark, and rain tore the glow from the streetlights. *Thwack thwack.* It felt as though the house were an aquarium in reverse, as though it could rise like the balloon that landed Raleigh Gaunt on Loyalty Island's black shore.

THE NEXT DAY I had to press my ear to the cold vent to hear Patsy Cline. I felt almost jilted and left quickly, so quickly that I almost missed the spoon. It lay in the sink, a pool of water in its bowl. I didn't dare touch the blue plastic handle teetering on the edge of the drain. There was a faint white rind on the rim, a flake of rust on the chrome trim. I catalogued each detail as evidence. I knew that, as I lay in bed that night, I'd need these details to remind myself that I hadn't made it up.

A DAY LATER I fell asleep on Jamie's couch as we watched *The Hidden Fortress*. He shook me awake and handed me the telephone, stretched on its cord from the kitchen. "Cal?" the voice said.

I could almost hear the music in the background. I found myself listening for it instead of to her.

"Cal, can you hear me?"

"I'm here," I said. "Don't hang up."

"I wouldn't," my mother said.

I put my hand over the receiver and raised my eyebrows at Jamie just as I'd seen my father do when an important call came in and he needed privacy. But I nearly called Jamie back into the room when he left. His voice was more familiar now than the one on the other end of the line.

"Are you there?" my mother asked.

"I'm here."

"It's good to hear your voice," she said.

"I guess," I said.

"Do you know what I saw today?" she asked.

"No."

"There was a man playing the violin part from *Quartet for the End of Time* outside the bookstore on Pacific. Do you remember when we danced to that album? Do you remember that?"

"Where?" I asked.

"We danced in the kitchen," she said.

"Where did you see the man?"

"On Pacific," she said. "Near the bookstore and the diner we go to."

The next question trembled in my mouth. I couldn't make my lips move. "This phone," my mother said. "Cal, can you still hear me?"

"Where are you?" I asked.

"Where? Santa Cruz."

"You've been there all this time?"

She didn't answer for a moment. In the silence I heard her teeth click together. I tried to imagine her lying on a deck chair on Meg's front porch, a tarp of sunlight at her feet. Meg's bushy black hair whispering against the doorjamb as she brought my mother something to eat.

"I asked you to come," she said.

I slid from the couch to the Norths' living room floor. The phone cord stretched like a tightrope. There was a brushed-glass shade on the ceiling fixture in the shape of a nautilus. My eyes unfocused and the shell tripled.

"Just a second, Cal. Hold on."

I heard the static of her hand on the phone, heard her say, "I'm going upstairs. No. No. I'll be fine. They're just stairs."

I couldn't help but see her opening the basement door, emerging into the kitchen on Seachase. She was out of breath.

"Right now, I feel like the world isn't caving in anymore," she said. "That's a really good thing. Can you understand that?"

"No," I said.

"You'll have a baby sister soon," she said. "She's due in two weeks, but it could be any day."

"Why haven't you called?"

"I did call." She paused. "I'm sorry. How do I answer that?" She paused again. "I was ashamed about what you heard me say that night to your father. And I was ashamed about what you said to me, and ashamed that when I called before, you hung up. You might not believe any of that, or that it could stop me from calling you. Because I'm your mother you think too highly of me."

"I wouldn't say that," I said.

"Okay. No, you wouldn't. I'm sorry. I wasn't thinking right. I still might not be."

"When are you coming back?" I asked.

"Would it be too much to ask how you've been doing?"

"Are you coming back?"

"You know you can still come down here."

"Are you coming back?"

"I don't know. Not until the baby is born. After that, I'll see."

"What will you see?"

"Well, Meg's offered to help me with her after she's born. I think it would be too hard alone. And for once your father and I agree on something."

"Fine," I said. "Everything's fine here. Have you heard about the season?"

"I haven't spoken to anyone other than you."

"They're making money hand over fist up there. The season of a lifetime, supposedly."

"Everybody must be happy," she said.

"Obviously. That's sort of the point of going up there. To make money."

"So everyone is happy."

"Everyone, except Richard."

"What about him?"

It hadn't occurred to me that she wouldn't know he was dead, but as I realized she didn't, I felt my hands tingling. There is a rush of power in being the first to break bad news. I wanted to level her with it.

It was a bright, cloudless day, I said. Unusually calm. One minute he was smoking a cigarette in the stern, admiring the sun, the next, he was gone. No one heard a splash. I'd invented the details, of course. "Are you still there?" I asked.

"Are you sure?" Her voice sounded as though it had dropped into a ravine. "Are you sure?"

"Everybody knows," I said.

"Okay," she said, after a long space of dead air. "Okay, just let me call you back in a few minutes, all right? Let me just call you back."

We didn't speak again for three months.

LATER THAT NIGHT I sat at Jamie's desk, a stack of his paperbacks spilled across it. The books were old, third- or fourthhand. They smelled sweet, and the pages crackled as I flipped them. *The Stranger*, *The Trial*, *No Exit*, names suited, I thought, to horror novels. I didn't really expect them to help, but I'd reached a dead end and I was still young enough to believe that the important questions had been answered somewhere. It was the illusion, I guess, of a solvable life.

I'd returned to the house late that afternoon and pressed my ear to the vent. Nothing. I thought the question I was asking now was pretty reasonable. When you find nothing where *something* is supposed to be, what do you do? Of course I couldn't follow a word of what I read.

The door swung open, and I swept the books to the floor, jabbing the pile under the desk with my foot. Jamie raised both eyebrows as if there were an audience to play to. "Should I give you and Camus a few minutes?"

"Who?"

"Ca-*moo*, he wrote the book you're grinding under your foot, right?"

A couple of weeks before, I would have ripped the paperback in two (and I could have, the spine was brittle yellow). Instead, I returned the books to the shelf, just as I'd found them. "If you can answer a question," I said, "I'd appreciate it."

"Yeah?" He scanned the shelf and shuffled the books, but when he turned back to me he still hadn't managed to hide his smile. "Let's go outside."

The night was freezing, but Jamie was right. It had come to seem fitting to talk about the big stuff on the roof. He threw me an extra jacket, a peacoat big enough to be his father's, and we crawled through the window, two experts now. Stamping my feet to keep warm, smoking furiously, I explained my crisis under a bleary moon.

"I was looking for something," I said. "It turns out there wasn't anything there."

Jamie paced the roof. In the oily glow from his bedroom window, I could see him tugging his earlobes as if trying to pull a thought into place. "It would help if you could tell me what you were looking for."

"I can't."

"This thing, is it real, is it physical?"

"It's supposed to be."

"Okay," he said, "because I think they were talking about spiritual nothingness, like living in a world without God. Is that your problem?"

"Not really," I said.

Jamie examined me with clinical eyes. "Then I'm sorry, but I don't think Camus can help."

I turned back toward the window, but Jamie cut me off. "On the other hand," he said, "there was a lot I didn't understand in there.

I probably need to read everything again. But let me take a look, maybe something will click, you know?"

The screen door below us creaked and banged shut. Before I realized what was happening Jamie was on his belly, forcing me down by the sleeve. I had to pull my face back when my nose scraped tar and I felt gravel divot my cheek.

Betty North streamed across the patio in an icy-blue nightgown. She rattled the metal legs of a patio chair and sat down at the table in moonlight that seemed to lend her body a blurry double. I assumed she'd come to scold us inside, but she only sat, staring into the trees. We were frozen with her, pasted to the roof.

"What's she doing?" I whispered.

"Shut up," Jamie spat. Her arms were crossed and her back was straight, but she shivered in the cold. I couldn't tell if her eyes were open or closed. Her nightgown rippled vaguely in the wind. She looked like a fountain at the moment the pressure is cut.

Slowly she seemed to relax. She leaned down onto the patio table, making a pillow of her crossed arms the way I did when I slept on my desk at school. She lay that way for another ten minutes, narrow back pulsing with breath, while my chin dug into the roof.

Once the back door banged shut again I followed Jamie through the window. He turned the light off and climbed into bed.

"What was she doing?" I asked. "Jamie?"

"Did you know," he said after a minute, "that back in the whaling days, nearly every woman in Nantucket was addicted to opium?"

"So she just shot up or something?" I said. Immediately I regretted it. If Jamie had said that about my mother I would have killed him. I climbed into bed, trying to erase my words with rustling sheets.

"Sorry," I said.

"My point is, don't get all judgmental about it. She goes out there sometimes. Not as much as she used to."

"We can pretend it didn't happen," I said.

His flashlight clicked on below me. The beam played across the ceiling and slashed down the wall.

"Be quiet." He sighed. "One night, last year sometime, I figured out how easy it would be to get out onto the roof. I was lying in bed, and it dawned on me, you know, just step on the dresser, lift the screen."

"I know."

"So I did. And one night I saw her come out. I didn't say anything the first time because I didn't want her to know I was on the roof. But she kept coming, not every night. A few times a week, though, she'd go out there and just sit, in the rain, in the cold."

"What did you think she was doing?"

"Will you just listen?" he said. "She went to bed around nine-thirty. I stayed out on the roof for a few whole nights, waiting. She never came out past eleven."

The flashlight floated across the wall like the slow beam of a lighthouse. In the spaces between the words I could hear rain on the window, whipped by wind, heavy and cold. Almost sleet.

"She had this sort of ritual when my dad wasn't around," Jamie said. "Good night to me, then check the locks on both doors. If the door wasn't already locked, she'd lock it. If it was, she'd unlock it first and lock it again. After that, she did a crossword puzzle at the kitchen table. Unlocked and relocked the doors and went to bed. So I picked a night, and when I heard her locking the doors I hid in the bedroom closet."

The flashlight darted across the wall opposite the bunk, crossed back, looped two circles. A bright spot, a dancing keyhole. I laughed. Not into the pillow, which would have been just as easy, but into the dark where I knew Jamie lay below. "Shut up," I said. "You didn't hide in the closet. Why didn't you just ask her?" The beam slashed the wall again, hovering on the spines of books I now knew he'd never read. Surprisingly, he laughed too.

"I don't know. I just did what I did."

"Jamie, kill the flashlight," I said, and the spot on the wall vanished.

"So I was on my dad's side of the closet, sort of crouched by a pair of his old boots and sandwiched between an overcoat and a suit I'd never seen him wear."

Outside, the sleet had turned to snow. That was the difference between rainstorms and snowstorms. You could hear the rain from miles away, see the gray billows, hear the grunts of thunder. But snow came in a hush. Suddenly it was just there.

"The light was out when she came in, and she didn't turn it on, just got into bed so I couldn't see anything, but I could hear the blankets and all that. I'd planned to wait until eleven and leave if nothing happened, because, as I said, it wasn't every night. But I didn't have any light, so I couldn't read my watch. I'd think hours had passed, and then I'd decide it had only been seconds."

He stopped, expecting me to say something, I'm sure. Only, I didn't have anything to say. I'd begun to think of my own mother, and I was trying not to. I wondered how long the snow had been falling, if it was sticking, if there was a layer on the sidewalks yet.

"It was one of those times when you lose all sense of where your body is, you know? Like, you still know that your arm is connected to your shoulder like normal, but it doesn't feel that way. It feels like there's you and there's this nothingness and your body is somewhere on the other side of that. Then someone was screaming. It wasn't really that loud, but I could feel all the breath behind it. I sort of fell into the bedroom, and there was just enough moonlight to see. She was in bed still, but sitting up. Her back was straight like she'd just been electrocuted. She had one of those eye masks on, and she was screaming into her hands.

"And she just kept screaming in bursts, like she would scream all the air out and then she had to catch her breath, but as soon as she did, she'd start to scream again. I tripped over a corner of the bed, and she still had the eye mask on, but she must have felt someone was there because she flew out of bed, dragging the comforter, still screaming into her hands. But when she got to the bedroom door she just stopped. She opened the door slowly and sort of tiptoed into the hall. I heard her on the stairs, and I heard her at the front door, but just barely."

He flipped the flashlight back on, dragging the beam across the bookshelf. I didn't want to speak, or prod him. But minutes passed, the flashlight beam trailing loops across the ceiling, and still Jamie said nothing.

"Jamie?"

"I never spoke to her about it," he said.

"Why not?"

"I didn't just forget about it. After that, I went to the library, read about it. I think she has night terrors. She sort of sleepwalks, I think, out to the patio, quietly, so no one will know. Or so I won't."

"But don't you want to know for sure?"

"No. I wish that I could just forget it."

"So forget it."

"If I could I wouldn't want to, you know?"

"This is bullshit." I was suddenly furious. "You're making this all up. How could you not ask?"

"I'm not," he said, and I knew it was the truth. "Anyway, it happens less and less. Tonight was the first time in forever, so hopefully . . ."

"I hear all of my mother's records coming from the basement of my house," I said. "I was sure it was my mother. But I guess she really is in Santa Cruz, so I don't know what's happening. If I'm going crazy or believing in ghosts or I don't know."

Jamie clicked the flashlight off and on. A pattern of dots and dashes flashed over the room.

"Is that Morse code? Did you hear what I said?"

He clicked off the flashlight for the final time. "It's not Morse code. Daj always promises to teach me, but he hasn't yet. That *is* strange."

143

"That's it? 'Strange'?"

"Don't go back to the house."

"Are you serious?"

"I'm serious."

I couldn't have been more disappointed. I thought I'd told Jamie because of the story he'd shared with me, because he'd finally convinced me someone else might understand. I'd reached my own limits. A year later or a year before I might have been able to go further, to knock on the studio door, but not there, not then, not alone.

"Why?" I asked. "Why are you saying that?"

"It's snowing a little, right?" Jamie went to the window, though I was sure he'd noticed the snow before. His back was a silhouette against the blue glass. White sleet seemed to pour down on his shoulders. "I'm saying it," he said after a minute, "because if you go back I'll have to tell my father when he calls next time. I mean, he asked me to tell him if I saw you go back home."

I sat up in bed and jumped to the floor.

"What's happening?" I asked. "Is it my mother? Is she really there?"

"I don't know," Jamie said.

"Have you told him already?" I asked. "You knew I went back for the VCR."

The snow was falling fatter and slower, less like ice. It felt almost as if the window had disappeared and the two of us were standing in the blizzard. I wished we *were* out there, with snowballs and sleds, those winter things that pass through a Loyalty Island childhood as infrequently as comets.

"I haven't said anything. He just mentioned it, you know. He just said to tell him, but I thought that the VCR was no big deal. But this now, I mean, it just seems like I would need to tell him. Unless you promise not to go back. Will you?"

The window was icing up, trapping moonlight in strips along the sill. I thought I heard Betty's bedroom door open and close. Then wind crashed against the house, spitting frost, shaking windows.

"Probably no school tomorrow," I said. "I'm going to sleep, anyway."

"It's a lot to figure out," Jamie said.

"I know," I said.

"I can't call him, you know," Jamie said. "He'll have to call here."

"I know."

"He could call tomorrow, but it could be weeks. How long do you think you'll need?"

"One more day," I said.

THE NEXT MORNING snow powdered the sidewalks, and ice clung like a rind to the curbs. School was canceled. By the time I awoke the sun was out, the eaves dripped steadily, and Jamie was gone. I'd slept badly, dreaming about my mother.

I knew every step of the way from Jamie's house, but the streets were disguised by snow, and I found myself checking signs. The sun was deceptive, the air vividly cold. My footsteps crunched beneath me. Inside the house, the kitchen sink gleamed pale silver in window light. The spoon was gone, but not the blond wood door and the gold knob that opened it.

I walked the same route to my mother that John Gaunt must have, through the living room and kitchen, past the blond basement door, down the stairs, past the rusting furnace, through shafts of light from dirty windows, and through the basement itself, now crowded with the debris of a family and a childhood. I walked over boxes marked "Christmas Ornaments," and old pots and a blender, and coiled seines and pink buoys, to the mint-green studio door. My skin prickled. I stepped quietly. The studio door was closed, but "Kind Hearted Woman" seeped through the crack beneath it.

I had a plan. I'd knock on the door, loudly, confidently, and if no one answered after exactly ten seconds, I'd push it open. I was a step away before I noticed that my mother's silver padlock was still on the door.

I heard the knock in my head. I felt my arm glide through the wood, felt myself stumble through after it, into deep space, or a bleached road in the South, or a burned-out factory in the Midwest.

But I couldn't move my arm. I just couldn't. I was afraid, it was as simple as that. I put my fist back in my pocket and retreated. At the top of the stairs, I flipped off the light. Then I lay down on the couch in the living room. I'd never been more disappointed in myself, more disappointed in anything. The Robert Johnson record streamed from the vent, then cut out. The needle tore static, and the song began again.

The living room couch was older than I was. My mother had hinted a number of times that she found it ugly and uncomfortable, but my father refused to give it up. Now, because I didn't know what to do with them, I dug my hands under the cushions and felt years of grime under my nails.

I remembered my mother finding me in the living room when I was very young, threatening to make a sandwich out of me. The cushions were the bread, and she piled on newspapers and magazines, slices of pickle, tomato, and onion. As I squirmed between the cushions, she pretended to take a massive bite, chewing with effort, before wrinkling her nose. "Still too sweet," she said.

I gathered up the cushions. I had to hold them to my chest with both arms to get through the door. Outside, I wiped snow from the porch railing and beat the cushions against it. The railing rattled and the cushions puffed dust over the snow-caked driveway. Afterward they didn't look much better. When I went back inside, the record had changed. The song was still "Kind Hearted Woman," but a different version, this one featuring a broken harmony.

But the other voice. It started and stopped, faded in and out, stumbled over some words, rang out on others. "Now, it ain't but one thing that make Mr. Johnson drink," the voice sang, on the bridge, off-key, but bright and steely and rich.

And then there was another voice, my own. "Hello?" it said. "Hello" down into the grate. "Hello."

The record died. Silence. I felt the blood thick in my throat; my face was tingling and heavy. "Hello," I said again.

"Who's there?" The voice was hesitant, raw.

"Richard?" I called.

"Who's there?" Richard asked.

CHAPTER 6

I N A STATIC OF WINDOW LIGHT AND DUST I PRESSED
my ear to the studio door.

"It's you, isn't it, Cal?"

I should have taken some time to make a plan, but I'd torn
through the kitchen and down the stairs, slamming the basement
door behind me as if for emphasis. After so many weeks, after so
many hours spent thinking about this moment while I sat in school
or stepped through puddles in the streets, I'd arrived and didn't have
a clue what to do or say.

"Are you dead?" I asked.

"It doesn't feel like it," Richard said.

"What are you?" I asked.

"The other option. Look, what's the point? What are you doing?"

This was a hard question to answer.

"I heard the music," I said.

"So?"

"I heard the music."

"Are you *complaining*?" he asked.

"What?"

"What? What? I've been fucked with enough, right? What do you need? What're you doing here?"

I knew it was the wrong answer, or not an answer at all. I knew it would be better to say nothing than to say again, "I heard the music."

Richard banged the door, and my breath vanished. My eyes were stinging. I jumped back into a shaft of sunlight.

"Stop saying that," he yelled, but then his voice thinned. "Wait a minute. Wait a minute. Tell them I said I'd turn it down. I mean they don't have to take the record player or anything."

"Tell who? Who would I tell?"

"What?"

"Who would I tell?"

"Wait, just wait," he said. "Do me a favor and let me just think."

"Richard," I said.

"Let me think."

So I did. I sat down on the corner of a cardboard box labeled "Halloween Stings" in green marker. I knew we'd decorated the house once on Halloween, but I could hardly remember it. I was very young, three or four probably, but I did remember standing over this very box, my arms tangled in cottony spiderwebs. "I've got the Halloween stings," I'd said. "Things," my mother had said, laughing.

"How did you know I was here?" Richard asked.

"I heard the music," I said.

"Shut up about the fucking music."

"So, that's it," I said.

"You didn't know? Nobody told you?"

"Like who?"

"Fuck. Fuck," he said. "Open the door, then, Cal. Open the door. Obviously they wouldn't tell you. Cal, open the door."

But I was paralyzed. I imagined my father, back home from Alaska, sitting at the kitchen table, nicks on his chin from the last pass of a dull winter razor. "Cal, why the hell didn't you let him out?" he said. "That's how you treat someone? That's what your instinct tells you?" Or, "Cal, how could you let him out? Did you understand what you were doing at all?"

"Cal?" Richard said. "Cal, Cal, Cal?"

"The padlock," I said.

"What about it? Open the door."

"There's no key." This was true, though the padlock wasn't large; bolt cutters could've sheared it. I could hear the relief in my voice.

Richard smacked the door again, not quite as hard this time, as if he were kissing it good-bye. "You're fucking with me. Yeah, you are. You are." I thought about him shouting at the door, his voice crashing into it, dissolving in the wood like foam in sand.

"I'm not," I said. "I'm not." And I would have said more except that through the snaking pipes, through the plank floors, through the orange kitchen tiles, I heard the back door swing open and feet shake the floor. Both Richard and I shut up. For a blink, and a blink only, I dreamed that it might be my mother, finally returning home.

You could hear everything down here. The feet stamped, knocking off snow, on the doormat. They crossed over my head. The kitchen tap began to run.

"Cal," Richard said, "can you hide somewhere? Cal, if you're not lying, then you should hide."

The words bounced off his tongue. I was scared of that tone, the panic in Richard's voice. I stood, frozen in front of the door in a vise of nausea. The footsteps thumped across the orange tiles, a beam creaked, shafts of icy sunlight slashed through the basement from a grimy window that hadn't been opened in years. I whirled, following the path of sun, and then sprawled on hands and knees in the murk behind the octopus furnace. There was light enough to see the black on my hands. I crouched on a soft flattened box next to a gray tennis ball and a few scattered foam peanuts.

The kitchen tap ran. I could almost see the footsteps, their impressions in the ceiling, circling like birds. The basement door opened, and I stepped backward into the darkness and kept stepping, nearly in time with the thuds on the basement stairs, my hand waving through blackness as I turned, reaching for a barrier. The steps slowed; there was a creak, a pop of old wood. A rustle of frayed runner meeting boot sole and still I walked into blackness, praying that I wouldn't trip or tumble.

When my fingers finally scratched the back wall it was cold and smelled of sweet grease. The boots smacked concrete through the basement, but not in the direction of the studio. Then nothing. Then a hollow clink of metal. Then boots again, walking the slalom of boxes. The padlock was wrestled off. The studio door finally opened. But I couldn't see a thing.

Time seemed to stop and start, to flow through space that contracted, bent, and almost burst. Years later, as I sat in a college lecture on Einstein, I'd think of this moment. Space-time, relativity, it seemed only a way to describe the feeling of being afraid in the dark.

Yet, as my eyes began to adjust, I realized that if I could inch forward a foot or two I'd have a view of a good portion of the basement. I remembered Jamie's story about his mother, and though I was afraid, I didn't want to be like him, missing everything, left to guess. I crawled through generations of dust and peered around the corner of the furnace in time to glimpse a figure in the studio's open doorway.

He held a plate of white-bread sandwiches, level with his shoulder, like one of the waiters at Belinda's. I was breathing through my nose, my lungs aching already, on the verge of a coughing fit, and I could smell, I think, the chemical mint of Ben-Gay. As he stooped to lift a jug of water from the floor, I glimpsed his face: sallow skin, eyes puffy as fried eggs, his lips pressed like he'd just swallowed hard. The waddling dwarf. The villain of my childhood. The greatest storyteller in the world. Don Brooke.

There were icicles in my chest. I remembered Betty North, her head tipped back, a rivulet of white grape juice at the corner of her mouth. "Don Brooke just called," she said. "Richard went overboard in the Inside Passage." I thought of Don's voice coming up the stairway from the kitchen. "Sam, you better slow down," he'd said. "I still think Richard will understand, if he just sees it," my father had said.

I didn't think I'd left tracks. I'd been too excited even to take off my jacket. The ratty cushions were back on the couch. I didn't imagine Don would notice that they were missing a decade of dust. I could feel the key to the back door outlined in my pocket. I'd locked it when I'd arrived that morning.

The seconds didn't seem to pass so much as flare up like kernels of popcorn. I listened, straining to keep from coughing, for what Don and Richard said to each other. At some point Don appeared in the doorway again, squinting into the dim basement. Or were his eyes closed? He froze for just a moment, before gently closing the door behind him and slapping the lock back into place.

He'd left the water and sandwiches and picked up a blue bucket with a yellow hoop handle that my mother had bought for me one summer in Santa Cruz. He was just a few feet from me, close enough for me to see the red N on the sneakers he wore (not boots after all), close enough for me to see an unshaven patch on his round chin, and close enough for me to smell the piss sloshing in my old summer bucket. Don crossed to the back half of the basement, the half I couldn't see from my place behind the furnace. Then he slowly climbed the stairs.

Once I heard the back door clap shut—it was spring-loaded,

so it snapped with the crack of wood to wood—I counted out fifteen minutes, one second at a time, before crawling out and taking the stairs two at a time. I ran out the door, down the drive, down Seachase, and halfway back to the Norths' before I stopped, hands on knees, panting into my shadow.

I needed to think, to get it all straight before I went back. But that night and the next day, I hardly considered what my discovery meant, or what its consequences might be. All I could think was that I knew Richard was alive and no one else did.

Will Percy, who passed in his rusted brown Volkswagen, rolling down the window to let out his pipe smoke, thought Richard was dead. Frank Bender, who sat next to me in school the next day, scribbling lineups for next season's Mariners on the flap of his chemistry book, thought Richard was dead. Mrs. Lowry, who taught the periodic table in a lime-green pantsuit, thought Richard was dead. Jamie North, who asked nothing but watched me with curious eyes, thought Richard was dead.

I WOULD HAVE SKIPPED school the next day, had planned to, except I realized at some point in the night that I'd never run into Don before because he came when I was at school. Ritual and repetition, to Don, to my father, were gods. Don drank a cup of coffee every morning at 6:35 from the same yellow mug. According to my father, even if Don was in bed, coming off forty straight hours, he'd get up specially to drink that cup of coffee before going back to sleep. If he was coming to feed Richard each day, he'd do it squarely.

By the time school let out, the snow had melted except for a few muddy white patches on the lawns. The cloud-scattered sky mirrored the ground. I rounded the block three times before letting myself in the back door.

The kitchen was warm and reminded me of an old dream I'd had where the neighborhood, the town, the world, had been taken over by witches. In the dream, I'd gone to my friend Paul's house to find an ally, but two skeletal women with black teeth answered his door. I sprinted home, diving into a kitchen filled with menacing tropical steam.

As I descended the stairs, the cooler air of the basement splashed me awake. I tapped the mint-colored wood with my knuckles.

"Richard," I said.

"It snowed," Richard said.

"What?"

"Yesterday. It snowed, didn't it? Did you bring the police?"

The sunlight had melted with the snow. The basement windows looked sooty-gray. My head felt dirty and hot. I hadn't considered the police.

"I'm locked in here against my will by men who may kill me." His voice sounded tired, as if he were obliged to say this but knew it wouldn't do any good. "Call the police, all right?"

"What men?" I asked.

"Let me out and I'll tell you about it."

"I can't," I said.

"You can," he said. "Really, you can."

"The lock, I mean."

"Don keeps the key down here. Inside something metal, with a door. Is it in the dryer?"

"I don't know," I said. But I'd heard him drop it into something metal too. It only took a second to find. I walked to the other end of the basement and opened the dryer. It contained a black sock and a silver key the length of a pinkie.

"It's there, isn't it?" Richard called.

I walked back to the door with the key in my pocket. "I don't see it," I said.

"Has it been snowing?" Richard asked.

The weather. These last weeks while I'd trudged to school or ridden my bike along the boardwalk smelling pine, salt, and exhaust, what had Richard smelled? Only white-bread sandwiches and his own waste. What had he touched? Only the mohair on the bench and the shag of the rug. What had he heard? Only the ceiling creaking above him. And the records.

"I've been thinking about you, Cal," he said. "I wondered if you'd come back. I thought you would, because that's what I would have done. And you probably want to do the right thing, but what is that? Right? You don't know. Because you *do* know who put me in here. You could let me out. That's what you should do. But what would happen? You just don't know, right? So it's better to do nothing. When in doubt, do nothing. Am I right?"

"No," I said.

"You found the key."

"Yes."

"Two keys?"

"One."

"That makes it easy for you. I promise you, if you open the door, I'm not going anywhere. They've got me chained to the sink. Please. I promise you. Did it snow yesterday? At least tell me that."

In that moment I would have done anything, would have given up all I'd found, if only I didn't have to decide whether to open the door. I imagined a blade jabbed in my neck. I saw Richard cowering in a corner, his cheeks shiny with sweat, his leg green with infection. I saw the two of us plunging into a roadside ditch filled with cloudy water, chained together at the ankle.

"Cal, tell me. Did it snow?"

I stabbed the lock with the key.

Inside, Richard lay across the bench seat, his head propped against the wall, one leg on the floor, the other bent at the knee. I'd expected a Ben Gunn sort of beard, but his cheeks showed only a few days' stubble. Strings of black hair hung over eyes that were alert and bright, light brown, nearly golden. His skin was the dirty white of old snow.

He looked healthy enough, but his expression—mouth half open, eyes half closed—was that of a starving man.

He wasn't lying about the chain, though I didn't see it immediately because it was wound around his ankle on the floor. It looped the ankle twice, pinned by another padlock, then snaked the length of the room and looped and was locked again around a pipe under the sink.

"Have you been the one walking around up there?"

My tongue felt too thick to use.

"What did you think was happening down here? Didn't you want to know?"

The question seemed directed at some other being. What *had* I thought was happening? I could hardly remember.

"How long have you been here? Since the beginning?" Richard asked.

I couldn't speak.

"Let me out of here, please."

Here meant a plate of half-eaten white-bread sandwiches on the floor, two plastic bottles of mayonnaise and mustard, and a plastic butter knife, broken in half. An empty gallon water jug. Two full jugs next to a jar of purple Kool-Aid powder. A mattress flipped on its edge and lined up against the shelf. A path worn into the orange carpet between the far wall and the bench.

"I can't," I said.

He sat up, and the chain whispered against the pipe.

I thought of the words I'd exchanged with my father before he'd pushed me into Betty North's station wagon. *Did you really change Richard's mind?* I'd asked. *I didn't have to,* he'd said. He'd stared into my eyes. The old rules, the old motors that I'd always felt running under the sidewalks, keeping the world in place, had snapped their belts and were spinning out of sequence.

Richard looked at me. I saw something like pity cloud his eyes. Was it possible that as I stood in the doorway of his cell he actually felt sorry for *me*?

"Then sit down," he said. "Don's already come. He won't be back until tomorrow." He licked his dry lips and added, "Please."

I stayed in the doorway and sized up the chain link by link. Did it have enough slack to wind around my neck? Did the broken knife have enough of an edge to cut my throat? He seemed so tired, though. The flat way he'd asked the question, inserting *please* after the lapse of a second.

"Did it snow yesterday?"

"Yes."

"Thank you." He looked legitimately relieved. "Don told me it did. But I can never believe what he says."

"No, I guess not."

"I *could* tell him you were here, you know. Do I have anything to lose?"

"I don't know."

"Sit down, all right?"

I sat down Indian-style on the floor, close to the doorway.

Richard lay back slowly on the bench.

"Okay. Good. Okay, thanks," he said softly. "There are sandwiches."

I shook my head. He wore a black hooded sweatshirt; he pulled up the hood now. "Do you want to hear some music?"

"All right," I said.

"Let's see, let's see." Richard rose from the bench and hobbled a few steps to the shelf. He was wearing baggy black pajama pants, wide enough for the leg to fall over the chain around his ankle. He scanned his finger along the record spines, settling on Ornette Coleman's *This Is Our Music*. "I really like this one. You've heard it before? Is it too loud?" He crouched next to the record player, the orange from the vacuum tubes glowing on his face. "We can try something else."

It was the kind of record I always begged my mother to take off: squealing saxophones, a melody like a car crash. All of which made the moment feel even less real.

"Yeah, I like this one a lot," Richard said, "quite a lot." He closed the turntable's plastic hood carefully. Then he darted toward the door, the chain slithering behind him. I scrambled back, hoping to hurl myself out of the room, but my feet refused to unpin. I threw my shoulders back, trying to somersault. My elbow banged the doorjamb and I fell awkwardly to my side.

He knelt, but didn't go for my throat. Instead, he tapped his hands on my knees to the rhythm of the drums. His crooked mouth hissed with the ride cymbal, *tsssst tsst tsst tsssst*.

"I've never had a lot of time to listen to music until now." His face was only inches from mine, and I could smell mustard on his breath. I knew I should scramble away. There wasn't a reason in the world to trust him. But I couldn't take my eyes off his face, the pale, high-boned cheeks beneath bright, mad eyes.

"I've heard you listening," I said.

"That's right," he said. "Upstairs you've heard. So you know. Actually it wasn't like I didn't have time for music before. Time had nothing to do with it. I just wasn't interested, you know what I mean?"

"I didn't know that," I said.

"You don't have to sit on the floor," he said. He got back on his feet and threw himself onto the bench. "I wish I could have figured it out sooner, because I think I would have liked to be a musician." He pushed out one palm as if he expected me to object. "Now, I don't say that like how you normally say it. You know, like when you fly on a plane, of course you're going to think: I'd like to be a pilot. Or you happen to see some movie with a crane shot or something, and you think: I'd like to be a cinematographer. But I think I would have been *good* as a musician."

"Why?" I caught a whiff of urine and spotted the beach pail under the sink.

"I can't hide anything, which has always made things hard for me. The problem was, I didn't know there was anything wrong with that for a long time. That's one of those things that they don't teach you. You're not supposed to say what you think. Even after I figured that out I still could hardly ever stop myself. Do you think there's any pursuit where that's actually a strength, a good thing? I can't think of any except music."

Richard reached for a half-eaten sandwich on the plate at his feet. He grabbed the plastic knife too, but, after smearing mustard across the face of the sandwich, tossed it back. Then he picked up a plastic jar of green olives.

"Where have you been living?" he asked.

I told him.

"What about your mom? Where's she?"

I told him.

"She just left without saying anything? That's hard. My mom died a long time ago."

"I know," I said.

"My dad also died," he said.

"I know."

"Does your mom know that I'm here?"

"I don't think so."

"If you told her she'd call the police. That's all you'd have to do. But," Richard said, as if it were his decision to make, "then your father would be in a lot of trouble."

"He put you here," I said.

"How's school?" Richard asked.

"How did you get here?"

"You're wondering why they didn't just kill me? Do you want me to answer? I'm just asking. People used to say things about *my* father. About women. Affairs, things like that." He reached from his place on the bench and jacked the volume on the stereo. He wrapped one finger in the drawstring of his hood. "I hated his guts, and I already knew everything, and it still killed me to hear it, you know?"

A fly was frozen on a crust of the bread. There was mustard on Richard's lip. I stood up and turned down the volume on the stereo. Richard sank into the corner, tugging the tassels of his hood. He frowned like he'd just bitten his tongue.

"You could have said it was too loud. Didn't I ask you?"

"My father put you in here," I said.

"Would you believe me if I said he didn't? He and Sam and Don came to my house."

"Then?"

"Then this." He yanked the drawstrings, and the hood scrunched around his face like an anemone's mouth. "Not now. Ask me anything else, go ahead."

"Have you really been in here all this time?"

"Don comes once a day. He brings food. Books, if I want them. What else can I tell you?"

I wanted to know what had happened. I told myself I didn't care what the truth was, what it broke. I wanted to know. That, I told myself, was my right.

"Are you all right?" I asked instead.

"See that?" he asked. "The ceiling over the sink, there. The water spot."

There wasn't much to see. A yellowing of the plaster in the corner of one wall near the ceiling, a faint shape.

"What do you think about it?" he asked. "What does it look like to you?"

"I don't know. Like a rabbit, maybe?"

He blinked in what appeared to be genuine amazement. "That's it? That's all you see?"

"What else is there?"

"A leak."

"A leak?"

"It doesn't look like much right now, but sometimes it's very bad. It's all the water from the rain. It builds up. It drains down here. Maybe you heard it dripping. No? It does, and a few times it sort of broke like a dam. There's no warning, really. The water just comes rushing into the room."

"Really?"

"Really. The room's small, so it fills up quickly. I stand up on the bench in the corner, but the water's at my mouth so fast, and there's just a little bit of time when I can only breathe through my nose. But the water's over my head soon enough, and all the records have floated off the shelves and out of their jackets, and they look like a school of black fish.

"The door bursts next, and the sink and the chain and everything floods out and the basement is flooded to the ceiling. So I float through it, trying to make it to the stairs. And all those boxes out there, they're floating, and the water has stripped the tape, so all that stuff you've collected is floating around me, and I'm struggling through it, trying to float up the stairs to the door before I run out of air."

"Really?" I asked.

"Well, I *see* it like that sometimes, you know?"

THE WEATHER STAYED BAD. The mountains tore strips from passing clouds. The rain stained the windows and soaked the color from the trees. It was, by then, that vicious stretch of November when the sea wound itself around Loyalty Island like a gray snake, squeezing. That night I called down to Jamie from the top bunk. I could tell he was awake, but he didn't answer. It was just as well. I had no idea what I wanted to say.

I could say it felt like a dream, but it didn't. Foreign, mysterious, yes. But there was none of the effortlessness of dreams. I've always thought that people cherish their dreams because, in them, they act but rarely have to *decide* how to act.

I could say I felt sick, but that's not right either. I felt fine. Rather, I felt like I was observing sickness, walking, immune, through a cloud that had descended and would not pass. I walked over sidewalks and across lawns and up the bluff to Seachase feeling the guilt and anxiety of the healthy.

Mostly, though, I felt isolated by what I knew. Under the floor, there was a cowering, half-crazy man. That was the secret, the solution to the mystery. I shouldn't have been stupid enough to imagine some happy reconciliation, some warm remedy. I should have known that at the root of any mystery that's all you find: people doing unspeakable harm to other people. What else on this earth is there to hide?

When I returned to the basement the next day, there were pillows on the orange carpet in the spot where I'd sat the day before. The records were back in their jackets, the books stacked next to the bench. The sheet and quilt, which had been thrown over the upturned mattress the day before, were folded. Richard shot from the bench as if he had been coiled there, and greeted me with a grin. He offered me a white-bread sandwich stuffed with inches of yellow turkey.

"Have you ever really *heard* a harmonica?" he asked.

"You promised to tell me what happened," I said.

"I will. But if you've never *heard* a harmonica, you need to, immediately." He spoke in a quaking voice, the voice of a man who hadn't had a conversation in a month. "Sonny Boy Williamson makes my teeth hurt. You just have to listen."

When the record ended Richard filled the space with chatter about the novel he was reading, for the third time in two weeks: Walker Percy's *The Moviegoer*.

The book was mine, taken from the private library my mother had provided. She'd spent more money on books for me than we probably had to spare. She would come home from Seattle with shopping bags full. I'd read a few—*Dr. Jekyll and Mr. Hyde*, the rest of Stevenson, Kipling, and Hamilton's *Mythology*. But most of them—*Silent Spring, Darkness at Noon, Victory*—were impossible. My eyes glazed over just reading the back covers.

These are investments, she said when I complained. One summer, the week before the Fourth of July, she demanded I finish one whole book or else I couldn't watch the fireworks over Greene Harbor. Pick any book off your shelf or mine, she said. There was no getting out of it, but I picked a book from my father's shelf, from the very top of the cabinet in the living room. Joshua Slocum's *Sailing Alone Around the World*. I read it in a day and a half. Afterward, for a few weeks anyway, sailing around the world became my sole ambition. I informed everyone of my plans, to appreciative laughter. I mapped my voyage in my mind—*sailing alone around the world*—but, though I imagined the Roaring Twenties, the Doldrums, the Horn, and the Loyalty Islands, I mostly thought about the day I'd return home. Stepping off the boat in Greene Harbor to a torrent of applause, whipped by wind and browned under a tropical sun.

"It's not just about movies, I guess," I said to Richard. "That book."

He rolled up the paperback like a newspaper and stung me on the shoulder with it. "Ha!" he said. "Do you want to know what it *is* about?" He was so eager, so impatient for my response, and this made me sadder than anything else.

"It's about 'the sad little happiness of drinks and kisses.'" He described the novel almost page for page, talking about the narrator, Binx, as though he were a real person. Binx, pressured by his aunt to become a doctor, instead walks the streets of New Orleans, looking for something, but what? All he has is time to pass, and he passes the time on long drives with his sunburned secretaries, or in suburban theaters where he finds in movies a poignancy not present in his own life. And suddenly Richard was telling me about his own life, about the first year he lived in New York.

"Finally," he said, "I was living outside of this rainy fucking shadow. But I'd still get these long letters from my father. He'd write to me all about his childhood, his college years, all this stuff he'd never *told* me." Richard rose from his place on the bench and began to pace the room, ten and a half steps in either direction, the chain slithering behind. "He wrote letters, but he never called. Never. He said that the time change made him nervous, that he never knew when he might wake me up. I had an apartment on Bleecker next to a Chinese laundry that sold Lucky Strikes and soap powder. *Just* Lucky Strikes and soap powder. The apartment was shit, but I was hardly there because finally there were people, I mean real people. I lived at the bars. I used to think about how it would be to get my mail there, like how those intellectuals in Paris got their mail at the cafés. They'd sit around the tables, plotting revolutions a thousand miles away. I thought about them all the time. I couldn't name a single one, but I just had that image in my mind.

"And the girls, Cal, that was something too. I met these wonderful, crazy girls. One time, I was at a bar talking to this very bookish-looking brunette, sexy-librarian, plaid-miniskirt kind of thing. We'd been talking all night, and suddenly I was kissing her. She was kissing me, really. The bathrooms were downstairs, and it was just about bar time. Come downstairs with me, she said. No thanks, I said, my friends are leaving, I have to go with them. Come downstairs with me, she said, or I'm going to stab you in the throat. Stab you in the throat! Oh my God. Heaven."

"Richard, why are you telling me this?" I really wanted to know. The ugly pride on his face seemed to signify something, but what? I thought the question might offend him, but he laughed.

"I don't know. You're right. I don't know why. I'm just saying I couldn't believe how fantastic it was. It's like, if I'd spent my whole fucking life chained up in this room, I probably wouldn't mind it so much." He paused. "I think I've changed. But I don't know. What do you think?"

"How have you changed?"

"Like I said, I don't really know."

"Well, how do you feel?"

His smile dried up. He tugged the strings on the hood of his sweatshirt.

"I feel afraid," he said. "I have a question for you, and you have to be honest, right?"

"Right."

"What do I look like?"

"What?"

"What do I look like? I haven't seen a mirror in a month."

Richard wasn't yet thirty, but he already had the face he deserved. He'd always had that face: A crooked, saber-sharp nose. A gaze that sliced like a dorsal fin through water. I wouldn't call him handsome, but he was distinctive.

If anything, he'd gained a little weight; his cheekbones didn't push as much against his skin. He wasn't asking for that kind of description, though, and the answer was bad news. I could almost see the cloud of fear moving under his skin. The metallic rind on his tongue. He looked poorly made, like he wouldn't last much longer.

"You're holding up," I said.

"Really?"

"Pretty well," I said.

I stayed another hour, delaying the walk home, the sky dark and dripping cold rain. But finally I couldn't put it off anymore. When I told Richard I was expected back at the Norths' he smiled and nodded, silently. I followed his gaze as he scanned the narrow room, as if trying to prepare himself for what it would look like once I left.

I locked the door and returned the key to the dryer. At the top of the stairs I had to fight the urge to go back. No one had ever been that sad to say good-bye to me.

WHEN I RETURNED to the Norths', Jamie was standing in the kitchen doorway with the phone to his ear. I tried to catch his eye, but he only looked down at his feet. "Sure," he said. "He's right here, actually." I froze in place. Betty glanced up from the kitchen table and smiled at me before returning to her crossword puzzle. As I stood there stupidly, Jamie said only, "Uh-huh. How much are they offering? Mmh-hmmh. Really? How big?" I knew this conversation. I'd had it countless times with my own father.

I went up to our room and waited, but Jamie never appeared. He spent the rest of the evening at the kitchen table with his mother, reading a magazine. I announced that I was going for a walk, but he didn't offer to join me. When I returned he was in bed with the lights out. I whispered, "Jamie, are you awake?" He didn't answer, but I knew the faint whistle of his sleeping breath. I knew he was awake.

I climbed out the window. Jamie didn't follow. Outside, I shivered and smoked until my lips were numb, sure that I'd been betrayed. I could no longer imagine what possible reason I'd had to tell Jamie I'd been going home. I crumpled up the rest of the pack and hurled it into the waving hemlocks.

The next day after school I waited for him, leaning against the flagpole under an iron press of sky. When Jamie pushed through the double doors he looked different; it took me a moment to figure out why. Usually when he saw me he smiled.

We fell into step on the cracked sidewalk and drifted onto the wet road winding up the bluff from town. The rain sputtered on, and we sped up to rain-walking pace.

"Did you tell him?" I asked.

His startled eyes met mine before dropping back to the street. "No," he said. "No, I didn't. You thought I did?"

I'd heard somewhere that you could always see a lie on a face. Jamie looked bewildered, hurt—is that what a liar looked like? I didn't know. The rain picked up. Before I could answer, Jamie broke stride and shouldered off his backpack. He looked at me fiercely as he bent down and pulled out a gray umbrella.

"What are you doing with that?" I asked. I didn't carry an umbrella; hardly anyone in Loyalty Island did—not the men, anyway.

He looked at me as if he'd been waiting for this question. "What's your problem? I don't like getting wet, is that so crazy?" He shook open the umbrella and held it over me. "Try it," he said. "You might like it."

And suddenly I was sure that he hadn't betrayed me, and almost as sure that he never would. We walked silently down the middle of High Street. A green sun beat through the clouds as we slalomed puddles and ascended the bluff into fog.

"Why don't people use umbrellas, do you think?" Jamie asked.

"I guess it's a good question," I said.

"For example, we run into each other downtown, it's raining, I have an umbrella, you don't, we're going the same way."

"Okay."

"If I don't offer to share, it's rude, right? But if I do offer to share, we have to walk right next to each other and think of something to say. But we can't say too much, because we might not be going the same place, and then it would be even worse because we'd be stuck breathing into each other's faces while we finished our conversation. So people figure it's better just to get wet. That's what I think."

He might have been right. Generations of fishermen had shaped the customs and language. I'd noticed it, listening to my father and Don and Sam and John Gaunt around our kitchen table. They'd veer from topic to topic in wide loops. Don might begin a story about a beautiful but far too virtuous Aleut girl he'd met in Dutch Harbor and suddenly drop it; but then the Aleut girl would reappear hours later without any obvious prompt. I thought of it as "long talk."

I told my father this one night, and he smiled, pleased, almost proud. "I like that," he said. "I'll have to tell everyone that. It comes from the work, I guess. You have twenty minutes to eat between strings, and someone starts telling a story, and the work won't wait for the story to end, so you spend the next eight or twelve hours waiting for that next break. Everyone does. It doesn't matter how long it's been or what's happened. Story has to get finished."

"What do you think?" Jamie asked. Rain slashed across the street under clouds booming thunder. "What do you think of my theory?" His smile was double-framed by the gray tent of umbrella and the gray tent of sky. I felt both jealousy and pity, as I had so many times before. Jamie didn't understand a bit of what was happening. He had no idea what people had to do so that he could develop theories about umbrellas and quote dialogue he didn't understand from movies he hadn't seen.

He liked to quote a line he'd read in his film magazines from a movie called *The Rules of the Game*. "The awful thing about life is this," he would say. "Everyone has his reasons." Maybe this was true. Richard had his reasons for threatening to sell everything. My father and Jamie's father and Don Brooke had their reasons for locking Richard in a basement and telling the world he was dead. But what Jamie never realized is that we do all have our reasons, but that isn't the tragedy. The tragedy is that, except in the rarest cases, we do things—good things, bad things—without ever really knowing why.

"What about that theory?" Jamie asked again. "It checks, right?"

"Maybe," I said, "but what difference does it make?"

Jamie spit into the gutter, and we continued stride for stride under the umbrella as it drifted past Spring Street and beneath branches draped with leaves like wet rags. The umbrella wound down the bluff, drawing water as Jamie switched it from hand to hand. It passed Spruce and shook in a gust of wind and spat water and righted itself like a channel marker. At the next block the umbrella turned right on Seachase Lane, then cut through the rain into my driveway.

The house's paint was graying, the gutters pasted with pine needles. Could I pretend that the rain had flooded out the streets, that the current had dropped us there?

"You were mad at me because I made you lie to your father," I said. We hadn't spoken in blocks.

"I guess so, yeah."

"If I show you what's inside you'll have to lie more."

Jamie kept the umbrella level, didn't move his arm at all, only turned his head to look me in the eyes.

"If you tell him," I said, "I'll say you knew the whole time."

He stepped back, his face blank. "Knew what?"

"I'm about to show you," I said.

The way Jamie smiled, I almost decided to call it off, to lead him home, to keep him in the dark. Anyway, we stood a few extra moments at the foot of the driveway under the shelter of his umbrella.

AS I UNLOCKED the studio door my guts felt frozen and brittle. I wanted to tell Jamie that he didn't have to go in, that it wasn't too late, but I could only jab at the open door with one finger. I hadn't even knocked. Jamie leaned the umbrella against the wall and stepped into the light.

"Who am I looking at?" I heard Richard ask. Nobody spoke. "Do I know you?" Still no answer. The thought that the moment could last forever forced me to throw myself through the doorway.

Richard was coated in sweat and tugging a white T-shirt on. I just had time to notice the splatter of a yellow-purple bruise on his stomach. The stereo was on low, some piece of piano music.

He went to the sink, panting, and splashed his neck and chin. Even after he turned off the tap he remained with his back to us, bracing the wall with both arms, chest heaving. I hoped Jamie would say something, because I couldn't.

"Finally, the police," Richard said.

"He's not the police," I said.

"No shit." He spun around, jerking the chain against the pipe. "This isn't a fucking zoo."

The disbelief in his stare was devastating. All I had to do was explain why I'd brought Jamie. But I couldn't.

"I see a guy could get confused, but it isn't," Richard said.

"I'm sorry," I said. I looked at Jamie. His mouth was a line, his arms crossed over his chest as if he'd just stepped into cold weather.

Richard leaned back against the wall, as far from us as he could get, arms outstretched like a scarecrow's. I thought about cornfields and about how I'd never seen a real scarecrow. I had nothing to say.

"I'm Jamie North," Jamie said. His voice was quiet, but impressively calm.

"Sam's?" Richard asked.

"Yeah."

"Sam North's?" Richard squeezed shut his eyes.

Jamie wiped his hand on his shirt and extended it to Richard. Richard opened his eyes and burst out laughing. "You're offering to shake my hand? Are we at a country club? Sorry about the low ceiling and pardon the chain around my ankle." He turned his eyes to me. "What's the etiquette here? When introduced to the son of the man who's chained you to a sink do you shake hands or do you just let him kick you in the balls?"

"Depends who you ask," Jamie said. "I think Vanderbilt says handshake, but Emily Post says balls."

"Very good," Richard said. "I've always preferred Vanderbilt. My mother had her book. We kept it on the shelf in the living room after she died."

"Mine too," Jamie said. "She isn't dead, though."

"That's wonderful news," Richard said. "Anyway, we don't need to shake hands. I've met you a hundred times."

"But not like this."

"No, not like this." Richard lay down on the bench. "I guess I shouldn't even be surprised, the three of us here—the spoiled, lucky victims of Loyalty Island. So, Jamie North. What do you want to know?"

It wasn't until Jamie took his seat on the floor, just as I had days before, that I realized how afraid I'd been. Afraid that Jamie would cut the chain or slam the door behind him and replace the lock for good. Afraid that, unlike me, he would know what to do. But he was as cautious, as confused, and as paralyzed as I was.

I sat down beside him. I knew what Jamie would ask. They were the same questions I'd asked, and I watched him, his elbows resting on his crossed legs, the lines around his eyes and mouth creasing as he began to understand.

"Tell me what happened," Jamie said.

"Not now," Richard said.

"What's going to happen? Will they let you out?" It was a question I'd asked myself many times. Maybe that was why I'd brought Jamie: I needed him to ask the questions I was afraid to.

"They can't keep you down here forever," Jamie continued. "If

178

they wanted to, they wouldn't have put you down here in the first place."

"I couldn't say," Richard said. "Call your father and ask him."

"They would've already ... done it," Jamie said. "They have to let you out."

Richard sat up. "Maybe it's not so easy," he said, "to do that. When they first came for me they *meant* to do it. I know they did."

"I don't believe that," Jamie said.

"No? Why not?"

Silently I prayed Jamie would have an answer. But Richard answered instead. "Because Sam North could never kill a man? Is that about right?"

"I don't know," Jamie said.

"No?" Richard asked. He struggled to his feet and ran his fingers across the records' spines. "When they first locked me in here I had no watch. That was the worst thing in the beginning. No time. These records were my only way to tell time, to know that it was passing, right? Honestly, I probably never would have turned on this stereo otherwise, but I'd put them on, and I'd know, for example, that 'Tangled Up in Blue' lasts five minutes and forty seconds. So I'd know that I'd just experienced the same five minutes with the rest of the world.

"You wouldn't think it'd be so bad, would you? Not having time, not having it to worry about. But it was bad. You can go months without speaking to another person, without touching another person, but if you're sharing the same time, if you both know that it's six o'clock, for example, then that's something, right? Like those monks who take a vow of silence, they're always ringing those bells. They never miss a quarter hour."

Richard paced to the end of the room, pausing with his back to us long enough for Jamie and me to share a look. It was chilling, the intensity on Richard's face.

"You hear," he continued, "I used to hear people always complain about the loneliness of the city. If you live in the country, you have the sun and the seasons to keep you in touch, it doesn't matter if you live miles from your nearest neighbor. You see the sun at the same time, you're intimate that way.

"But the city has no seasons and no sun. The city has to work so people don't go fucking mad. They have to manufacture time to fight loneliness. Big clocks on banks and in Times Square, ha, see, yes. Rush *hour*, lunch *hour*, happy *hour*. Why not save us all some trouble by staggering work, why not save the roads? Because we need a schedule so we feel part of the same thing. Can you imagine the desolation of a deserted train ride to work each morning? We want traffic jams. Because you're frustrated, you're pissed, but you know that hundreds of people around you are feeling the same way, and there's a lot of comfort in that."

He'd been talking to the ceiling, the shelves, the floor. He looked back at us now and sighed. He crumpled onto the bench and pinched his lower lip between his thumb and index finger, as if it had disappointed him.

"All right. Forget that. You're wondering what this has to do with your question, huh? Your fathers. How many times have you heard them say, 'Yeah, it's dangerous, but I could never punch a clock, so it's all I have'? What are they saying? When they're working there's no daytime or nighttime. No mealtime, no sleep time, no work time, no playtime, no quiet time. It's all one smear. They've arm-wrestled it, pretzeled it. But they get to do it together. I think that's what love really is, this thing that just wrecks time. You don't need time anymore. So. Do I think they're capable of doing anything to protect that? Yes."

JAMIE AND I TRUDGED the crooked streets under a sickly dusk, silent accomplices. I'd half hoped that it was all a dream, that Jamie would open the door to an empty, mildewed room. Now Richard's kidnapping, his captivity, was real. Did it seem real to Jamie? I wondered. As we passed Spring, Jamie drifted off the sidewalk and into the middle of the street. I had to quicken my steps to keep up.

"Hey," I said, but he only went faster.

"Jamie," I said, but he didn't look back. He lengthened the distance between us, taking long strides under the fir trees on Martin, heavy with rain. I couldn't blame him for trying, but it was too late to run. He turned once to see me two boat-lengths behind and broke into a run anyway. I let him vanish into the twilight, feeling sorry only for myself. I'd hoped that I wouldn't have to make this walk alone again. It started to drizzle, but I rounded the Norths' block four or five times before I went inside.

When I opened the front door, stamping my wet feet on the mat like my father used to, Betty North was standing in the hallway smoking a long cigarette. "Oh, honey," she said. Her eyes were red and wet. She flicked her cigarette at the ashtray on the side table and bit her bottom lip.

I felt the blood drain from my limbs. "Oh, honey," she said again, as she put a clumsy arm around my shoulder and pulled me in, "you're just a few minutes too late." She looked me in the eyes, smiling. Her teeth were white but outlined in yellow. "Your mother just called. She's at the hospital now. A girl."

I was too relieved to speak. In the silence Betty started to cry.

"What's the matter?" I asked.

"A healthy girl." Betty sniffled and ran the back of the hand holding the cigarette under her nose. "I'm sorry. You should really hear that kind of news from your own family, shouldn't you?"

"It's okay," I said. "I'll call her."

"She didn't leave a number. She said she'd call back when she got home."

"She's coming home?"

"Well, not home," Betty said. "Wherever she's staying right now is what I mean. Isn't it wonderful, though?"

"Has anyone called my father yet?"

Betty shook her head in a cloud of smoke. "I don't know. I should have asked, but it was such a surprise."

"What about the name?"

She made a face, defeated. "I don't think I heard it. I'm so sorry. Really."

I could suddenly see, in Betty's every expression and gesture, a bone-deep kindness. And yet she passed through the rooms of her own house like a specter, sadness on tiptoes.

Somehow it was all connected: Jamie's running away and Richard in the basement and my mother in California and our fathers on the Bering Sea and John Gaunt in his grave and Betty North and I standing a foot apart against either wall of the narrow hallway, talking about joy but absolutely hating ourselves. She stamped out the cigarette and turned back to the mirror.

"Don't be sorry," I said. "I like the suspense."

JAMIE SHOOK me awake in the middle of the night. The radiators were up too high. The sheets were damp. I'd been dreaming I was awake, lying there, thinking about the basement.

"Why did you show me?" he asked.

I flipped toward the wall. "Fuck you," I said. "I shouldn't have."

The bed rail creaked and I felt Jamie's weight on the mattress.

"I'm sorry about running, but you understand—"

"Not really," I said. "Get out of my bed."

"It's my bed," he said. "You get out."

"Or?"

"I'm fine peeing all over my own bed."

We both started to laugh. Jamie sat up, and I lay on my back, staring at the shadowy poster of Sigourney Weaver.

"Couldn't you have found a better-looking chick to put above my bed?" I asked.

"She's a great actress," Jamie said.

"I have no idea what to do." It felt good to actually say it, to have someone to say it to.

"I'm glad you showed me," he said.

"Are you?"

"Aren't you glad you know?"

"I don't know," I said. "I really don't."

"It doesn't matter if you're glad or not, I guess." Jamie climbed out of the bunk and dropped to the floor. I heard him zipping his jacket in the darkness.

"Roof?"

"I don't think so," he said.

We padded down the living room stairs and out into the street. The clouds were heavy with moonlight, the sidewalks empty all the way down the bluff. Jamie was right. What we had to say didn't belong on the roof. I wasn't sure if that was because what we were about to say was too secret even for our sacred place or because it was too horrible. From the Norths' it was fifteen minutes downtown. We passed the tiny Safeway, dark; the library, dark; Belinda's, dark; Eric's Quilt, dark; and the Fisherman's Memorial, drowning in a pool of streetlight.

The harbor was dotted with boats, but it looked vacant and harmless with the big ships gone for the season. Jamie sat down on the edge of the dock, dangling his feet over the lapping water. He lit a cigarette and leaned back on one hand, blowing thoughtful clouds. He shook another cigarette from the pack and stood it up on its filter. "I feel sick," he said. "I've been feeling sick all day. How are we supposed to solve this? What are we supposed to do?"

I chewed on the tip of the cigarette filter and looked out at the bobbing boats as I auditioned answers.

"We could let him go," I said.

"We could."

"But then."

"But then?"

"They'd put everyone in jail, wouldn't they?"

"Who's everyone?"

"Your dad and my dad and Don, at least," I said.

"What if we made Richard promise not to tell anyone? What if we made him promise not to sell everything?"

"I've thought of that," I said, "but, I mean, he's dead, isn't he? He can't just reappear."

"No," Jamie said.

"Anyway," I said, "he hates them. If he got out, what would he do?"

"But he doesn't seem to hate us."

"No."

In the distance a freighter lumbered through the channel, though it was too dark to see anything but lights on the bow and stern. I'd watched ships like these cruise the channel en route to Seattle from Singapore, Tokyo, or Taiwan all my life. Something about them still made my stomach leap. They spoke of just how giant the world actually was. In comparison to these monsters, the *Laurentide* was tiny.

Jamie flicked his butt into the water. Everything smelled like early memories of my father, before he quit smoking, when he came home after summer work and stroked my hair with damp yellow fingers.

"Is it right," Jamie asked, "what they did?"

"What else could they do?" I said. "He was asking for it, wasn't he?"

"No." Out of the corner of my eye I could see Jamie shaking his head. "I don't know. Maybe he was. I always hated him. But today he seemed—"

"I know," I said. "You know how I found him? He was singing."

Jamie didn't answer. The clouds broke and moonlight dropped onto the waves. I thought of all the times as a kid when I'd played on the front lawn and a breeze whipped the ocean smell past our house, of that slight change in temperature, in the elemental composition of the air.

"Jamie?" I said.

"It's sad. That's all. It's sad to think about him in the basement singing by himself."

"I know."

"Maybe he's changed."

"So what if he has?"

"So what?"

"If we let him out, if we call the police and it's not the right thing, we can't undo that."

"And we know he's in the basement," Jamie said. "We can't undo that either."

"So, we'll wait, okay?"

"And go back?"

"I guess we have to."

We sat in silence until we were both shivering, until the first birds swooped across the bows of the moored trawlers, and, slowly, the night came apart.

CHAPTER 7

W E CAME STRAIGHT FROM SCHOOL EACH DAY, our backpacks sagging with unread books. We hid our bikes under bushes in Henderson Park and stumbled through the forest into the backyard. We hid our wet sneakers under the bushes next to the porch, so as not to leave tracks in the kitchen, then stood waiting, our socks cold and damp, as I knocked on the mint door.

The first day, Richard sat cross-legged on the floor, the needle popping on the turntable, a mystery novel of my father's open in his lap, a cigarette stuck in his smile. One of my mother's triangular ashtrays lay next to him on the ground, half full.

"Things are looking up," he said. "Don wouldn't bring me cigarettes until suddenly, today, he did."

"He was feeling like a humanitarian," I said.

"Maybe," Richard said. "Maybe he wants cancer to kill me, or maybe he finally realized I'm not going to burn myself alive." He flicked a plastic lighter and held it up like a torch to demonstrate. "Of course, if I was gonna do it, I'd have drowned myself, right?"

"What has Don said?" Jamie asked.

"Not very much. He brings a gun when he comes," Richard said. "One day he told me he killed Dan Fosse. He told me he pushed Dan overboard."

"Why?" Jamie asked.

"He'd seen a lot of guys die over the years, and he wanted to know if it felt any different, knowing that he was responsible for it. He said it didn't. Anyway, Don only comes in the morning, so there's nothing for you to worry about. If you're going to keep coming. Are you?"

We both nodded. Richard tipped back his head and exhaled through his nose, just as he had that day on the boardwalk, when he had worn the shiny red shirt, when he had been right to be afraid. Then he smiled.

"Too bad Don doesn't have any kids," he said. "We'd have a fourth for bridge."

Nobody laughed.

Richard looked at us with mock seriousness. "I don't play bridge," he said. "It's a game for spoiled East Coast pricks and fags. But spoiled West Coast pricks don't play much. Sit down anyway."

We took what would become our customary places on the floor. There wasn't much room, so we had to cross our legs like Richard.

"Don could kill us too," I said, "if you're sharing those smokes."

"Not sharing," Richard said, "but wagering, sure. I could teach you how to play bourré. Do you have any cards?"

"Upstairs," I said. "I can get them."

"Good. I learned to play in New Orleans. The number one rule is you got to follow suit, and this isn't just a rule of the game. It's a rule of honor. I used to play with the line cooks I knew down there. That might not sound like much, but there were more knives than teeth in that kitchen. And if you laid down a card and heard, 'Did you jus' boo-ray? Hey, man, you boo-rayed, you fuckin' boo-rayed, man,' you were about to meet one of those knives."

"Should I get the knives from upstairs too?" I asked.

"You can play without them." Richard shook two Winstons from the pack and held them out to us. "Here, play with house money, and until you figure it out you're on the same team, all right?"

Jamie North and I. We spent our afternoons with Richard in the basement, but when I locked the back door and replaced the key in its magnetized slot under the grill, it was as if a switch had been thrown. We walked home talking about Harrison Ford and home-work. We walked to school in the morning talking about Beth Garson's white legs and purple high heels. We sat at lunch talking about Katherine Cloons, who had just cut her hair short and come to school for the first time without her glasses, looking very pretty and very blind.

What we knew kept us busy, I guess, trying to act like we knew nothing. We didn't talk about Richard, or Alaska, or our mothers, or our fathers. We lived two lives, and, strangely, I remember the second of those lives as happy. It's probably wrong to think about my own happiness while a man was locked in my basement waiting to die, but my own happiness has always come before a lot of things.

The second Indiana Jones movie came out, finally, at the Orpheum. Jamie and I skipped school to catch the Friday matinee so we could be the first to see it. As we handed dollars to Will Percy he chewed the end of his pipe disapprovingly; then he tore our tickets and turned his back. "I didn't see you boys. If you have to, tell people you snuck in while I was fixing the reel, got it?" I knew if it had just been me he would have peered over the rims of his glasses and told me to get back to school. But Jamie was at the Orpheum almost every week. Even if he'd seen the movie already he'd come just to talk to Will.

We sat in the first row of the empty theater. Afterward, squinting as we stepped into a bar of sunshine, I looked at Jamie and said, in my best imitation of Roger Ebert, "Well, Gene, thumbs up or down?"

Jamie's eyes shone for a moment. Then he looked at me cautiously, trying to decide if I was making fun of him.

"Gene?" I repeated.

He bit his lip, but he couldn't help but slip into that open-mouthed smile. "Well, Roger," he said, "I'm sorry to say, thumbs down. Tremendous action sequences, vintage Spielberg, and the mine-car chase was almost worth the ticket. Almost. The racism here was just too much to overcome. This film strikes me as an apologist's take on imperialism."

"For once, Gene, we agree," I said, and even tried to puff out my cheeks. We shook on it, but still we returned to see the movie the next weekend and the next.

We rode our bikes over the bluff, belting out "London Calling" (which Jamie had introduced me to) as loudly as we could without disturbing the cigarettes stuck in our lips. We checked out Frommer's guides to Europe from the library and planned trips: French girls with beauty marks, enormous steins of beer, quaaludes and riots and dirty alleys full of prostitutes and new friends. Jamie spread the map across his desk, and we traced a line from Portugal to Prague, each saying, "I have a goat. He gives me cheese and butter," in imagined versions of local accents. We watched *The Ten Commandments* on television and farted every time someone said "Moses."

Why do I remember these things? Because, in spite of what was happening in the basement on Seachase, in spite of what was happening with my mother in California and my father in Alaska, these hours with Jamie felt important. The secret of Richard bound me to him. He already knew the worst thing about me: There was a man being held prisoner in my basement, and I was doing nothing about it. And neither was he.

If only there had been a way to become that close to Jamie, to anyone, without the lasso of a secret. I wonder if already I could see what would happen later, and if, in some kind of retribution for it, I tried to be who Jamie wanted me to be. I'd like to think so, but I've never known anyone try to be someone else *for* someone else and be happy, and for those weeks, as fall bled into winter, as our bikes sped past the storefronts on Canal, the silver of the handlebars reflected in the picture windows—I was happy.

We invited Katherine Cloons to see *Indiana Jones and the Temple of Doom*, hoping she would show up without her glasses. She arrived chewing her nails, hair still spiky but starting to wilt because she'd walked the whole way from her house way out on Cordon. Jamie and I split the cost of her ticket, and she sat between us, a Cherry Coke in her lap. We'd memorized half of the script by then and barked dialogue into the darkness. "This Nohachi sure is a small guy," I said. "I cheat little. You cheat very big," Jamie said. Katherine actually laughed, and when the Thuggee priest pulled out the man's beating heart she didn't even gasp.

"How do you like the movie?" I whispered.

"It's really great," she said.

I leaned back in my seat and let my eyes unfocus, trying to see the movie the way she did, the screen a sheet of swirling color. "Fortune and glory, kid. Fortune and glory," Jamie quoted. Katherine smelled like sweet oranges. I asked for a sip of her Coke and reached into the pocket of her jeans. She stiffened but didn't take my hand away.

The next afternoon after school when we visited Richard, I told him all this.

"And then what?" he asked. He'd been hitting push-ups every day and was no longer the willowy figure I remembered. The veins on his neck stood out like the veins in an old person's hand.

"The heart burst into flame," I said.

"What did *you* do? In that pocket." He reached into the baggy pocket of his sweatpants, jabbing his hand against the fabric. "You mean you had your hand inches from this girl's dewdrop, and you just quit?" He jumped to his feet as if to suggest that this wrong was so outrageous that he personally had to fix it.

"It was further than he got," I said, pointing across the narrow room at Jamie.

"What was I supposed to do," Jamie said, "put my hand in her other pocket?"

"There you go," Richard said. "Exactly. You'd already fucked up the whole thing for both of you. Hand in her pocket? Are you serious?"

"Sorry," I said, "didn't mean to disappoint you."

Richard sat back down. "It's not your fault," he said gravely. "It really isn't. The good news is I can help. Give me some time, and I can show you. The high school girls will think you just busted out of Spanish Harlem."

"Is that a good thing?" Jamie asked.

"Definitely."

These were the things we talked about in the basement: what we did when we weren't with him, how we lived. Richard asked us questions about music we'd heard, or movies we'd watched, or girls. One afternoon, at Richard's prodding, Jamie told the story of his doomed love for Andrea. Richard absorbed the story with a solemn, regretful expression, the kind of face the confession booth is designed to hide on a priest.

"I'd say you did the right thing," Richard said.

"Yeah?" Jamie looked up. "It doesn't feel like it."

"So you were wrong about her. Let me tell you about wrong. When I was living in Savannah for a summer, I used to see this complete beauty at a café down the street from my apartment. She had this classic style, wore one of those big sun hats. And she always wore a skirt with those nylons with the back seams, know those? She was at this café every day, and whenever I walked past she'd always raise her eyebrows like she knew me, like we were in on something together. You know? I was living alone, so I had a lot of time to think, and I thought *a lot* about this woman.

"At the end of the summer, just as I was about to leave town, I finally asked if I could sit down at her table. She said, 'Sure, Richard, please do.' And for a second I thought: This girl knows my name somehow. This is it. This is fate. And then I realized that the girl was my landlord's *son*, who I'd met a bunch of times because the sink kept breaking. She was a fucking drag queen."

"Shut up," Jamie said.

"I wish it weren't true," Richard said.

Jamie and I rolled on the floor, laughing.

"Usually the lines aren't that bright," Richard said. "It's not a question of if you were right or wrong about someone, but how wrong you were. Too wrong? Were you too wrong?"

In this way, the three of us agreed silently to pretend. We said nothing about the chain wrapping around Richard's leg and snaking along the length of the room and coiling around the pipe under the sink. We said nothing about the plastic bucket. We said nothing about the pallor of Richard's skin, skin that hadn't seen daylight in two months. Nothing about the body that hadn't had a proper shower, or the ears that hadn't heard a human voice other than Don's and ours. Or the soul—I don't know what other word to use—that was captive and idle. Or the life that the world thought was over.

Instead, we brought games down from the living room, Trivial Pursuit, Monopoly, Parcheesi, Connect Four. Richard taught us hearts and we kept playing bourré. Any trump game we played from then on, we'd always shout *boo-ray* when someone didn't follow suit, standing up, throwing our cards down in disgust, adopting that New Orleans accent Richard had first used. "Did you just boo-ray? You just fuckin' boo-rayed, man."

Jamie told us about Andrea. Richard told us about an irrational fear he'd always had of losing a limb, how he didn't think he could bear the expressions he'd see on the faces of strangers for the rest of his life. He told us about his father, about what he'd revealed in the New York letters. I began to talk too. I told them about my mother, about how I hadn't spoken to her for weeks, about how I wanted to but was too angry with her for leaving. And I told them about *Treasure Island*, about my father's stories of the good Captain Flint— I didn't realize until the words left my mouth how important that memory was. There was silence after I finished talking, then Richard said, "Man, I'd have loved to hear those. *Treasure Island* was my absolute fucking favorite."

According to Richard, Don still came every morning, but, as the afternoons passed without a sign of him, we played the records louder and louder. One afternoon we listened to both sides of *The Black Saint and the Sinner Lady* without saying a word. I lay there, looking at the jar of pennies back in its place beside the record player, thinking of my mother for the first time in some days, how she must have done this very thing so many times, how it had kept her sane. And I thought of Richard's father sitting almost exactly where I sat, maybe. And I wondered why I had never asked to come in, why I had never sat down in this spot with my mother. Perhaps I was just respecting her privacy, but privacy is a convenience, a way to politely ignore what doesn't interest you. When it came to these records, to this basement, I wasn't interested. I never had been.

When the album was over, Jamie lifted the needle, but Richard stayed on his back. "I just wish that I could know nothing but this music," he said. "That I had really grown up right here. That all I knew I learned from these records. I wish that."

And Jamie and I said we wished it too.

OF COURSE we were still scared. A passing car, a rattling window, a creaking floorboard sent Jamie and me streaking into the basement, diving under the stairs. We brought plastic bags to carry out our butts and ashes, and checked and rechecked the same list. Key in the dryer. Basement door closed. House key in the magnetized slot under the *left* side of the grill.

One day we cut school to check up on Don's routine, to make sure we never crossed paths. We spotted his truck on the far side of Henderson Park. With its rusted grille and cracked windshield it looked dangerous just parked on the street.

"He must walk through the woods to get to the house," Jamie said. "Just like us."

The thought of Don following the same path we followed—winding around the rusty swings and pushing his way through branches—made my stomach hurt. I felt as if he'd stolen something from me.

The morning rain had stopped, and sunlight tumbled down, turning the windshields to mirrors. There was a steady trickle in the gutter, rain dripping from leaves. A dog barked. I felt a spasm of fear and had to force myself to turn around and look. A big black Lab was tearing down the street, a man running behind him.

"Who's that?" Jamie asked.

I knew the answer but was too startled to speak. The dog's name was Dutch. The man's name was Bill Rathke. He'd worked with my father on the *Laurentide* until a sliding pot had crushed his left arm. Even though he hadn't been on the boats in years, he still subscribed to the *Dutch Harbor Fisherman*, and there must have been a part of his mind that still went to Alaska every season. There were a lot of people like Bill Rathke in Loyalty Island.

"I won't tell," Bill said as he approached. Dutch was nosing Jamie's hand. Bill caught his breath and knelt to put a chain on the dog. "You two look worried," he said, "but I won't tell."

"We should be in school," Jamie said.

"I was thinking that," Bill said. "Just don't make a habit of it. Good news about the season, isn't it?"

Years before, Bill had tried to give me an old BB gun; my mother hadn't let me accept it, but I'd felt grateful to him ever since. And yet, as we stood in the middle of the street I could barely find my voice. I could only imagine Don rounding the corner, and, at his signal, Bill's kind face turning mean, the dog's teeth bared and snapping.

As we rode down Spruce I had a fantasy—and not for the last time—that the whole town knew, that they were all in on it. Sometimes in the weeks that followed, while walking the boardwalk or waiting in line downtown, I'd be talking to Belinda or Will Percy and suddenly be afraid that while I'd meant to say, *School's fine, the Norths are fine*, what I'd really said was: *Richard is alive.*

I began to wonder what people would do if they knew. What would Bill, with his crippled arm and big dog, do if he found out that Richard was captive in our basement? He would help, I thought, he would consider it the right thing to keep Richard there, to keep him from ever reappearing. I guess I had to think this. I had to think that my father was no worse than anyone else.

THE ONE THING we didn't talk about in the basement was what had happened the night Richard was taken. But I continued to think of the ring of yellow and purple around his midsection. Who had pounded it there? Jamie never raised the question again, but I felt I had to. One afternoon later that fall Richard sighed, defeated. "You really want to know?" he asked.

I had to nod my head.

"The night they came for me," he said, "I was lying in my father's bed thanking God he hadn't died in it."

He described the bed, the thick grain of the mahogany, the four posts and their spade-shaped knobs, the wide wooden slats at the headboard. He told us he had vague memories of his mother sweeping back the comforter, smoothing a space for him between flannel sheets. Later, after his mother died, he'd played on the bed on Saturday mornings in the summer, his father at the head reading the newspaper, Richard at the foot filling in a color-by-numbers book. He remembered raw window light and the aroma of chicory coffee.

He told us he brought his first real girlfriend into that bed, and she bit him on the shoulder. He was in high school by then, and John was away for the season, one of his last. "Bit you how?" Jamie asked. "Is that common?" And suddenly I realized we'd been tricked. Richard would never describe the kidnapping, no matter how many times I asked. And I felt a surge of relief because Richard had been right. I didn't want to know.

Richard told us that the night John left for the season, he asked Melissa, his girlfriend, to lie to her mother. "Tell her you'll be out all night, make up a good reason for it."

"Why should I?" Melissa asked. She was a year younger than Richard but five times as smart. Already he was preparing to lose her.

"Because we've got a big house now. It's ours. We can lie to anyone."

He'd rehearsed the line and was ready for her to laugh at him. She did laugh, but he could hear the blush in it.

Later, Richard lit candles, ruined a pot of razor clams, and stole a bottle of his father's sauterne. They ate on the screened-in porch overlooking the glassy bay. It was warm but breezy enough to blow the napkin from his lap. He tucked it into the collar of his shirt, and she laughed. He carried her into the bedroom after dinner, and she laughed. In bed, she wouldn't let him take off her underwear, but he didn't mind. He felt dazed by his first glimpse of what it might mean to have money and time and a father who was gone half the year and who would do anything he asked.

"Nice?" he said to Melissa. They were done fooling around; the drapes were open, the moonlight puddled on the floor. She turned, mostly asleep, said nothing, but bit him on the shoulder. Richard told us he would always remember that feeling. After she'd broken up with him in a polite voice as he stood at the foot of her parents' driveway. After he'd gone away to college. After he saw her in Eric's Quilt around Christmas and Dan Fosse made fun of her because she'd gained weight and looked broken and tired. After Dan Fosse died and Richard came back to Loyalty Island hoping for a familiar, understanding face. By then she'd moved to Spokane with a boyfriend who sold pharmaceutical equipment. Richard never saw her again, and though he could hardly picture her face anymore, he told us that all these years later he still remembered the feeling of that bite, her teeth, their ridges and dips, pressing, not quite hurting.

ON THE LAST WEEKEND of November, *Indiana Jones and the Temple of Doom* closed its run at the Orpheum. At the final screening, Jamie and I, having tried nearly every seat in the house, chose the second row. I knew the movie almost shot for shot, and by then the pleasure in watching came not from the movie itself but from the comfort of knowing exactly what came next. But when the film ended and the lights came up, Jamie whispered, "Don't turn around."

The theater had been full that night, and I listened to the rustle of footsteps as it emptied, all the while staring into the dead screen.

"Okay, look."

I turned in time to see Don Brooke push through the heavy purple curtains and into the lobby. My throat went numb. I'd known that we could run into Don at any time, that he must live like the rest of us, buying his dinner at Safeway and finding some way to escape the empty evenings, but to actually see him, to actually imagine him buying a ticket, enjoying a movie, was unnerving, almost painful.

"We should wait here a few more minutes," Jamie said. "Will won't mind."

"Was Don alone?" I asked.

"I think so."

"Was he watching us?"

"He was probably watching the movie, wasn't he?"

"Or he was following us."

"But why would he follow us here?"

"I don't know, but we should be more careful."

"We shouldn't see any more movies?"

"No. We should be more careful," I said. "Who knows what he'll do."

My father's affection for Don had always been a mystery to me. I knew that he and Sam weren't innocent, but I was sure neither of them could have opened that basement door day in and day out. I imagined that Don had insisted he be the one to stay behind, because only he was cruel enough to last. Had my father always known that one day he'd need someone capable of such horrible work?

WE CHANGED OUR ROUTINE, varying the time we arrived, following different routes through the neighborhood. If we'd really wanted to be careful we would have stopped going to the house at all. But we didn't stop. We couldn't.

Without natural light, Richard's skin had grown appreciably paler, accentuating the dark circles under his eyes. But the eyes themselves had grown luminous in response, so that, as he spoke, he seemed to peer at us like some nocturnal animal. Richard had also begun to reveal the one thing he had in common with the fishermen of Loyalty Island: He was a storyteller.

We'd sit in a triangle, Jamie and I on the floor, Richard on the bench, as he described dodging a train in a tunnel outside Green River, Wyoming. Or the diner where he worked in Lawrence, Kansas, that sold illegal fireworks and tropical birds out of the back of the kitchen. Or an acquaintance, no, a friend, a Broadway director, who held suicide parties at his mansion in Westchester. Or a man in Chicago who wore a Japanese demon mask on the El every day at rush hour.

Were the stories true? It didn't matter then, so I guess it doesn't now. We treated Richard's stories as if they were true; we acted like they meant something, Jamie especially. "That's amazing," Jamie would say. Or, *"That's* amazing." Or just, *"Amazing."* I'd never heard him so inarticulate. For once he could afford to be. Richard was already saying everything Jamie wanted to hear.

His stories were dispatches from a kind of life we had never encountered. It's not that they were more thrilling or dramatic than our fathers' stories of Alaska, but those stories were gray, drenched in icy slime. They made you gasp but not smile, and the men who told them smiled—if at all—only at the gasps.

Richard's stories told us something else: There are other ways to live. I know this now, but did I know it then? Obviously I'd known there could be a life for me outside of Loyalty Island. What I didn't realize was how different the world was on the other side of Puget Sound, on the other side of the Cascades. I didn't realize that staying in Loyalty Island and earning a place on the boats with my father was not to have everything, that it was, in fact, to miss an incalculable amount.

Loyalty Island was peculiar in the sense that, with its economic heart two thousand miles north in the Bering Sea, if you dreamed of living there your whole life, you also dreamed of leaving. Richard Gaunt, like so many others, left Loyalty Island at eighteen. He'd continued to hope, at times anyway, that his father would at last offer him a place on the boats, that his father had been testing him all this time, and that, despite these sour years, he'd passed the test.

But he had too much pride to bring it up, and when graduation day came John pressed a thousand-dollar check into Richard's hand. He bought Richard a sheet cake and gave him the keys to the Volvo. He told him how handsome he looked in his cap and gown.

After the ceremony they ate a late meal together on the screened-in porch. John brought out a bottle of Laphroaig, and they sat up late, quietly getting drunk. It was the kind of night for reflection, for reconciliation. There was something about the whiskey, the breeze, and the tap of John's foot against the stone floor that told Richard he could ask him anything. Yet they spoke only in little bursts and about little things.

Richard didn't go to Alaska. He went to the University of Washington. He cheered at the Apple Cup, got kicked out of his freshman dorm for smashing a bottle in the hallway, pledged Sigma Chi, hosted snow parties, read *Civilization and Its Discontents* and a few other books, broke his wrist falling from a roof, and dropped out the summer before his senior year.

Why? Because he couldn't sleep. Because he'd smoked his fingers yellow. Because he'd learned that he never had to make up his mind and he wanted to prove it. Because Dan Fosse died that spring, giving Richard a good excuse to leave. Because Richard had decided for no good reason that he'd made the wrong decision in going to college in the first place. Because that's the thing about coming from money. Decisions don't matter because they can always be undone.

He drank Greyhounds at a bar in Ballard and called his father from a pay phone outside. It was after midnight, and he'd hoped to wake John up, to have that advantage on him, but the voice that answered, though irritated, was clear and level.

"I'm not going back to school," Richard said. John sighed, and Richard smiled.

"What *are* you going to do?" John asked.

"Nothing," Richard said.

"And where are you going to do this nothing?"

"Anywhere. I don't know."

There was a pause. Richard thought he might hear his father finally explode, finally tip and snarl that he was spoiled, stupid, lazy, all the things Richard had aimed to be, but John said, "Good. Travel. Take some time, and if I can help let me know."

Richard slammed down the phone, but left school in spite of his father's blessing. He hitched a ride out of town, a shy mop of dark hair with good teeth and bad posture, living off his father's money. Around Yakima he caught a bus east and watched the earth begin to dry out, the skies to clear. His hair grew into his eyes, and he tamed it with a ponytail. He found college friends in Bozeman, Montana, ski instructors who said he could stay at their resort cabin as long as he paid his own way. Their names were Davey and Carol. They offered to teach him to ski.

"No thanks," Richard said.

"What will you do all day?" Carol asked. She had sunburned cheeks and hair as blond as swan's feathers. Richard had always wondered what she was doing with Davey. "I think I'm a painter," Richard said.

He never actually painted anything, but he spent three happy months in that cabin. Every night the three of them stayed up drinking and playing a game Carol had invented called Blackmail Jack. Once, though it was only part of the game, Richard got to kiss her. And, each morning, as the sun rose, the darkness lifted like a stain from the white fields.

When the ski season ended and Davey and Carol packed up and went west, Richard, who'd planned out the words he'd use to persuade Carol to go with him, but never actually said them, went east. First to Minneapolis, where he lived for a month in a long-stay hotel on Hennepin Avenue.

His room was cleaned each day by a bulldoggish, diabetic Swede, who kept oranges on a tray atop her squealing cart. She pushed the cart slowly down the hall, unlocking every door as she went, then worked her way backward room by room, so that the doors at the head of the hall remained unlocked and vacant for hours.

The first time Richard sneaked through one of the unlocked doors, the room was empty and, except for a blue stain on the comforter, identical to his own. The next day he grew bolder. In the third room he checked, he found an open suitcase on the unmade bed. He found three black T-shirts, a howling timber wolf silk-screened on each; a cribbage set; a nearly destroyed copy of *The Fellowship of the Ring*; and four tubes of toothpaste rolled to the spout.

Richard began to frame his days around the squeal of those wheels, the tumble of the locks, the Swede's crackling voice as she greeted each empty bed with *"Tjena, tjena."* He spent the next few weeks cataloging the belongings of strangers, their contours and smells, their myriad significances. In one room he found stiff shirts smelling of rummy aftershave, a smooth leather belt with the initials NFD stenciled in faded gold. He found a sticky comb, a real estate brochure from Burlington, Wisconsin, a box of baking soda held shut by a rubber band. Richard could practically see the man who lived here, threading the belt through the loops of brown slacks, fanning himself with the brochure, leaning across the table to better hear a question. A man who pronounced only half the W when he cupped his ear, saying, "Vhat, vhat?" He'd recently retired and had come to the Midwest to buy a bit of land, something that reminded him of his childhood in Hungary or Poland.

In another room he found a leather motorcycle helmet with earflaps, a collection of postcard prints of the paintings of Filippo Lippi at the Uffizi in Florence, a bottle of spicy perfume, its missing cap replaced by a plastic bag tied with purple ribbon. These items summoned the image of a slender woman with salt-and-pepper hair. The woman's daughter was missing, a runaway. A friend of a friend of a friend saw her, maybe, working the counter of a dry cleaner's in Dinkytown. The woman had come all the way from Connecticut to find out.

"I wondered what I would think about my own room if I could walk into it as a stranger would," Richard told Jamie and me. "What would I say about my belongings?"

He'd been tempted to steal the Lippi cards or the cribbage set as souvenirs, but he never did because he felt loyal to the images these items had helped him create. Instead, on his last morning at the hotel, he stole an orange from the Swede's cart.

After Minneapolis, Richard followed the spine of the Mississippi south, the river, sky, and road sliding past tinted Greyhound windows, the summer coming. He'd made vague arrangements to stay with an old fraternity brother, a legendary University Avenue drinker who'd moved to New Orleans to play piano in a bar. When Richard arrived the drinker was no longer a drinker or a piano player. He sat at the open window, smoking a cigarette and wiping his wide, sweaty face. His name was Mickey. "I'm a cook now," he said. "No shit. If you were anyone else I'd offer to get you work."

"And why not me?" Richard asked.

His friend shrugged. "Anyway, there's a prep-kitchen spot if you want it," he said. "I don't mind lying for you."

Richard sweated away the next four months in the kitchen of a restaurant for tourists on Canal Street. He learned to peel prawns and shuck oysters, to skin catfish and bone chicken. He learned to smoke a cigarette in ninety seconds and to deal bourré. He didn't learn to appreciate food, but he learned to disappear into the work, into the rhythm of the chef's knife clicking on the board like the needle of a sewing machine, into the clock of boiling water.

He met a pastry chef with a filthy mouth who was almost a decade his senior and moved into her studio on Conti Street. He lived there for three months, sleeping through the heat on a mattress in the middle of the floor. She drank a bottle of dessert wine before bed most nights, and Richard woke in the blast of a squeaky fan to find her thrashing on the damp sheet.

On a rare day off from the restaurant he and the pastry chef packed a picnic and drove to Biloxi along I-10, the sun blowing in through the open windows.

"What's that smell?" Richard asked.

"That's the ocean, fuckhead," the pastry chef said. But it wasn't the smell of the ocean. The smell of the ocean was the smell of Greene Harbor: gasoline and engine oil, fish and dry ice. The sun was too bright here, the water too green. Richard thought about the smell of Loyalty Island for the rest of the day; though he tried to smoke it out with Camel after Camel, he couldn't. He was homesick. He wanted to go home. So he did.

That decision was the first stitch in a pattern that stretched over the next decade of his life. He'd pick a place: four months in Boulder, six in Savannah, eighteen in Chicago. Sometimes he'd work in restaurants, sometimes he'd do next to nothing. Sometimes he was happy, and sometimes he was miserable. But he found that it didn't matter either way, because eventually he would be drawn back to Loyalty Island.

Though he always left by car or bus, he'd return by plane: touching down in Seattle; taking a cab to the terminal on Pier 53 and the ferry across the Sound; staring east from the rail in the aft; tossing butts into the wake; thinking about time and the universe;

disembarking at Bainbridge, where his father would be waiting for him, smiling, perceptibly older.

He'd sleep in his old room, drink with his old friends at Eric's Quilt, drive his old car. He'd sit on benches under squabbling birds. He'd watch the water and breathe in air that was so damp, so thick, it seemed that the solid earth, the streets and the buildings, were hardly more substantial.

"Why?" I asked. "Why did you always come back?"

"If I knew that, you know . . ." He shrugged and turned up his palms. "One night I remember I was at a dinner—it might have been in this house, Cal, I think it was—and Don was drunk, surprise, surprise, and he sort of cornered me outside while I was waiting to drive my father home. 'I know what you're doing,' he said, and jabbed me in the chest. He thought I was coming back so I wouldn't get cut out of my father's will or something. Fucking asshole. But what could I tell him? I just had to come back. That was it."

"But don't you hate it here?" Jamie said.

"I read somewhere," Richard said, "that the only reason to hate your home is because you hate yourself."

"Don't you?" I asked.

Richard smiled as if he possessed some secret. "You know," he said, "you're both like me, but especially you, Cal. Jamie, see, he'll never be one of them, but he knows who he really is. Not us, though. We'll never be one of them, but what else is there for us to be?"

He waited for an answer, his expression soft and sad, as if his deepest regret was that he should have to pity me.

AS THE DAYS PASSED, Jamie and I spent less and less time wandering the boardwalk, less and less time at the Orpheum, less and less time anywhere but his bedroom and the basement on Seachase. When Delia Dole stopped us downtown and asked about school one afternoon I couldn't find the words to answer. I hardly knew what she meant. When Heiner the policeman passed us on his bike and poked at me with his nightstick, laughing, I spun away. I couldn't laugh, though I knew I was supposed to. The faces I had known my whole life seemed to appear before me as if reflected in warped mirrors. And the boardwalk, the movie theater, Belinda's, already seemed like the ruins of those places.

My mother called twice in November, both times when she must have known I'd be in school. There'd been some complications that had kept her in the hospital for a week, but she was home now, Betty said.

Betty wrote Meg's number in purple pen and stuck it to the refrigerator with a magnet shaped like a frog. "She said to call as soon as you can." She squeezed my shoulder. Only the lamp above the stove lighted the kitchen. "And don't worry about the long distance, talk as long as you want."

I missed my mother, I did. I wanted to know how she was, how my sister was, who my sister was. But, in comparison to afternoons in the basement with Richard, these thoughts were distant and dim.

I couldn't bring myself to call her back, and, for the first time in my life, I wanted to talk to my father even less.

In first or second grade I had returned home every day with one question for my mother. Did Dad call? Did Dad call? No, she'd say, no, no, I'll tell you when he does. But I kept asking. Finally, one night over dinner, my mother snatched the paper napkin off her lap and put a pen to it. "These are phone wires," she said, scratching a series of lines, "got that?" She drew a round little boat. "Know what this is?"

It looked nothing like the *Laurentide*, but I got the idea.

"Well, these lines don't go to this boat, or any boat. So please stop asking."

But I couldn't stop. Something took my father away for most of every year, something more important than I was. So when he sacrificed that thing for a few moments to call from the cannery, I'd hang my week, or my month, around the conversation. I thought I needed the person who had left and, of course, that wasn't very fair to the person who'd stayed. I wondered if my mother would be satisfied to see me flinching every time the phone rang at the Norths', afraid it was my father.

JAMIE CAUGHT THE FLU in early December. We decided that I'd continue to visit Richard alone, and when I arrived after school I found him waving a paperback at the wall. A black fly had found its way into the room, and Richard and I spent twenty minutes trying to corner and swat it, tripping over each other, laughing. Afterward he put on *Money Jungle*, and we sat down to cards. Without Jamie we couldn't play hearts or bourré, so Richard suggested gin rummy. He taught me how to deal and keep score.

"You know," Richard said after a few hands, "I'd forgotten it, but my father taught me how to play this game. I must have been eight. One weekend he said in this stern voice, 'I have something *important* to talk to you about.' And we sat down at the dining room table, but all he did was teach me to play gin rummy. About a month later he told me again that he had something *important* to talk to me about. That time he sat me down and told me he'd never let me on one of his boats. He must have been planning to tell me for weeks. He must have been afraid. That's a funny thought, that he was afraid." Richard smiled to himself as he reshuffled the deck. "Know what I did then? I went into his office and started smashing these bottled ships my great-uncle had made. Pretty dramatic, huh? Maybe I should have just asked him why."

"He never told you?"

"Not until I was in New York. He'd started with those letters and in one of them he said maybe he'd made a mistake. He said he'd been thinking of himself at my age. That he realized he'd loved his own father through the work they did together, through what he'd been allowed to learn from him. And he said that he understood why I'd hated him all this time, for the one true reason to hate anybody."

"There's only one?"

"Because you want to love him and he won't let you."

"Did you hate him?"

"I did."

We kept playing. I stayed later than I'd planned and grew hungry enough to accept Richard's offer of white bread, mayonnaise, and turkey. As we paused to build the sandwiches I asked, "What else can you tell me about him, your father?"

According to Richard, the John Gaunt who appeared in those letters was a man more conflicted than Richard could ever have guessed, a man Richard wished he had known. After the war he'd been a music major at the University of Wisconsin, where he'd studied composition and gone to bars with friends, talking early into the morning about the future, as if it were yet to be determined. But for John, nothing was further from the truth. He'd worked the summer salmon boats with his own father since junior high and by eighteen had acquired the curse—the dual mind—of the offshore fisherman: Alone, life on land and life on the water were unbearable, but each was the antidote to the other's poison. So, even as he crossed the snowy quads in Madison, racing to keep his guitar tuned in the cold, John longed for the sting of salt in his nose, the vibration of a diesel engine under his feet.

Morley Gaunt died when John was forty, leaving him an impressive trawler fleet and a dying salmon fishery. It was John's idea to push the fleet north, to refit the old trawlers for crab. He was proud of this decision because, though much had changed, he'd managed to preserve the rhythm of generations. Five years later, the money coming back from Alaska was unlike anything Loyalty Island had ever seen. Five years after that John borrowed on the Magnuson-Stevens Act to build the *Laurentide* and the *Cordilleran*, along with three other smaller boats. And five years after that, without warning, he announced that he wouldn't be going to Alaska again, that he was going to quit.

"He wrote that he was proud he'd been able to step down, proud he'd been able to stay home," Richard said. "It wasn't the kind of thing he'd normally say. I guess he saved it all for those letters."

"Why? Did he explain why he quit?"

"Maybe because he met your mother. That's what you're asking, isn't it?"

I couldn't meet his gaze.

Thankfully, Richard spared me from answering. "He used to come down here, didn't he? He used to sit right here."

"Do you know something about them?" I hated how the words sounded as they left my mouth, hoarse, almost desperate.

"See that mason jar over there?" Richard pointed to the jar full of pennies that my mother had brought up to the kitchen after John died. "My father must have brought it."

"How do you know?"

"It's an old tradition," Richard said. "Every time you visit a woman whose husband is at sea you put a coin in the jar. Don't think I haven't wondered what it was like for him to sit here. I've thought about it a lot. Imagined it. Haven't you?"

That was the problem—I never had been able to imagine them together. When the basement door closed they stepped into oblivion. But after all these weeks spent in my mother's studio, sitting where she once sat, listening to the music she once had, finally I could picture it. As Richard talked, I saw John standing on the pi.arly September, amid whistling wives and crying children, waving the big boats away. Facing, for the first time in his life, the cruelest feeling in Loyalty Island, the feeling of being left behind. I saw him pacing up our front walk with the mason jar, rapping on our front door with his cane. I can see him even now, smiling as she opens the door, holding the jar out before him.

As they take their seats in the studio she says to John the same thing she used to say to me, "Do you want to hear the best thing ever?"

The piece she means is Ellington's "Lotus Blossom" from ... *And His Mother Called Him Bill*, the album cut by the Duke Ellington Orchestra just weeks after Billy Strayhorn died.

My mother drops the needle, closing her eyes and listening to the lilting, down-tempo piano, the rainy chords and minor arpeggios. And, as he listens, John learns, relearns maybe, what I refused to let my mother teach me—that music marks time while remaining outside of it. That the 3/4 signature of "Lotus Blossom" could carry you along for the rest of your life. And perhaps—sitting next to my mother, the lights off, the orange vacuum tubes pulsing like veins— John feels strangely and finally at ease, his mind drifting through nameless feelings just as his eyes, for so many years, drifted over nameless miles of water.

The piano plays on. Eventually my mother says, "This is the best part, listen to this." A baritone sax emerges, laying long, golden notes on the chords. The solo follows the melody but seems to come from another place entirely, from another room, outside the door, outside the earth, outside life.

If there are ways to love someone without betraying others, isn't music one of them? Could music have been all there was between my mother and John Gaunt? Probably not, but I can *almost* convince myself. Because I can see them so clearly, my mother explaining to John that on the original album the take with Harry Carney on saxophone hadn't even appeared. It stayed hidden in the RCA vaults for years, until someone stumbled on it and included it on a reissue.

"Can you imagine that?" I hear her saying. "All those years locked away and no one knew anything about it. Can you imagine what else must be lost?"

JUST BEFORE CHRISTMAS VACATION the weather turned. For three nights it rained ice. Then the skies cleared and the temperature plummeted. One afternoon Jamie and I arrived at the house blowing on our wind-bitten hands. We walked through a basement that seemed to shudder against the roar of the octopus furnace. The studio was blazing hot, and we found Richard lying shirtless in the middle of the floor, his long hair splayed out like a black halo.

"What can we do?" Jamie asked. He knelt beside Richard, but I stayed by the door. "Cal," he said, "grab that T-shirt there and run it under cold water."

I did as he said and then watched as, with the light touch of a nurse, Jamie dabbed the wet shirt to Richard's forehead. "It's ridiculous in here. There you go. There you go," he said.

Eventually Richard sat up against the wall, the T-shirt wrapped around his head, falling onto his shoulders like the cape of a Legionnaire's cap. His cheeks were flushed. As if in answer to a question, he said, "It's been hot in here before, but not like this. I wish your mother had thought to put a thermostat in here."

"She didn't build it." I could feel sweat slide down my neck as I spoke. Richard closed his eyes and leaned his head against the wall.

"Are you okay?" Jamie asked.

"If I were an Indian, I'd be chief. Chief of the sweat lodge. Did you know that people used to say I was part Quinault?"

"No," I said, though I'd heard this any number of times.

"Well, they did. Because of my cheekbones, see?" He drew a finger across each one. "And because they hated me. That was also part of it."

"No one hated you," Jamie said. The sight of Jamie standing under the light of the unsheltered bulb, wringing out the T-shirt, made me uneasy. "We're worried about you," he said, glancing my way, inviting me to say something, to help.

"I think I'm up to cards," Richard said.

Jamie and I stripped down to our T-shirts. We played a listless game of hearts, staying an extra hour as if in solidarity.

"We should go back early tomorrow, make sure our friend's all right," Jamie said later as we lay stacked on the bunk bed. "Are you awake?" he asked. "We should go back early. Are you awake?"

"He's not our friend, Jamie," I said.

"Then what is he?"

He wasn't our friend. But he wasn't our enemy either. What was he? Despite the cards, the records, and the stories—despite everything—he was still our prisoner. You can't look at your prisoner with the kind of light Jamie had in his eyes. You just can't. Only, at the time, I couldn't find the words to explain how I was beginning to feel, so I said nothing.

When we arrived at the house the next day the furnace was off. I unlocked the door to find Richard shivering in a blanket, perched on the bench with his knees pressed to his chest.

"Is Don doing this on purpose?" Jamie asked.

"I don't know."

"He gives you cigarettes, then he tortures you?" I asked.

"I don't know."

"Is he trying to torture you?"

Richard sucked a breath through clenched teeth and shivered. He looked nearly insane. Maybe Don had done it deliberately, or maybe his twitching hand at the thermostat had bestowed two days of agony by accident. In such circumstances insanity might be a blessing. The things we can't control in our lives—where we happen to be born, what weaknesses we happen to discover, who happens to fall in love with us—outnumber the things we can control by a factor of ten. But we live day by day, choice by choice, and comfort by comfort, forgetting that, when all is said and done, we've really had no choice whatsoever. Shivering in the basement, Richard could no longer forget.

"They're going to kill you this way," Jamie said flatly.

"You need coffee," I said.

"Please, not coffee," Richard said.

"Hot chocolate?" I asked. I took his silence as a yes. Upstairs, I boiled water in my mother's blue kettle, pinched in cinnamon and nutmeg from their foggy jars, and mixed up a packet of the instant cocoa I used to drink when I lived in the house. I hadn't yet convinced myself I liked coffee either.

When I returned to the basement with a torpedo-shaped thermos wrapped in a dish towel, Jamie and Richard went silent. I had the bitter feeling they'd been saying things they didn't want me to hear. I stood there, unsure of what to do, and when Richard dropped his blanket and reached his hand out to me I wasn't sure why.

"For me?" he asked. He rubbed his hands over the thermos and held it under his face for a moment before taking a sip. "It's good. Thank you."

"What were you talking about?" I asked.

"I was talking," Jamie said. "I was saying we just turn on the heat."

"If Don's doing this on purpose then he'll know we were here," I said.

"Maybe it doesn't matter if Don knows."

Jamie's voice was small. I knew he wasn't sure if he meant what he was saying. "Doesn't matter?" I said.

"He's freezing to death," Jamie said. "That matters, doesn't it?"

Jamie's face, always open, always ready to listen, was at full attention, waiting for me to explain myself. But I couldn't.

"It's up to Richard," I said.

Richard shivered, his hands clasping the blanket just below his chin. "Leave it off," he said quietly. "I don't know what he'd do if he found out."

"Look at yourself," Jamie said. "What more could he do?"

"I don't know. Didn't I say that?" Richard's voice was louder this time. Then, as if he'd used up his last bit of energy, he leaned against the wall and closed his eyes.

Jamie bit his lip, perhaps wondering if it was wise to continue. "I'm afraid of him too," he said. "I hate him too, but we can't just let you freeze."

Richard pulled the blanket tighter around his shoulders.

"Richard?" Jamie said.

"I appreciate the thought, Jamie, really."

That should have been the end of it, but Jamie wouldn't stop digging until he hit rock.

"I hate him too," Jamie repeated.

"I don't hate them," Richard said, just loud enough to be heard.

"What?"

"Sorry to wreck your theory, but I don't hate them."

"Them?" I asked.

"You know who I mean," Richard answered, his head still glued to the wall. "I mean, I do hate them for who they are. But not for what they've done to me. I'm too weak for that. When Don walks in here with those sandwiches I feel grateful."

"You'd be grateful for some heat," Jamie said.

Richard mumbled a response.

"What did you say?" Jamie asked.

"I said just let it go."

"Okay," Jamie said, finally giving up because I think he had heard, the first time, what I'd heard.

Richard had said, "Just let *me* go."

AFTER THAT WEEK the heat returned to normal, but Richard never quite did. Increasingly, he told his stories with his eyes closed, as if reliving them exhausted him. As December wore on, we'd arrive to find him lying on his side on the bench, his arms crossed over his chest like a daytime Dracula. He would say no to cards and games. Those afternoons we spoke little but still sat with him for hours, crowded around the record player as if it were a fire.

I remembered what my father used to say about the look Alaskan fishermen got when they were about to break. The blankness in the eyes when the darkness of the winter and the madness of break-ing waves had unsealed the mind and seeped inside. They called it the Aleutian stare. It happens all the time, he used to say, dark days, no sleep, the weight of the water and the work and the low sky all pressing on you. The sea begins to feel infinite, and the boat you're tossed in painfully small, and the body you're tossed in smaller still. He once told me about a friend of his, a man named Wright—a big man, so they called him the Wright Whale—who got that look and, in the middle of a string, walked into the galley, set a pan of water on the burner, and, when the water was boiling, carefully poured it down the back of his flannels.

One afternoon, after not speaking for at least an hour, Richard raised his head from the bench and repeated something he'd said weeks before. "I just wish that I could know nothing but this music. That all I knew I learned from these records. I wish that."

We were listening to Sun Ra's *The Magic City*. The first time he'd said those words they had sounded spontaneous and right. Now they felt off.

"Nothing else?" I asked, but only because I felt like I had to say something, like Richard would be offended if we just let what he said fade in the silence.

"Wouldn't that be great?" he said.

"I don't know," I said. "Aren't you glad you learned how to chew, walk, that sort of thing?"

Richard smiled to himself. I could almost see his mind drift-ing into the place he must have gone to protect himself from the long hours alone. "I learned to hate music," he said, "because my father loved it. Of all the stupid things, right? I made a mistake." He propped himself up on his elbow. "I see that now. I defined myself against things. I spent all my time hating this or that. I don't know what I was getting out of it, do you?"

I looked at Jamie and shook my head.

"Freedom?" Jamie said.

"There's no freedom in that. I mean, define yourself against a cause, a war or something. I'd be at parties, and people would say things like 'Hey, Richard, what the fuck, man, lighten up.' And only then would it hit me that I'd been ranting about all the things and people and places I didn't like. I'd have to pretend I was joking. I'd say, in this Eastern European accent, like I was a crazy Polish expatriate or something, 'But you must understand! My natural inclination is to hate!'"

"What did you like?" Jamie asked. "There must have been something."

"I'm sure there was. But honestly, sitting right here, I can't even remember. I mean, it feels like trying to remember what someone else liked."

"But it wasn't someone else," I said.

"But that's how it feels. Sometimes I think, Who is this person in here with me? This person who lived somewhere, in some other place and time. This person with all these memories and all these things he hated. I remember him, but he's not me, understand? I remember him as *him*, not as me."

"Do you think that excuses you from what *you* did?" I didn't know where it was coming from, but suddenly I felt angry. Sometimes it's hard not to forgive. It was Richard who'd dumped the suitcase over our dining room table. It was Richard who'd brought us here. It was too late to take that back, and if he thought otherwise he was fooling himself.

The clarity returned to Richard's gaze. He arched an eyebrow at me. "And what did I do?" he asked.

"Just shut up, Cal," Jamie said.

"Let him talk," Richard said. "I'd like to know."

"Nothing," I said. "Sorry."

Richard let me drop it. He needed us, and we needed him. If only we didn't. It would have been so much better for everybody if we could have wiped the knowledge of Richard away, if we could have locked the door and, like our fathers, sailed away until spring.

BY THE TIME the semester ended in mid-December, I'd been living at the Norths' for almost four months. Approximately one-fortieth of my lifetime. I actually did the math. It seemed like so much longer.

At school we had a Christmas party with bubble lights and a

punch bowl. In English, we were asked to make a list of New Year's resolutions and explain them. I wrote: *Become a bitter speler. Obious?* We said good-bye, Merry Christmas, Happy New Year. Then we were gone, walking out into the yard.

"What about Sand Point tomorrow, for oysters? We can bike," Jamie said.

"Low tide's at like three a.m. right now," I said.

"I just thought because of the holidays you might want to," he said, shrugging.

Oystering at Sand Point was a family ritual. In the summers my father and I would pore over his tide charts, choosing the best morning, marking the calendar with a red pen. When the day came, my mother packed bottles of white wine and lemons. She sat in a white-and-green-striped bathing suit on a blanket on the gray beach, a book open on her lap and a wide-brimmed sun hat on her head no matter the weather. My father and I waded into the tide. He cut a special tape measure for me, two-and-a-half inches long because the native Olympias were off-limits and they seldom grew to that size. There were more than enough of the big Pacifics, crusted with barnacles, clinging to black rocks.

When my father and I had filled a mesh bag, we splashed back to shore and sprawled across beach towels. As my mother wedged lemons, my father shucked the oysters with a dull knife. There was never much sun, and there was no shine on the blade, but I remember it glinting in his hand; as I remember his eyes glinting as he tossed half of the shell back to the tide and handed the other half to my mother; as I remember her eyes glinting as she held the shell to her mouth.

Had I told Jamie all this? Could I have told him all this?

"We don't go in the middle of winter," I said.

"Then we need to go somewhere else, to talk. Where?"

"That depends," I said.

"This can't go on," he said. "How can it?"

Jamie's sudden certainty was jarring. He was right that to go on living these two lives bordered on madness—but the circumstances were mad, so, in a way, madness seemed sensible. It was Richard's fault. If he hadn't welcomed us in, hadn't told us jokes and played us music, hadn't acted as if we were all friends, could we have really gone on this way for so long? I would have had to let him go or let myself go, turning my back and pretending I had never found him. Either way, things would have turned out better than they did.

"The roof?" I asked.

"Not safe enough," Jamie said.

That night we picked our way down the bluff. The wind was just cold enough to sting. I followed Jamie for blocks along the waterfront, past waves that groaned and lurched into the moonlight. We sat, finally, on the bench in front of the Fisherman's Memorial.

"We have to let him go," Jamie said.

"We do?" It was an honest question.

"I think so," he said. "He doesn't deserve it, Cal. Maybe he did, but he doesn't now. He's a different person."

"Different than what?"

"Than he was."

"Maybe," I said, "but it's not who he is, it's what he did. And 'deserve it'? That's not what we're even talking about."

"Aren't we talking about doing the right thing?"

"Maybe there isn't a right thing," I said.

"What do you think they'll do when they get back, just let him out? Really?"

"We don't know. That's the point. They must have a better sense than we do."

"I'm not so sure."

"Come on."

"I'm not."

We'd each had this conversation dozens of times in our own heads, and there were, at least for me, no surprises now. We knew each other, knew where we stood, and that was part of the reason we'd never needed to talk about this. My eyes were adjusting to the dark. The memorial, nearly invisible when we arrived, was beginning to take shape, its gray lines turning solid as if filled in by pencil.

Richard had sat in this very spot, staring into the bay, drowning in anger. Jamie was right: He didn't seem like the same man now. The old hatred had burned away like fog. For the first time in as long as I'd known him he seemed able to treasure something other than his own resentment. Wouldn't it be wrong not to give someone like that a second chance?

But I also wondered if anyone really could change. When I thought of all the time we'd spent with Richard, listening to his stories, listening to music, I remembered lines from a Dunbar poem we'd read in school that year: *We sing, but oh the clay is vile / Beneath our feet, and long the mile.* Words and songs can help you forget yourself for a while, but nothing more.

"We're not so different," Jamie said.

"Who isn't?"

"You and me and him. Couldn't we have done the same thing?"

"As him? No."

"No? What would you have done?"

I couldn't answer. Even then I knew who I wanted to be, and I knew who I was. What I didn't yet know was that those two people would never meet.

I reached into the pocket of Jamie's coat and pulled out his cigarettes and lighter. The flint was jammed. My hands were shaking from the cold. Jamie took the lighter and held up the flame.

"The day John died," Jamie said, "you remember that? Your first cigarette, wasn't it?"

"What do you mean? I've been smoking for years."

"I always thought we should be friends."

"You never thought that."

"It's been good, sharing a room and all. Maybe I'm not supposed to say it or something, but it's been good."

"It has," I said.

"My dad used to always talk about you, you know? What a good guy you were, how good you were going to be at baseball. I think he was trying to get a rise out of me, but I always just agreed with him. I think he wanted me to be more like you."

"What am I like?"

"That's what I always thought was funny about it. He had his ideas about you, and I have mine."

"I didn't hit his pitch," I said. "I lied about that."

Jamie laughed. "Obviously. I can't believe he thought you did. I mean, I can, it's just funny what people will believe."

"It's sad what people will believe," I said. "Do you really think Richard's changed?"

"It seems like before he never had a chance," Jamie said. "Now he does, or could."

"But if we let him go what happens? What's your father going to do to you?"

Jamie looked at me with an expression I'd never seen, an expression that was both contrite and defiant. He said, very seriously, "He'd think I betrayed him. He'd never forgive me. He'd send me to Alaska and tell me not to come back."

Before I could reply, Jamie put a finger to his lips. He got up from the bench and took soft steps to the edge of the boardwalk and back. The wind had died. There was no moon now, only stars woven into the clouds like sequins. Once Jamie seemed confident we were really alone, he lowered himself back to the bench and leaned close.

"No one would have to know we let him go," Jamie said. "He could disappear. How would they ever know it was us?"

"This is serious," I said. "Do you realize how fucking serious this is?" I could see him blink in the dark.

"Why do you think I don't?"

"Because you're acting like this is some movie."

Jamie shrank back. I knew I'd hurt him.

"I'm sorry," I said.

"That's pointless," he said. "Do you want to see Richard dead?"

"Of course not."

"Then we have to let him go. We let him go, but we make him promise that he'll disappear, that he'll never come back, that he'll never tell."

"How could we ever take his word on that?"

"He's wanted to be free of this place his whole life, hasn't he? Now he finally has a reason."

I didn't know what to think. It was difficult to believe that Richard would just give up his inheritance. Then again, hadn't he already *tried* to give up his inheritance? I imagined Richard on a bus, streaking east on Interstate 90. The sun coming up, waking him. He shades his eyes and gazes at yellow fields that bow as the bus blows past. He smiles and rubs sleep from his face. He's crossed into South Dakota. Crazy Horse and the Black Hills and Chicago and New York are ahead. The Cascades are miles back, Puget Sound even farther, already memories he can blink away like dreams.

"We have to know," I said. "We have to make sure."

"Okay," Jamie said.

"When?" I asked. "When do we do it?"

"After Christmas," Jamie said. "It'll be easier to travel after Christmas."

"After Christmas. Okay. After Christmas."

We started back along the boardwalk. We'd gone a quarter mile or so when I felt the burn of headlights on my back. A car, indistinguishable behind the gleam, rumbled slowly toward us from the direction of the harbor.

"It could be the police," Jamie said.

"It could be Don."

"It could be anyone."

"But still."

Jamie and I took off running, and even after the headlights sliced across the road as the car turned up the bluff, we didn't stop. We bored through the cold wind, shoulder to shoulder. I wished we were still young enough that a footrace could tell us what we needed to know about each other. We ran on, tennis shoes slapping the boards, the black drum of the water beating to our right. As the end of the boardwalk approached in the dark, I raised my head to see if I was winning.

CHAPTER 8

I THOUGHT I'D NEVER SURVIVE THAT NEXT RAGGED week. Mornings, steel gray, spitting sleet, lasted nearly until dusk. I shuffled from window to window with nothing to do but worry. I even called Katherine Cloons one afternoon and left a message with her mother. I never heard back. Jamie wore away a patch in the green crushed velvet of the sofa, watching movies for the fifth and sixth times.

The afternoons on Seachase were no better. Richard had a steady cough. I watched Jamie watching him. I knew he wanted to ask Richard: Would he allow us to erase him from this place? But Richard looked less and less like a man who could offer assurances. Whatever new life or hope we'd brought him had drained out and sunk back into the cold floor.

Only the nights were bearable because we finally had something to do—we had an escape to plan. As the moonlight pressed the windows, we paced. The desk lamp threw our shadows to the floor as we discussed the details of the details. We scribbled pages of notes that we'd burn later during smoke breaks on the roof. We drew a map of downtown on the back of a poster for *Jaws*. (Why? What did downtown have to do with anything?) We talked ourselves into silence, then broke our silences with "But don't you think . . . ?"

We started over two or three times before deciding that the most important thing was to give Richard enough time before Don discovered he was gone. Night would be better, but since the last bus to Port Angeles left at four, we'd have to cope with daylight.

"What day?" I asked. "Shouldn't we pick a day?"

"Christmas is a Friday. We'd better wait for the twenty-eighth so he can use the weekday ferry schedule."

We mapped out our plan, dreamed out each minute, talking through it time and again until eventually it seemed like it had already happened. We saw ourselves arriving on Seachase in the last gasps of a foggy morning. Monday, the twenty-eighth of December. Hiding out in the wet bushes across the street from the park and waiting for Don to arrive and leave. We'd find Richard in the basement, probably sleepless but shot through with anxiety and energy. Would there be time for a last little ritual, a cigarette, a side of a record? Maybe. Hopefully.

Then the chain. Jamie unzips his backpack and takes out his father's hacksaw.

("Do you know how to use it?" I asked Jamie as we scribbled out notes in his bedroom.

"Don't you just kinda saw?")

Jamie sets to work, and the room starts to buzz. He slows after a few minutes, and I take over. We've practiced already on a link of chain we found in the Norths' garage—the same chain?—but with Richard's ankle so close, with his breath on the back of my neck, it's anxious work. My hands sweat and grow sticky with dull silver dust.

Richard's teeth are clenched. Eventually he takes the saw, and I fall back, my arms stinging. He works at the chain for—what?—another few minutes until we hear the link and lock fall to the carpet.

We all stand. Jamie pulls clean clothes from the backpack. We've bought them specially from Rainbow Resale: a pair of khakis, a red-and-gray flannel, a forest-green winter jacket, a pair of Nike running shoes. The sizes are approximate, but everything fits all right. Jamie hands Richard a baseball cap, University of Idaho Vandals. A pair of sunglasses, mirrored. A spray can of Old Spice. Richard douses himself. He stretches. In the new clothes he could be a logger headed back east, a college student. He looks frail and white, but so do a lot of people. He'll pass. We take his filthy sweats. We'll burn them later.

("And then?" Jamie asked.

"Then we start for the bus stop.")

It should be about eleven by now. There's a bus to Port Angeles at noon. Does Richard spit on the floor? Does he kick over the plastic bucket? We're curious to see how he says good-bye to his prison. We leave the door hanging open and take the basement stairs one at a time. At the back door I wrap my hand in the sweats and punch through the window.

("Then?"

"We leave.")

The fog has burned away, and we walk through sun-drenched streets, filing down the bluff, Seachase to Goose to Morland. A twenty-minute walk, give or take, depending on how fast Richard can go. What does his face look like when he sees the sun for the first time in months and the streets of Loyalty Island for the last time in his life?

("What if someone recognizes him?"

"He'll be disguised. Anyway, no one is going to *want* to recognize Richard Gaunt walking around.")

With the bus stop in sight—the low green bench, the bare steel pole—Jamie hands Richard a wad of bills, all we've been able to scrape up, about two hundred and fifty dollars. He tells Richard to keep the backpack, that there's a change of clothes in it and a few sandwiches we've made ourselves.

The bench is empty, and so is the street. Jamie and I sit on either side of Richard. We tell him that we couldn't figure out how to get him an ID or passport, that's up to him. He nods as if he's expected this. We tell him that the Seattle ferries are running on the hour. We ask him if he remembers how to transfer to the Bainbridge bus once he gets to Port Angeles.

"Don't worry," Richard says, "no one knows how to leave this place like I do."

And then the rumble, squeal, and clatter of the bus, and there's no time to say more. Richard gets up to go, but just before he steps on the bus, he turns and shows us his teeth. They're the color of the sunlight. Then the bus pulls away, leaving only sunlight in its wake.

("And then?" I asked.

"Then, that's it," Jamie said.)

That was the plan. We agreed it was a good plan, except for one problem. We hadn't told Richard anything about it.

ON CHRISTMAS EVE, Betty North cooked pot roast. She wore a blue dress and hung three fuzzy stockings from the mantel. She lit green candles that smelled like pinecones and spread the table with a red cloth. She opened a bottle of sparkling apple juice and made a show of pouring it, letting the bubbles foam up just over the rim of each shallow glass.

"Merry Christmas, gentlemen," she said as we toasted. "It's a privilege to spend Christmas with two such handsome young men."

She'd cooked more food than we could possibly eat: the roast, steamed broccoli, Brussels sprouts smothered in melted cheese, buttery mashed potatoes, a green-bean-and-tomato casserole.

As we chewed, Betty asked us about school. She reminded Jamie that his father would make every effort to call the next day, but that if he didn't it was only because he couldn't, not because he didn't care.

"I know that," Jamie said.

Betty smiled. "I'm sure your father will do the same, Cal."

"My mother reminds me of that every year too," I said, though she didn't. She never had. "The dinner's great," I said to Betty. "Thank you."

Betty put down her knife and fork and dabbed her mouth with her napkin before answering. "Well, I used to want to be a chef," she said. "When I was about your age my friend Miriam and I always talked about how we were going to open our own restaurant here."

"You should have. My mother always complains about the restaurants," I said.

Betty twisted her lips. "Well, I don't know if we'd have been up to her standards. Anyway, Miriam moved to San Diego during high school. She's an interior designer now."

"You'll have to do it yourself, then," I said. "She can help you design, at least."

"I'm afraid not," Betty said. "Miriam only designs for private jets."

Was she joking? Were we supposed to laugh? Jamie shook his head and pushed around his sprouts.

"Once," Betty said, "she was working for a woman, an heiress to a company that made drill bits, who planned to buy some paintings by some Scandinavian artist for her plane. The woman couldn't make up her mind, she kept choosing one then the other. So Miri told her that she had a friend with an eye for Scandinavian painting and that if the heiress wanted an answer she really had to fly up and show her. She meant me."

Betty flashed a mischievous smile and cut a sprout in half.

"Are you serious?" Jamie asked.

"Mm-hm," she said, chewing.

"I've never heard this before. You're an expert on Scandinavian art?"

"Yes," Betty said. "Well, no. But the heiress didn't know that. I got a call from Miri saying that this woman had landed at the private strip in Port Angeles and would I mind driving over and pretending to be a Scandinavian art expert. They let me drive right onto the tarmac, and when I got on the plane the heiress pecked me on the cheek and just pointed at the paintings. I could barely even tell them apart. They both had squiggly gray designs, but one was green and the other was blue. The woman sort of flapped her hand at the paintings and said, 'Which, darling, which?' I looked at her, and I said, 'How could I ever tell, darling, when the plane is on the ground?'" Betty laughed out loud, as if all these years later she was still surprised at herself.

"And she threw you out?" Jamie asked, laughing.

"No," Betty said. "She said, 'Of course you're right, of course you are.' We flew over the Cascades and back before I finally picked one of the paintings, and, a week later, she sent me the largest fruit basket I've ever seen, with a note that said, 'You simply must show me *your* Oslo someday.'"

We all laughed. It seemed that Betty had just enough strength to ignore for a few hours at a time, maybe a few times a year, whatever was haunting her. In that brief window you could see what kind of person she might have been, charming and graceful and funny.

After we'd finished eating, Betty carried three bowls of real plum pudding to the table. The candles burned low but still smelled like Christmas trees. I took a spoonful of my pudding and immediately bit into something hard. I spit a tiny ceramic anchor into my hand as Betty beamed at me from across the table.

"Honey, you've got luck," she said. "You found the prize on the very first bite."

Later that night, as Jamie and I lay in bed, Betty opened the door and stood in the rectangle of hall light. She wore the same blue nightgown she'd had on the night we'd watched her from the roof. "Are you awake?" she asked. "I just came to apologize. I was in bed, and I realized I forgot the crackers this year."

"It's okay," Jamie said. "Next year."

"Really. I'm very sorry."

"It's no big deal."

"Good night, then," she said.

"Your mother's kind of great," I said, after she shut the door.

"Yeah," Jamie said. "A few times a year."

"What are crackers?" I asked.

"They're a British tradition," he said. "Like the toy in the pudding. Sometime back she decided we'd be British. I don't know why."

"Probably to make you feel better about your bad teeth," I said.

"Yeah, well, anyway, since we didn't use the crackers we should bring them to Richard tomorrow. We should bring him something. You do want to go, don't you?"

"We'll have to go somewhere," I said. "I can't be here if my parents call."

"Me too, I guess."

"No," I said. "You're much luckier than I am."

WE ARRIVED the next day to find Richard with his eyes closed and his ear pressed to the underside of the sink as though it were a seashell. The poor man. How did he find a way to survive in that room for so many weeks—Richard, of all people? But if Don or Sam or my father had thought that he would break, they were wrong. Nat King Cole's *Cole Español* played low on the stereo. Richard wiped his cheek. "I wasn't expecting you today," he said. "It is Christmas, isn't it? A day to be with your family."

"Options are slim these days," I said.

"Yeah," he said, smiling. "They sure are." He got to his feet. "You even brought gifts."

Jamie handed us silver parcels that weighed next to nothing. There was a twist of thick paper at each end, like a candy wrapper. These were the famous crackers.

"What do you do with it?" Richard asked.

"Pull the ends," Jamie said.

"And?"

"Well, they crack. But first you make a Christmas wish."

I expected Richard to snicker at wishes, but the small gift, the small fact that we'd come on Christmas, had clearly cheered him. His expression seemed to have lost the ravaged quality of the last few weeks. He rattled the cracker next to his ear and shrugged. He was in too good a mood to criticize anything.

"Wishes first," he said. "Everybody ready? Here, I'll turn down the music."

The crackers popped weakly and fell apart. Inside mine there was a cat-shaped eraser and a slip of paper the size of a Chinese fortune.

"Question: How do Santa's elves greet each other?" I read aloud. "Answer: Small world, isn't it?"

"Because elves are short, I guess?" Jamie asked.

"Obviously that's why. I like that one," Richard said. "Here's mine. Question: What's a ghost's favorite ride at the carnival? Answer: A roller ghoster. Jamie, you gave me the fucking Halloween cracker. Trade you, Cal?"

I folded Richard's slip and put it in my pocket. I carried the joke with me for a long time afterward, years actually, until it was stolen along with the rest of my wallet in Chicago. I'd just come to town, had no friends, and without money or ID I had to sleep the next few nights in my car. Still, the only thing I really regretted losing was that strip of paper. It had lasted longer than anything else from my time with Richard and Jamie. It was the last piece of proof that I hadn't just made it all up.

"We're forgetting the crowns," Jamie said.

"Who wears crowns?"

"Tradition is tradition," Jamie said. He pulled out the tissue lining the inside of my half-destroyed cracker, unfolded it into its rightful shape, and placed it solemnly on my head. We sat down to cards that way, wearing our tissue crowns. Richard's was violet, Jamie's baby blue, and mine pink.

"Trade you?" I asked.

"Sorry, nothing doing, Queenie," Richard said. We all laughed.

"What did you wish for, Richard?" Jamie asked.

We still hadn't told Richard about our plan, and Jamie probably hoped that Richard's wish would offer a portal. But Richard only shrugged and dealt the cards for bourré. "Don't act like you don't believe in bad luck, Jamie," he said. He produced a sealed pack of Winstons from the pocket of his sweatpants. "Here, extra Christmas rations from Don. Don't be sore. Help yourself."

Richard lit his and Jamie's cigarettes with the same hissing match, but shook it out as I leaned in.

"Sorry, Cal. Three on a match is bad luck."

"Since when?" I asked.

"We're superstitious up here," Richard answered. "It comes from too much freedom, you know? Everybody needs boundaries to stay sane, and since there aren't any on the ocean, they have to make them with superstition. They'll steal them from anywhere. That's a Great War one, I think."

Richard put on *Diamond Dogs*. I lit my own Winston, and we began the game. I took the first two hands. In the third hand Jamie burned and chased it into the fourth, which I also won. I let myself enjoy the taste of the cigarettes, which I'd finally come to like. I let myself enjoy the feel of the cards in my hands, the sound of the guitars, the lilt of the singer, and the rhythm that the three of us had settled into after so many hours together in the small room.

What must we have looked like? What would an outsider have seen? I watched Jamie's face as he played, his forehead crinkling under his tissue crown. He must have noticed that Richard had come around, that he felt like talking, yet he still didn't say anything about the escape. Maybe he knew, like I did, that there wouldn't be many more of these games, these afternoons, and he didn't want to break the trance. Maybe he knew that as soon as the word *escape* left his mouth we would never be able to lay cards down again.

"The Great War, was that the one with the trenches?" Jamie asked.

"That's right," Richard said. He smiled and put down his hand. "There's a story I've always liked about that one, about the Christmas truce in France, or where was it? A professor I had in college used to call it the last day of the nineteenth century."

"What story?" Jamie asked. "What happened?"

"On Christmas Eve the soldiers came out of the trenches on both sides, exchanged smokes and booze, kicked a ball around, promised not to shoot each other for a few hours. I always liked that because back in those days, see, you knew what you were."

"Didn't they know they were soldiers?" I asked.

"No. No. They weren't soldiers. I mean, they were, but they weren't soldiers first. If you were a Brit, from a certain kind of class, there was a way you acted. For example, you didn't need someone to tell you that you stopped shooting on Christmas Eve."

"Why?" Jamie asked.

"Well, because, even if you were at war, you still had more in common with a rich German than you did with a poor Brit. Then the twentieth century came and fucked up everything."

"The whole century did that?" I asked.

Richard showed an impish smile. "The entire century. That's right. Back in those days, you were born into something. Let's say you were a butcher. Maybe you're a butcher and you see a carriage roll past, carrying a duke—purple curtains, white steed, all that—and for a second you feel jealous, but what are you going to do? You're a butcher. You go back inside, hack up a pig, and forget it. It wouldn't even occur to you that you could ever *be* that guy riding in the carriage.

"That's how it was, always. But somehow, in this century, things changed. I think we have to blame America for it, actually. And western America in particular. We didn't know how big this country was, how much of it there was, so when we came over here we didn't have enough dukes to fill it. And all of a sudden, for the first time ever, people had room to maneuver, they could change. Here, the butcher could actually become the duke. That was actually possible, and that's some great thing, right?"

"Isn't it?"

"No. Give it a couple of generations and that freedom turns into an expectation. So now you're thinking to yourself, I'm a butcher now, but if I'm not something else by the time I die, I've failed. And here's the problem. People can't change. It's impossible. So even if you make all the right moves—you make a fortune, you're the butcher and you become the duke—you're *still* the butcher. Now you're just riding in the carriage. And you're miserable. You miss your cleaver and your apron. You'll finish your life waiting for someone else to open the door and throw you from the carriage back into the street."

Richard paused and looked at us. Whatever he saw made him smile.

"You're wondering what this all means? A lot of anxiety is what. Nervous conditions, and, ultimately, probably, nuclear war. There you go: Richard Gaunt's take on world history. Quote whatever, but credit where it's due, right? Now let's put on some music."

Jamie flipped the record. Richard picked up his cards, looked at them as if in distaste.

"What you said the other day, Cal. I've been wanting to ask you. Did you mean it? Do you think I belong here? I'd like to know your opinion."

"I already apologized," I said.

"Because I might agree with you," he said. "I've thought a lot about it. Maybe I do deserve it."

"How could you deserve this?" Jamie asked.

"I don't know. It's hard to say who deserves what."

"We can help you. We'll help you," Jamie blurted, so fast that the words mashed together. I understood him only because I knew he was going to say it.

But Richard seemed to understand too. He looked at Jamie, his head tilted to one side. "What will you help me do?"

"Escape."

Richard tugged at his bottom lip. He seemed to be considering the meaning of that word, *escape*, its implications. "You'd do that?" he asked. The expression washed from his face. "You can't do that," he said, raising his pitch on *that* as if he were still asking a question. "What if I go to the police?"

The soft angles of Jamie's face hardened. He'd finally said the word, and now he had to work fast. I knew he'd already written the script in his mind and polished it to a mirror. "You wouldn't do that," he said. "You'd have to promise that you'd disappear. You'd owe us that much. Could you promise that?"

Richard threw his cards into the pot. He rose from the floor and sat down on the bench. He ran his hands through his hair. The whole while I watched his face. He looked intensely lonely but gave nothing else away, like a house shuttered against a storm.

"You've come here every day for weeks," he said. "Have I asked you to let me out? Have I asked you for anything? And now you two—fucking kids—think you can decide what happens to me? You think that's your choice?"

Nick Dybek

"We want to let you go," Jamie said. He was smiling, but the smile looked sadly out of place.

"So I owe you something? Maybe you owe me," Richard said. "I've done you a favor, you know that, right?"

"I don't see, I don't see how."

"You two are lost, you know that? Without me you'll be even more lost."

"I'm not really sure why you're saying this," Jamie said. The gratitude he expected was clearly not coming. And I realized then that I'd known it wouldn't come.

I'd known that it wasn't as simple for Richard as escaping or not. In order to really help him escape, we'd have to help him to forgive everyone he had ever known, himself especially. The chain wrapping around his ankle stretched back over years and over miles of water.

"Richard," I said, "maybe you're not thinking all that clearly. You've been in this room too long."

Richard got to his feet and scraped his hand along the record spines. "Yeah, look at this room," he said. "You think your father wanted your mother because she was some great beauty, Cal? He married her because she had all this, she knew about all this shit that he never would, and he knew she wouldn't have a kid who didn't think her way. My father was the same. He *made* me do whatever I wanted. That's what I think, anyway."

"What about my mother?" Jamie asked.

"Now, she *is* a great beauty," Richard said. "Sam probably married her for the shape of her mouth."

252

"That's really shitty," Jamie said.

Richard sat down hard on the bench. He scratched his ankle under the chain. The record had ended. The speakers hissed warm static. "Yeah, but so what?"

All these years later I can still see the wounded expression on Jamie's face, and still I feel sorry for him. How could he have known that there's a vacuum inside most of us? How could he have known that some people live their entire lives in the moment when the heart has stopped but the blood is still rushing?

"Richard," I said. "We want to let you out. We want to help you escape. Don't you want that?"

"Yes," he said. He sighed, as if to admit that he wanted to live was to admit defeat. "Yes, of course I want that. I'll promise whatever you want me to."

"That's all you had to say," Jamie said. And then he froze. The sentence disappeared. We all heard it at the same moment. Upstairs, someone had come in the back door.

I REMEMBER THE PANIC, but only flashes of everything else. I remember running from the room, starting to slam the door, but catching it in the last instant by jamming in my hand. I remember the blizzard of pain that followed and Jamie pushing me aside to close the door softly and click the lock. Somehow we remembered our coats. Somehow we returned the key. And somehow we stood for precious seconds at the foot of the stairs as if waiting to greet the man in the kitchen, before I snapped to and, with my good hand, dragged Jamie behind the rumbling furnace.

We stumbled through unbearable heat all the way to the back wall. I fell to my knees and didn't dare move again. I couldn't see Jamie in the dark, but I could hear his shaky breath. I held my hand to my mouth. I felt like crying out—in pain, in fear, I didn't know which. The furnace roared like an ocean. Above us, the stairs creaked under footsteps.

I imagined the gun Don carried. If he knew we'd found Richard, if he even suspected, wouldn't this be the moment to use it? In my mind I heard the explosion. I imagined his slow, shuffling steps as—finished with Richard—he came for us. I imagined his pale face, peering into the darkness behind the furnace.

I was sure that my father and Sam would never have been able to kill anyone, but Don was a different story. That's what I thought about good people back then, that at a certain point their muscles knew right from wrong. As a child, this was the question I'd always wanted to ask my father about the good Captain Flint: Even if his mind had been consumed by greed and evil, wouldn't his body—his bones, his nerves—have resisted? If his body *let* him kill innocent people, hadn't it been evil all along? I knew Don could pull the trigger. It was all Don could manage, I thought, to hold that gun and *not* pull its trigger.

Sweat rolled into my eyes and over my ribs. Otherwise I was aware only of searing heat and darkness as the nightmare cycled through my mind: gunshot, footsteps, face. Jamie tried to whisper something, but I stopped him with a hand on his slippery wrist. I didn't let go. Some time passed that way. How much? I heard sounds. A slamming door? A crash? I couldn't tell. And then I heard a sound that was familiar. The stairs creaking under heavy feet. The door at the top of the stairs opening, closing.

Jamie tried to stand, but I pulled him down. How much time had I spent this way, crouching, waiting, as life unspooled before me? It felt like I hadn't done anything, like it had all just happened to me. After some time I felt Jamie jerk away. I followed, and we stumbled out into the basement, where I fell to my knees again.

"Richard?" Jamie said.

"He's gone," Richard said, his voice soft through the door.

"Did he know?" I asked. Richard didn't answer. "Did he know?"

"He gave me a stocking," Richard said.

"A what?" Jamie asked.

"There's an orange in the heel," Richard said, laughing. "You have to see." Jamie went for the key and opened the door. Richard sat on the bench, the contents of a red Christmas stocking—a few packs of gum, the orange, a chocolate bar, a tin of peanuts—dumped out beside him.

"That's it?" I asked. "He stopped by to give you a stocking?"

Jamie and Richard began to laugh. I wanted to laugh too, but there was something about the way Richard looked that stopped me. Something was wrong. It took a few moments of staring before I realized what it was.

"Fuck," I said. "Oh fuck."

"What," Richard said. "What, what?"

All I could do was point at his forehead. He was still wearing the paper crown.

WE LAY IN OUR BUNKS that night talking about all the terrible possibilities. Could Don have missed the crown completely? It was possible. Could he have noticed it and not said anything? Also possible. Did we really know what he was capable of? Could we ever know what he was capable of?

We climbed out to the roof. I smoked the feeling from my mouth and lived a lifetime of panic, but, in the end, all the speculation was pointless. We decided nothing. Should we break Richard out that very night? Should we wait an extra week for things to settle down? We just didn't know, and since we didn't know, we decided to stick to our plan. We'd wait two more days, until December 28. We went back inside, and I fell asleep without realizing it, sometime before dawn.

Jamie was gone when I woke. In the early morning he and Betty had taken the ferry to Whidbey Island to visit Betty's parents. They'd asked me to come, but I couldn't stand the thought of sitting with strangers, eating Christmas cookies that tasted like paper, acting as if everything were fine.

It was the day after Christmas, the emptiest day of the year. I slept late, until eleven, maybe. At first I heard the knocking in my dream, a second hand on a clock. I got out of bed but was still half asleep, aware of cold wood against my feet and not much else. I had a vague idea that it was Jamie at the front door, that he'd come back, that he'd locked himself out, but of course it wasn't.

Don Brooke stood on the Norths' porch in a canvas jacket with a bit of shearling still clinging to the collar. The remains of his hair stuck to his scalp in oily ropes. "Your hand's ugly," he said.

After slamming it in the studio door, I'd told Betty I'd fallen off my bike. She'd wrapped and iced it, and now my fingers puffed out of an ACE bandage. Don and I watched each other through the screen door. He rocked in place.

"If you saw Jamie's face this morning you wouldn't think so," I said.

"It's been like that, huh?"

"You know. Christmas." I shrugged.

Don smiled. "I told your father." He paused; I felt pins explode in my back. "I told your father before he left that I'd look in on you. Take you out somewhere sometime. Guess I should have come earlier."

"It's no problem," I said. "I don't have to kick Jamie's ass *every* day."

Don looked me straight in the eyes then for the first time, maybe the first time ever. "Has it been hard," he asked, "being away from home?"

"Sort of," I said. "You get used to it."

"Yeah." He rubbed the back of his head sleepily. "You do get used to it. But it's harder when you're alone. I don't see their car. Are you alone?" He put his hand on the door but didn't pull it open. He was chewing purple gum. "It's not bad out," he said. His forehead shone faintly in the sun. "We should go out somewhere. Since we're both alone."

I could have slammed the door and run out the back. Maybe I should have, but there was something in Don's voice that held me in place. He'd noticed the crown. Of course he'd noticed the crown, but he wasn't sure I had anything to do with it. For a moment, before my head cleared fully from sleep, I was sure that Don was just as scared as I was.

The weather was warm. I slid into the cab of Don's dust-colored pickup, through the driver's side because the passenger door was rusted shut. There were silver beer cans on the floor, tall boys. The cab reeked of the stuff and of flowery cologne.

"Where do you want to go?" Don asked.

"Nowhere I can think of," I said.

We turned onto Spring Street, splashed by sun and empty as midnight. The radio was on, staticky, low, buzzing like a table saw. We swung onto 101 and picked up speed, flying out of town. Don rolled down his window and switched on the blower.

"I haven't been home for Christmas in a long time." He had to raise his voice over the wind. "It's not how I remember it."

"Me either."

He glanced at me, then turned back to the road. "I always liked toys," he said. "You're probably too old already."

"I try to be."

He grimaced and shook his head as if this were important and disappointing news.

"I used to buy them for my sister's kids, little army guys and cars and things. Good for nothing. But I like that. I think one day a year it's good to get stuff that's just pointless. Especially on a hard day like this. What do you think?"

He didn't look at me, and I didn't answer. As we sped east toward Port Angeles, Don's expression was slack, but his eyes were hard, like knots in rotting wood. "Of course, you're too old for that," he said. "I know that. By the time I was your age I'd been to Alaska already."

"You went on the boats that early?"

"The first time I drove all the way up with my father. We started on this same highway."

"What for?"

Don smiled and spit out the window. "Who the hell knows? One night, I was about four probably, this man walked into our house and kissed my mother. It took me a minute to figure out that it was my father, back from the war. He sat down at the kitchen table, poured a cup of coffee, and started to talk. He didn't stop until he died from a stroke fifteen years later."

"What did he talk about?" I asked.

"What do you think?" Don asked. "Alaska."

Instead of Okinawa or Normandy, places whose dangers needed no explanation, Don's father had been sent to the Aleutian Islands—Fort Mears. You guys just don't understand, his father would say to the silently nodding men at the barbershop or the gas pump. To Don, who didn't yet know his father was a drinker and a braggart, these nods, these silences looked like signs of respect. Alaska isn't a place, his father would say. It don't end. It's just this endless thing.

Don told me that he found out for himself when he was eleven. When his father declared one morning that he was planning to earn some extra money in Alaska that summer, Don begged to come too. He'd never driven before, but his father told him to slide behind the wheel, that if he was going to come, then he was going to come as a partner. They took the Alcan in three straight days. The nights were a nullifying black. But at sunrise the land was still flat and dirty-green, and the same crack still snaked down the dash. And Don, blinking to stay awake, wondered if anything in this life ever changed.

They set up camp in a two-man tent on a bluff above the Porcupine River. It was late summer, 1952. The coho were spawning in riverbeds all the way to the Rocky Mountains. Don knew this, everyone knew this, but it wasn't until they'd unloaded the guns—two Weatherby rifles wrapped in oilskins—that he realized they hadn't brought fishing gear. Don recognized the guns. He'd seen them on the rack in the pickup truck of one of Loyalty Island's richest men, Morley Gaunt. His father sometimes ran deliveries for Morley, but Don, young as he was, wasn't able then to put it together that his father had stolen them.

They rose near dawn and trudged down the bluffs to the river, carrying the freshly oiled rifles. They kept on through purple light until they reached the bank. Don's father flopped onto his belly in slippery clay, amid brown summer bushes. They looked out over a ribbon of water clear enough to show the coho rushing past. Don could almost hear them, the force of their muscles murmuring against the current. He had seen salmon runs, but nothing like this, this solid mass flooding the liquid. By then the sun had risen and was dripping light like juice from a lemon. Don's father licked his lips.

"Do you see?" he asked.

Don nodded.

But his father jabbed Don's shoulder and pointed. "Over there. Over there."

Don raised his eyes, following his father's bristly finger. The opposite bank, no more than thirty yards away, was lined with white-headed birds, so large that their size had hidden them from Don at first. His father pointed up at a tattered second sky of birds, seeming to hang as if nailed in place.

"Eagles," Don said.

"They're here for the salmon," his father said. "Fish and Wildlife pays three dollars a head. You keep half of what you shoot, okay?"

"Shoot how?"

"What do you think? With this gun." Don's father tapped the gleaming wood of the stolen rifle.

The eagles on the bank flapped their wings lazily; they swayed and nodded their white heads, preened a few steps and fell back to rest. The ground was scattered with offal, red gills turning brown in the morning sun. They'd caught these birds just after breakfast.

His father's gun went off, and Don shrank from the report. He heard his father curse, then he heard a second shot.

"Let's go, Don, let's go."

Don broke after his father, not wanting to lose sight of him as he scrambled over the lip. The Weatherby cracked again and again, deadening Don's ears. It seemed that Don's father had turned the gun on the circling birds above, rather than on those perched on the bank. Another shot. And only after feeling the rifle jerk back into his shoulder did Don realize that the shot had come from *his* gun. The eagles began to beat their wings. *Wump, wump, wump.* They looked like hunks of ground taking off, rising so slowly that they seemed to levitate more than fly. The sky above molted streaking clouds; it was giant, exploding.

Don looked down just in time to see the gun smoking in his father's hand, his father stepping then slipping in wet clay that bled from brown to gray. As his father fell, sliding down the bank on his back, he got off another shot. He was up a moment later, caked in mud. He splashed into the shallow river, then began to shout.

Out of frustration? Triumph? It was hard to tell. It was hard to tell what was happening at all. Don let off three more shots at the eagles on the opposite bank. He crossed the river at his father's heels, pulling the trigger and the bolt as fast as he could. Could he feel the salmon running between his legs, slashing past his ankles? Did he burn his chin on the hot gun barrel? Did he see his father trip again and fall headfirst into the water? The moment he paused to consider an event it seemed to have never happened at all.

High above their heads the birds circled like blades of a fan. And when it was finally, mercifully obvious to Don and his father that they could stop firing, the murmur of the river and the coho returned.

It took Don's father a moment to notice the eagle lying twenty yards down the bank. The wing had been clipped by one of the thirty-ought-six rounds, and the bird wriggled in a shower of brown-white feathers. They approached cautiously. Don's father poked the bird with the barrel of his gun, then drew back his shaking hand. The next shot clapped. The bird made a sort of coughing sound. The damaged wing was gone, blown off. The bird tried to twist around, got a foot planted in the earth, and fell back. Its eyes looked in no particular direction.

Don's father took his third shot from just a few feet away but managed to miss completely. He looked over his shoulder at Don and shrugged, as if Don was supposed to laugh. The next bullet didn't go in true, and his father had to wrestle with the bolt. All the while the eagle writhed on the ground, coughing, trying to stand.

When his father finally got the cartridge right, he took two more steps toward the eagle and put him down. Don looked away in disgust. When he turned back he found his father panting, bent over with his hands on his knees, his hair wet, his face streaked with clay. He looked up at Don and smiled. "Well, it's a start," he said.

And if it was a start, where would it end? I'd been looking out the window as I listened, the white sky of Washington turning to the white sky of Alaska. But when I looked back at Don—driving the same make of Ford his father probably had, his nubbed finger dreaming of the old grooves in the steering wheel—I remembered that he'd inherited every nasty quality of his father's he'd just described, the shiftless, thoughtless nature, the weakness for drink. The real Don was the man taking his time, letting the bird suffer. Not the boy looking on in horror. I turned back to the window, rested my head against the cold glass.

"Your man ever take you to the Dungeness Spit, the park there?" Don asked.

"My man?"

"Your old man."

"No," I said. "I mean, I've been there, though."

We hadn't passed a single car by the time Don hooked left onto Beach Road, on the outskirts of Sequim.

"Hungry?" Don asked.

"Probably not much open," I said.

"Probably not," he said. "Hand me a beer, though, yeah?"

I pulled a warm Olympia from the half-empty case on the floor. Don drank it and threw the can at my feet. We pulled into a lot, empty except for a muddy jeep, and got out. Don slammed another Olympia as I tied my shoes.

"You drink these?" he said. "Want one?"

I shook my head.

There were puffy pink circles around his eyes. He belched softly and wiped his mouth with the back of his mangled hand.

"I have a gun." He said it matter-of-factly. He patted the right front pocket of his jacket as if to assure himself he wasn't making it up.

I thought about running, just taking off, but I willed myself not to. Maybe he was testing me. I thought he was stupid, or at least not as smart as I was. I thought if I acted the part I could convince him. We walked side by side, over the black asphalt, through a pine forest and onto gray sand.

The spit jutted five miles into the strait, crowned at the tip by a lighthouse. To the right stretched a murky tideland speckled with tufts of yellowing grass. To the left dim waves tumbled onto the sand. It was too cloudy to see much else. We trudged through gray—gray water, gray air. Every step seemed a step into a steel safe.

"Have you talked to your father?" he asked.

"Not in a while," I said. "Have you?"

"Have to. It's been a big season, really big. Always the luck I had. My hip keeps me home the year they make more money than Christ. We can thank Richard."

"Yeah?"

"When a man goes overboard it's good luck. Nobody talks about that much, but it's true."

I didn't risk looking at him. We walked on beside thudding waves. The middle of the beach was littered with tangled white driftwood that ran the length of the spit like a spine. Gray birds hopped among the snarled branches. Don walked unevenly, steadying himself once with a hand on my shoulder.

"Have you thought much about him?" Don asked.

"About Richard? As much as anyone else, I guess."

"How do you know that?" Don's voice was suddenly hard, offended. "How do you know how much anyone else has thought about him?"

"How much have you thought about him?" I asked.

"He's dead," Don said.

"I know," I said.

"No, he's dead now," Don said.

Before I could stop myself, I met his gaze; it must have mirrored my own, horrified, sick. We kept on down the bar. I watched Don's boots press the sand. He bent to pick a twig from the ground and tossed it into the flats. He couldn't act unless he *knew*. I just had to keep a distance. He sucked in through his teeth and groaned. Beside us the ocean struck dull notes. Richard was dead? I was too afraid to believe or disbelieve.

We continued side by side until Don, without warning, peeled off and picked his way through the driftwood that divided the ocean side of the beach from the tidelands. We walked parallel paths up the beach, until Don yowled in pain and stiffly bent down.

"This fucking hip," he said. "Come here, I wanna show you something."

I was too confused to object. I crawled over a white log and crouched beside him. He was peering into a tide pool.

"Look at this, huh? Pacific Blood Stars, that's what you call these." Don pointed to three sea stars on the shaggy green bottom and splashed a ripple across the water. The sea stars were blood-red, no more than three or four inches across. "Do you see?" He picked one up and held it out to me in his palm. "Look at this, huh?"

He held the star by one coarse arm and dangled it in front of my face like a hypnotist's watch. "This is what I'm talking about," he said. "These things. What are they good for? What do they do? I mean, why are they here on earth living with us? It just makes you think. Touch it, come on."

The sight of him holding out the sea star, his mouth half open in a grimace or smile, was more terrifying than anything else. I got to my feet. Don tried to stand too, but his leg gave out, and he tipped to one side. He reached out to steady himself, grinding the hand holding the sea star into the sand. I started walking. Soon I was ten, then fifteen feet ahead of him. Don was up, though. I could hear him puffing behind me, trying to keep pace.

"Hey," he said. "Hey. This was our time together."

I walked into the gray mist.

"Come back," he called. "Hey, slow down."

But I kept walking.

"Hey, Cal. Hey, Cal." There was panic in his voice, a panic that told me to go faster. I could walk all the way out to the lighthouse, but then what? Still, I quickened the pace that carried me farther and farther out into the sound.

"You have to wait for me," Don shouted, pleading. "Hey, you *have* to."

I started to run. I'd gone maybe ten steps more when the gun went off, a flat crack. A log's worth of birds lifted and scattered across the clouds.

I thought at first that he'd shot me, but I felt nothing. I turned around. Don lay on his side, curled in an S. I couldn't see blood from my angle, but I saw blood in my mind—bits of splintered skull and sandblasted brain. I sat down in the sand for a moment, got back to my feet, and started to run down the beach. I was planning, I guess, to keep running, to get back to 101 and Port Angeles. It didn't matter where I ended up exactly, just as long as I put distance between me and this.

But when I reached Don, I fell to my knees and turned him toward me. His eyes were open, and his skull was intact. He blinked. The gun was still in his hand. He lifted it and pointed it a few inches from my face.

"I pretended to shoot myself," Don said. We were both breathing hard. "I'll give you this gun if you help me up."

"Why?" I asked.

"Don't I deserve it?"

I felt like crying from pure confusion. As if in a dream, I pulled

Don to his feet, and he set to work brushing the sand from his shirt. He patted at his jacket pockets like an old man looking for his glasses.

"The gun's in the sand," I said.

"You hang on to it," he said.

I picked up the revolver and put it in my jacket pocket. It looked small, but it was heavy and hot.

"I've always had a head for pranks, not much else, but pranks, yeah. That's what first got me noticed by John Gaunt. I switched out all of the magazines on board with porno, guys doing it to each other. John had to teach me not to prank like that again." Don held up his hand and nodded at the missing finger. Then he burst out laughing. "See, got you."

He scrubbed his face and scalp with the knuckles of both hands. "I was trying to tell you something," he said. "I saw your face when I told you he was dead. I saw your face."

"Is he dead?" I asked.

"He's not dead. That was a prank too." Don took a step and winced. "When I drink these days my hip just locks up. I think I need your help."

The fog turned to a sprinkle as we walked back across the darkening beach, Don's elbow weighing on my shoulder. I felt as gray and flat as the sandbar; it was as if my reserve of feeling, my ability to be surprised, had been used up, and something cold had seeped in to replace it.

Don kept talking. "When we first got Richard down there I tried to talk to him, brought down the sports page and things. But he'd just ask in this little voice if he could turn the music back up. Your father had told me to take the stereo out of there, but I thought, what the hell, it might keep him company. I'd knock on the door, trying to be, you know, trying to see if he was okay. But I'd just get silence. He wouldn't say a word. And part of me thought, he's just gonna fade away, you know, and that was sort of for the best, considering . . . But six weeks ago, maybe, he turned around all of a sudden.

"He asked for cigarettes, he started doing push-ups, he started looking more like a human and less like some spooky fucking *thing*. And honestly, I was happy, happy that he looked like the living. And I was happy someone else knew, happy someone was kind of sharing the load with me. It's an awful thing what I've been doing. You know, one day's okay, but after so many."

"You knew it was me, six weeks ago?"

"Who would find Richard in that basement, and who wouldn't let him out? It had to be you."

"There were two of us," I said.

"That right?" Don asked. "It makes sense, I guess, but I didn't figure Jamie could do it like you did. It takes something to show up in that room every day, Cal. I figured you could, but not him."

I'm not sure Don meant this as a compliment, but I have to admit I took it as one. "What did you take me out here for?"

"You did a good job all this time. I thought you had found him, but I wasn't completely sure, so every day I could tell myself I didn't have to really do anything about it. Not until I was sure. Does that make sense?"

I nodded, not trusting my voice.

"Yeah, but then I saw that crown on his head. It seemed almost like a signal. So I came to get you this morning. I wish I knew why, exactly. I wish I knew why I've done anything I've done for months."

We reached the parking lot after another few minutes. Don was breathing heavily. "You drive?" he asked. "You know how? It's an automatic."

I'd driven only once before, around the parking lot of the high school with my father, but I thought I could do it. I helped Don into the truck.

"Has it been hard for you too?" he asked.

I pulled the truck onto the highway and turned back toward Loyalty Island. The sky had thinned out some, and I could see a sash of light in the west. The wheel felt slippery and so did the road. "Yeah," I said. If Don's stunt on the beach was a ploy, it had worked. It seemed pointless to hide anything from a man who had just pretended to shoot himself.

"Yeah," Don said. "Quit checking the brake. It works. You just got to be able to take to things. That's important. So, you've talked to Richard, you probably know most of it. We decided that if Richard was gone, well . . . But then . . ."

"You didn't want to?" I asked.

"Sam was supposed to do it. He said, all right, if nobody else will,

I will. I remember him saying those words. But then he couldn't and neither could your father and neither could I. So we panicked. We changed everything on the fly, 'cause we couldn't do that thing. We hated this guy, and all we had to do was fix it like he'd come on board and then gone overboard, 'cause it happens a lot. It happened to Richard's friend, even."

"Dan Fosse."

"Yeah, Dan Fosse. We never even knew what happened to him. That's what it was supposed to be with Richard, but we wrecked it. We put him down there. Then they left. Your father's smarter than I am, but we're all stupid."

"Why you? Why did you stay?"

"Oh, that's the question. I got a bad hip and no family to explain myself to. That's what they said, anyway. I didn't want to disappoint those guys. I really didn't." Don straightened up in his seat. He scoured his forehead with his knuckles. "That's why I'm telling you all this, I guess. Because I need you to help me."

Dusk hit the windshield. I pulled the tab on the lights, and they smoothed out the concrete. I nudged the wheel, hugging the double yellow line that wound around the edge of the United States. Knowing we were at the end of something, not on the way to somewhere else, was always comforting somehow.

"I can't help you kill him," I said. "I can't."

Don sighed. "We're really not understanding each other. That's gotta be my fault." He sighed again. "I need you to help me let him go."

I DROVE HOME THROUGH DARKNESS, Don snoring in the passenger seat. The dashboard was lit in stereo-tube orange, the partial moon brilliant above. We'd have to drive the first leg of Richard's escape—that should have been obvious all along. To put him on a bus in Loyalty Island, on a bus that ran nowhere but Port Angeles, was too much of a risk. Even the ferry was too risky. No, we'd have to drive him south—I'd drive—to Tacoma at the very least, Olympia or even Portland might be better. From there, Richard could go anywhere. I thought of him in sunglasses, fiendishly pale, nervously fiddling with the knobs of the radio. The airwave static. A sudden storm, a skid and a fishtail, momentary, but enough to get us joking about how tragic it'd be after everything if we both died in a wreck.

When we reached Don's bungalow on Monroe I had to shake him awake. The front door was unlocked. We made our way through darkness into his living room, his arm around my shoulder. I'd never been inside Don's house before and had imagined a chamber of horrors, smelling of blood. Really, it smelled like wet wool and tobacco.

"The couch is over here," he said.

I felt him lower himself onto it and then heard him fumble with the lamp. The bulb revealed loose-knit white blankets on both arms of the couch. A green easy chair with an actual doily spread like a fried egg on the ottoman. A cuckoo clock hanging on a knotty-pine wall. A half-completed jigsaw puzzle of *The Night Watch* laid out across the coffee table.

"It's my folks' old house," Don said. "I'm never here, so I left it the way my mother had it."

"The puzzle too?" I asked.

"The puzzle's mine. I like them." Don grabbed an orange pill jar from the end table. He swallowed two pills dry, then lay back on the couch.

"What do you want me to do?" I asked.

"When we talked about it, we always said it was worth it. We just had to get rid of this one guy."

"I know," I said. I'd meant, *What do you want me to do for you now?*

"And it wasn't just some guy. It was Richard Gaunt. If God or whoever had said to me five years ago, 'Don, pick a person and they die,' that's probably who I would have chosen. And I wasn't the only one. I mean, do you think we had a hard time convincing the rest of the guys on the *Laurentide* to lie about him going over?"

"But now?" I asked.

"Richard didn't want this, Alaska, fishing, all that. He never knew what he wanted. He's just a fucking guy, you know? You know that thing he always does? He'll pinch his lip and pull it out and twist it? You know that?"

Don swept his palm along one jowl, as if there were something to wipe away. "John should have just left Richard out of it. It was *his* mistake. Richard won't talk to me, but I don't want him dead. I can't do it. But you can talk to him. Explain it to him, explain to him that he has to disappear."

"What about my father?"

"Yeah, you'll have to lie to him, Cal. We both will. I'll do the hard part, I'll tell him and Sam that I did it, that I shot him. They won't want to know the details. All you have to do is pretend you know nothing, that this never happened. Can you pretend like that, can you get Jamie to?"

"I think so," I said.

"If Sam and your father found out, I'd have to tell them you knew, Cal. I wouldn't want to, but I'd have to do it."

"I get it."

"I'm glad you found him, Cal. I really am. I was afraid I was starting to go crazy, like I was making all of it up. That's really how it felt. You gotta take over a little, all right? Talk to Richard, tell him to disappear."

"What if he won't, what will happen?"

He winced again, trying to prop himself up on the couch and failing. "Yeah," he said. "Maybe it's a lot to believe that we'd never see him again, but I don't care. I honestly really don't care what's gonna happen. Just get him out of here."

Don closed his eyes. He hadn't taken off his boots, and as he twisted, trying to get comfortable, he stamped wet sand into his mother's sofa.

CHAPTER 9

THE NIGHT THEY CAME FOR HIM, RICHARD LAY IN
the four-poster bed, thanking God his father hadn't died
there. The bed, like so many objects in the house—certain
doors, certain windows—was built out of associations. And, as I
imagine it, Richard had time that night to be grateful that the bed
with the spade-shaped knobs was not his father's deathbed, but
still the place where he remembered his mother and his color-
by-numbers and the press of Melissa's teeth. He had time to wonder
how it was possible that he had so many loving memories of a place
he also hated.

He had time because the knock on the door didn't come until just
after three a.m. After my father destroyed the radio in the kitchen

on Seachase. After I retreated to my own bed to follow *Voyager* past Pluto. But Richard knew none of this.

I imagine his hands still smelled faintly of salty blood. When he'd returned home from the Memorial Day dinner two nights before, he'd thrown the Donald Duck suitcase in the corner by the back door. The smart thing would have been to pack, to leave town immediately, but he resisted doing the smart thing the same way one resists waking from an interesting nightmare.

He couldn't shake the memory of the faces squashed around our dining room table. He remembered the scrape of chair legs, the table seeming to explode before him. He'd resorted to such a melodramatic gesture because, just once, he wanted to look at the men and women seated around that table without feeling jealous.

But it didn't work. In the moment, as glass splintered and brine seeped through the tablecloth, he saw the fear on our faces. We were defenseless, terrified. Yet he still wanted to be sitting in one of our chairs instead of standing at the head of the table. He still wanted to be one of us, hating Richard Gaunt, vowing revenge.

So I imagine that when he hears the knock he goes to the door in his bare feet, shirtless. The hall light is on. The porch light is off. Outside three men stand, puffing smoke in the shadows.

"A little late at night for this," Richard says. He can't help himself. Looking at them, he feels the old hatred return. He smiles even though he doesn't feel like smiling. "But then, not much reason to be up early, is there?"

"We want to talk about that."

"Take your shoes off," Richard says. "The carpets."

The men kneel and unlace their boots. My father looks up at Richard. His cheeks are white, and the skin under his eyes is swollen and purple. "Do you want to put some clothes on?" he asks.

Richard shakes his head and leads them into the living room. He pulls the chain on an antique lamp with a square glass shade that was once his mother's. The three men sit on one plaid sofa, in nearly identical postures, elbows on knees. They exchange glances, as if they haven't yet decided who will speak or what they'll say.

Sam clears his throat. "Richard, what you did the other night, what you said you were going to do, we can't let you."

"Wait." Richard raises his eyebrows as though he is confused, as though he is really as clueless as Sam thinks he is. "Why?"

"Why?" Sam asks. "Why?"

My father puts his hand on Sam's knee, silencing him. And then, in carefully chosen words, he explains why. He explains the economics of it first, the cost of the ships and the gear and the licenses, and he explains the infrastructure for bait and fuel built over a hundred years of fishing. He explains Forks, down the coast, and how it's been gutted. And he explains Port Townsend to the east, and how the old diners and shops have become boutiques for tourists selling expensive junk and wine. And he explains what has been sacrificed over years and years, lives and lives. And of course it's Richard's decision, but, if he has any doubts at all, why not just put everything off until after king season when an entire year's money has been made?

Richard has imagined this conversation. He dodged their calls and fled to New York because he'd imagined it. And even though my father talks for a long time and says many things, his tone, and the way his hands stay perfectly in place on his knees, say something else, say that he knows Richard understands it all already and just needs to be reminded.

But it's too late. Richard wants to listen, wants to tell them he understands, that he agrees, but he can't. He just can't. He has no choice but to do everything he can to hurt and embarrass them. "Is that all?" he asks.

My father takes a breath and closes his eyes. "Most," he says quietly.

"Then that's all," Richard says. "Go home. I'm tired."

They don't move at first; they just exchange bewildered glances.

"Okay, Don," Sam says, standing up. Even in socks he's still huge, looming in the dim light. Don doesn't move. His hands seem stuck between his knees. My father's eyes are closed.

"Good. Now the rest of you get up and go," Richard says.

The command seems to jolt Don awake. He puts his hand in his jacket pocket and pulls out—with an expression on his face suggesting he has only just found it there—a black revolver. The gun looks comically large, like a stage prop. Don holds it in his right hand, the one with the index finger shortened at the first knuckle, and points it experimentally at Richard.

Before he can stop himself, Richard begins to laugh: Don, with his shortened finger, won't be able to pull the trigger. Richard puts up his hand as if to ask for a moment to collect himself, but he knows he won't be able to stop. He puts his hands over his face. If he looks at Don again it will only get worse. He knows how insane he must seem, but better insane than afraid.

Then Sam strikes Richard with his open hand, just below the ear. The blow sends him to the ground as pain splinters through Richard's eyes.

"Wait," my father says. Richard gets to one knee. Don is still pointing the gun, but looks as though he isn't sure how it works. Sam towers over Richard, breathing hard. He's put the hand he used to strike Richard in his pocket. His face seems far away, just a collection of shapes, deconstructed.

My father takes a step toward Sam and then a step back and then a step toward Don. "Give it to me, then," he says.

Richard gets to his feet but stumbles into the lamp next to the sofa, the glass shade shattering under his weight. He expects the room to go black, but the bulb remains intact. The gun goes off next: a thunderclap, a flash of light above the naked glow of the lamp.

The three men are looking at one another as if they've just woken up and are wondering how they've arrived in such a strange place. The gun dangles from Don's left hand; he looks like he wants nothing to do with it. Richard scrambles to his feet, still hearing the shot in his mind.

"Are you all right?" Sam asks. Richard isn't sure whom Sam is talking to. Sam reaches for the gun. Richard feels glass digging into his feet and tears surging for his eyes as he runs for the kitchen, turning out the lights as he goes. He feels the advantage of the darkness, knows that no matter how much time the men have spent in the house they won't know the corners and turns that have been burned in Richard's mind since childhood. He can get away.

Through the back hall, into the dining room, into the kitchen. He knows the kitchen door opens onto the screened-in porch where he sat with Melissa, and the screened-in porch opens onto the back-yard, the hill sloping into the forest where Jamie and I lay on our backs smoking cigarettes the day Richard's father died.

Maybe Richard didn't want Jamie and me to know what our fathers were capable of, but people like Richard, people like me, don't do much to spare others. We spare ourselves. And so I imagine this is what he never told Jamie and me: that he could have gotten away. All he has to do is run.

He can get away, but he imagines himself, shoeless, shirtless, running down the bluff, crying for help. He sees himself knocking on doors, on dark windows. He sees eyes in the peepholes and dim faces in the glass. Smiling. He hears the laughter. Cruel laughter, spreading from house to house to house faster than he can run. He sees himself sprinting in bare feet, covering his naked chest with his arms. He sees himself pass two Safeway clerks smoking in the mouth of an alley. They begin to laugh. He sees himself pass two old women walking an old white dog. They begin to laugh. He sees him-self pass two police officers, their bicycles leaning against a bench on the boardwalk, their eyes longingly turned to the sea.

There isn't a soul for miles in this town he has known his whole life who won't see the justice of this moment. To put his startled face to their startled faces and watch as they slowly begin to understand what is happening—he can't do it.

As he runs he remembers his father standing at his dresser in the bedroom. He remembers watching him from the four-poster bed as he stuffed a duffel bag, packing for Alaska. He remembers thinking, You have to ask, you have to ask. "Can I come with you?" He remembers his father sitting him down at the dining room table, remembers being held in his gray gaze as he said, "Not this year. And not ever."

He remembers the sloped necks of the clear glass bottles containing the model ships that his father treasured, that his great-uncle labored over. And he remembers the satisfaction of breaking glass and the blood streaming from his big toe because he'd forgotten to wear shoes.

But he doesn't remember feeling disappointed, and this he can never tell another soul. He'd heard stories of Alaska his entire life. They were incomprehensible and terrifying. They were irreconcilable with his life of Christmas mornings, baseball games in tall-grass lots, television, and soft sheets. This future, this responsibility, had loomed on the horizon as the price to be paid for his comfort. And when he learned that he didn't have to go, he was relieved, but also so ashamed of this relief that he felt his own bones and guts go as rigid and breakable as the glass bottles.

He is halfway down the hill now, the forest in sight. He slips, falls, struggles back to his feet, slips again, and lies still in the wet grass.

Sam reaches him first, skidding to a stop. He puts his foot on Richard's naked shoulder to hold him in place, but there's no need.

"He's here," Sam shouts. Richard watches the moon tear the clouds like a saber. First Don, then my father, arrive at Sam's side. My father holds the gun against his leg, his lips white in the moonlight.

"Here?" he asks.

No answer. Richard squeezes his eyes shut.

"Here?" my father asks again.

"Yes, here," Sam says.

"He's not moving. Is he even awake?" my father asks.

"What's the difference?"

"Richard," my father says. "Can you hear me?"

He bends down, and Richard can smell the coffee on his breath, the sleeplessness. "Richard?"

But Richard refuses to answer. He refuses to open his eyes.

Then my father punches him in the stomach, a diamond-hard, punishing jab. Once, then three more times. Jab. Jab. Jab. Each punch is a private explosion. Richard squeezes his eyes shut tighter. He feels the barrel of the gun against his jaw. It feels so much smaller, so much less dangerous, than it looks.

Richard only wants it to be over, but my father's voice softens. "Richard. Why am I about to do this to you?" Richard tries to roll away, not to escape from my father but from the question. The foot on his shoulder holds him in place.

"Explain it to me. How can you make me do this to you?" My father is nearly pleading. "Do you know what you're making me do?"

It's too bad, Richard thinks, that of all the senses, sight is the only one you can just shut off. If only he could blow out his ears now, if only he could spend just a few seconds in silence on the soft grass.

"Hank," Sam says, and Richard can hear panic in his voice. Rough fingers grab his jaw and turn his head back. "Come on," my father says. "Tell me."

"Hank," Don says, "I don't think . . ."

"We can't wait," Sam says.

"Fuck. Look at him crying, though," Don says.

Richard tries to sit up, but the foot holds him flat. He wants to shout one sentence. That's it—one sentence—then they can shoot him. *I'm not crying, how could I be crying? My eyes are shut.* But, as he opens his mouth, a sound comes out that he will hear in his head for months to follow. It's hollow, empty, wordless. It reeks of a fear so naked, so indecent, that my father pulls the gun away, as if in alarm.

AS I LEFT DON'S BUNGALOW, I imagined telling Jamie, the expression on his face, the disbelief, the envy. *Don wants to let him go. He wants us to help him let Richard go.* I started running once I reached Fir Street, imagining the next day, the chain undone, limp as snake-skin on the orange shag. As I ran, I became not myself but Richard, running from Don Brooke. I saw his escape in the crystal vision of my inner eye, the bus speeding away, a last peek through the tinted window at the two boys standing in the street, not daring to wave.

But instead of returning to the Norths' I turned on Seachase. I stood under the yellow fist of a streetlight, feeling a sickening buzz in my chest, telling myself not to go in. But I did go in. I flung my jacket on the kitchen table, flinching when the revolver, still in the pocket, struck the Formica. In the basement a slab of light jammed the crack beneath the studio door. Inside, Richard sat reading on the bench. He was wearing the crown, the spikes now wilted, the tissue dark with sweat.

"What time is it?" he asked.

"You're still wearing that?"

"Oh," he said, and took the crown off, "just trying to cheer up."

"He wants to let you go," I said.

Richard put the book down and leaned toward me. His face was so pale that even his smile couldn't bring life to it anymore. "They want to let me go?"

"Just Don," I said. "Jamie and me too."

"When?"

"The day after tomorrow. We have it all planned. But maybe sooner, maybe tomorrow."

"Tomorrow?" He touched his tongue to his lips. His voice, when it came, was hoarse and low. "He'd do that? You'd do that?"

"We told you already," I said.

"I didn't believe you before. I just didn't."

He was right not to have believed us. Don had made it all real and not just to Richard. Before, Jamie and I had been two kids playing at something, but suddenly it felt as though we *could* actually saw the chain, we *could* actually lead Richard into the kitchen and out the back door. For the first time I believed, in my core, that we could do it, and Richard believed too.

"But you have to swear, like Jamie said. You have to promise," I said. "You have to promise never to come back here. You'd have to give up everything and never come back. That's the condition."

They weren't my words, but I felt the power in them. Richard's expression changed. Had he forgotten? He was escaping back to life, and in life there is always an *almost* or an *except*.

"Have a cigarette with me, Cal," he said.

I leaned toward the flame that flickered from his hand. "You can never come back. You're dead, you know?"

"I want to leave. I just want to leave, that's it."

"Where will you go?" I asked.

"Do you want to find out?" he said. "Do you want to go with me?" We both laughed.

"Really," I said. "Where?"

"Anywhere, I guess. I'm still trying to imagine it. I didn't think I'd have the chance."

"But what do you think?" I asked. "Try."

He frowned at me and turned up his palms. "What the hell? Can you give me more than ten seconds to decide that? I'm not sure I know what I'll do. Or where."

"Sure. Sorry. I'm excited, that's all."

I sat down, and we smoked like two old friends. We didn't need to talk. There was no music on the turntable. And, in the silence that followed, I heard Jamie's and Don's voices in my mind. *Richard's been waiting for an excuse to leave Loyalty Island all his life,* Jamie had said. But that wasn't true. *Richard never wanted this; he never knew what he wanted,* Don had said. That wasn't true either. People like Richard, people like me, always know what we want—we just don't know who wants us.

"There's something I've wanted to ask you," I said. "Did you really plan on selling everything, selling the company, like you said on Memorial Day? Could you really have done it?"

"You're asking that now?" But he didn't seem angry, only amused.

"When else will I get the chance? Jamie and I have money on it."

A lie, obviously. I'd asked the question because I was looking for some hope, some excuse to deny what I knew to be true. Once we let Richard out, all he had to do was find a cop on a bicycle, but that wasn't the risk. I was convinced that he couldn't face police and lawyers and insurance companies and Sam and my father. I believed him; he really *did* just want to leave.

But then I imagined a black lip of highway running south, Richard stepping off the bus in San Francisco in the middle of the night and walking through a deserted downtown. Light clinging to skyscraper windows like beads of sweat. His old name, his old life, yellowing. He can't stay in San Francisco long. So, east along Interstate 80, the sky enormous, blasted with a buckshot of stars. He crosses into Wyoming, then Nebraska. In Des Moines the air is so cold that it seems to break against his mouth like glass. He could keep going, but he's already gone to Salt Lake City and Omaha and Des Moines unwanted. Can he face Chicago, Cleveland, and New York unwanted too? Loyalty Island will still be there. What will keep him away? A promise he made while chained to a wall?

I wanted to believe that if Richard actually could have sold everything, then we could trust him never to return. If he could have stayed away then, maybe he really could stay away now.

"It's funny, isn't it?" he said, as if the only surprise was that I hadn't asked sooner. He lit another cigarette. "It's funny what people are capable of and what they're not. Three months ago I never would have thought your father could've thrown me in here. And fifteen minutes ago I never would have thought Don Brooke would let me out. Why even bother thinking about it at all? There just aren't answers, except to a few things."

Richard must have known that there was no bet with Jamie, but I wonder if he knew I would have believed him no matter what he said.

"Did you?" I asked again, wishing I was already back in Jamie's bedroom, Richard's escape set, the future written. All Richard had to do was nod his head, say one word: yes.

But he said, "How could I have?"

The orange carpet was dirty with ash, the thick shag worn down. I noticed for the first time the long line the chain had drawn across the baseboard. This wasn't the room my father had built or the room my mother had run to. It was Richard's. Just as I wasn't the person they'd made anymore, I was Richard's. All I could do was ask the least important question. "Why didn't you tell them?"

Richard shrugged and shook his head, as if to say that there was no way to know, as if to say that if he did know, absolutely everything would be different. I stubbed out the cigarette and lit another. We didn't say much more, and eventually Richard put *Nefertiti* on the turntable. He sat on the floor, legs outstretched, head tilted back so that his black hair fell across the bench in waves. Now and then, he hummed a few bars of the music. I sat, smoking until my mouth stung, and when the record ended I stood up to leave. "Tomorrow," I said, "or the next day. You'll go, right?"

"Yes," he said. "I'll go. I'll see you then." They were the last words I ever heard him say.

I locked the studio door and dropped the key in the dryer. The furnace was off, the basement quiet. At the top of the stairs I clicked shut the door and stepped into the dark kitchen. I remembered the smells of my mother's cooking and was suddenly starving. The refrigerator was bare except for the old bottle of French's mustard. I unscrewed the cap and took a heaping fingerful, then a few more. The mustard was somehow both watery and crusty; it made my stomach hurt almost instantly. I left the bottle open on the counter and went to the kitchen phone and dialed the number stuck to the wall with yellow tape.

It rang three and a half times before a woman's voice answered, which surprised me.

"Pacific Cannery," she said.

"I need to get in touch with Henry Bollings," I said. "It's important. This is his son."

THE PHONE RANG around four in the morning. I was on the couch in the living room, not quite certain how I'd gotten there.

"Cal?" my father said. "What? What is it?"

I didn't say anything at first. I'd fallen asleep, and I was still half dreaming, still hearing the soft chords of "Lotus Blossom."

"Cal?"

"They want to let Richard go," I said. And to make sure I'd gotten the words right I said them again. "They want to let him go."

THE NEXT MORNING I replaced the key in the case under the grill as my father had instructed, and walked back to the Norths'. The good weather had held, and the few clouds in the sky looked warm and wrinkled. I felt tired and dirty, but not guilty, not yet. I walked, following my father's words like a path.

"Who knows about this?" he'd asked.

"Don," I said, "and me, and . . ."

"And?"

"Jamie North," I said. "He followed me one day. I had to tell him. But nobody else."

At first the only response was white noise. Static and crackles. I'd taken my shoes off—out of habit—and I felt the cold floor.

"Are you there?" I asked.

"I have to go," he said. "Leave and don't come back. Promise me."

"I promise."

"I have to go." Then, in a voice that ached for sleep, he added, "Cal? I'm sorry you had to make this call."

When I returned to the Norths', Jamie was standing at the kitchen counter drinking hot chocolate. He was wearing gray corduroys and a red sweater with a curly-shoed elf crocheted over the heart. His hair was matted and messy as an angry sea. Either he'd just gotten up or he hadn't slept at all. He put the mug down too fast, and hot chocolate splashed over the counter.

"I was about to look for you at the house," he said. "I had to lie to my mother. Where have you been?"

"I haven't slept all night," I said. I wasn't sure if this was true, but I felt like it was.

I don't know what Jamie saw on my face, but his smile dimmed. "What's wrong?"

The question seemed meaningless. All I really felt was an insane jealousy because I'd had to betray him and he hadn't had to betray me.

"We're on for tomorrow, right?" I asked. "I'm exhausted. Let me just rest up."

I went upstairs and crawled into the bottom bunk. When I woke the windows were dark. The overhead light was on. Jamie sat hunched at his desk, over an open notebook and two steaming cups. The room smelled like chocolate. The phone was ringing downstairs.

"How do you feel?" Jamie asked.

"Oh, better," I said.

He was still wearing the elf sweater. He saw me looking. "Present from Nana. I just wanted you to see what you missed yesterday before I burn this thing. Of course I've had it on for about twelve hours now. Where were you? You've had some sleep now. Where were you?"

His voice was high and tight. The sheet I lay on smelled like him. The corners of the *Jaws* poster glittered with new tape. The phone was still ringing. I had no idea whose voice would come out of my mouth, no idea what it would say.

"I was with Don," I said. "They know it was us."

Jamie must have been preparing for bad news, but still his face nearly came apart. He blinked, as if trying to beat back the panic. "Don? How did he know?"

"Richard must have told him," I said.

The phone stopped ringing. I felt the first waves of guilt as it occurred to me that the ruts left by this falseness would last forever. There had been no reason to make Jamie think that *both* Richard and I had betrayed him.

"Are you, are you sure?"

"No, it's just a guess."

"It's a bad guess," he said. "Why would Richard do that? Why didn't you tell me? We have to go, we have to get him out of there now."

"We can't," I said. Jamie's nose had started to run. I shook my head, kept shaking it to keep from having to look up at him. "We can't."

"What do you mean?"

I could never hope to explain what I'd done, but I didn't need to, at least not to Jamie. He could see it in me. And the worst part was that, as he rose to his feet, his hair and nose messy, the elf sweater tight across his chest, clearly knit for Jamie's size of a year before, he looked upset but not surprised. And I could see, without having to ask, that I'd never be forgiven. "Will you just take that sweater off?" I said. "You look so stupid."

He didn't answer, and I closed my eyes. Betty North's melodious voice called from downstairs.

"Jamie," she said. "It's your father. He needs to speak to you."

CHAPTER 10

I N MID-JANUARY, MY FATHER TOOK ME TO DINNER at a new restaurant smashed amid car dealerships on Loyalty Island's eastern edge. He'd been home for two or three weeks by then, at least since New Year's Eve. I knew this only because I saw his pickup truck splashing through a puddle downtown on the last afternoon of vacation.

His arrival at the Norths' was just as sudden as my own arrival there months before. He rang the bell one morning, and when I came downstairs he pulled me close to him, crushing me against his chest. "We should go home, huh?" he said. "Anytime you're ready."

My green duffel, his old green duffel actually, was already packed. I grabbed it from under the bed and left, squeezing past Jamie at his desk. We hadn't spoken since Christmas, but I'd felt his cold, silent anger each day. I'd heard him, one night, sobbing on the roof. The thing I most wanted at that moment was never to see his face again.

The restaurant was called Mr. Steak. My father and I ordered sirloins and baked potatoes. We sat, pretending to be too busy gazing at the wood paneling and the display-lit Ansel Adams prints to talk. After the food came my father tucked his napkin into his collar and said, softly, the way he said everything, as if the words didn't have a right to exist, "Do you have anything you need to ask me?"

"I don't know," I said.

The waitress came with Coke in a pitcher.

"I had Diet Coke," my father said. She apologized and left. "If you do have something to ask, it should be now."

"No," I said.

He closed his eyes and sighed. "Good." He patted my hand. His own hand was rough, calloused. "That's a good guy." And the way he said it, with his eyes still shut, I knew that Richard was dead. It shouldn't have come as a surprise. I'd left the revolver on the kitchen table myself, without having to be asked.

"You think your mother would like this place?" my father asked.

"I don't."

"Well, I like it. We should go when she gets back. I feel like I haven't eaten in a year. Are you sure there's nothing else?"

There was nothing else. In my mind, I could already see my father picking the gun up from the table. I could see him and Sam walking the same path through the basement that Jamie and I had walked so many times. I could see Richard even more clearly.

He's been alone for three days straight when he hears the knock on the door. He's expecting me, but, just from the sound, two heavy thumps, he knows it hasn't worked out. Sam and Henry look tired and windburned. They smell like the harbor. They don't say anything, and he's glad they don't.

Was he grateful that they'd given him this extra time, these months of extra breath, even if it was only of stale air? Or did he wish they had done it months before on the lawn behind his father's house?

The revolver pokes from the zip pocket of my father's corduroy jacket, but he doesn't touch it. He and Sam unlock the chain from around the water pipe but not from around Richard's leg. They put a piece of gray tape over his mouth. They gather up the chain, and Richard puts out his hands to hold it.

They drive through dark streets, Richard sandwiched between my father and Sam. The truck smells of cologne. The road is dirty white under the headlights. It's too dark to see much else, and Richard finds this unaccountably disappointing. They pass the harbor and pull off near Black's Beach. The tide's in, so there isn't far to walk.

He sits in the bow of the skiff as instructed. He waits as they wrap the chain tightly, but not painfully, around his legs, from the ankles to the thighs, and refasten the lock to hold it in place. This boat's a twelve-footer, not so different in size from the one that supposedly carried Richard's great-great-grandfather to the shores of Loyalty Island. My father sits in the stern, while Sam pushes them into the tide. After two pulls, the engine sputters to life.

Richard pulls the tape from his mouth—my father doesn't protest—and looks out into the water rippling invisibly along the boat. Here it all is: the sounds, the smells, the absurd perceptions from which there was no escape.

After ten minutes my father cuts the engine. "Stand up, Richard," he says. And Richard stands, almost automatically. Moonlight drops on the water like a woman letting down her hair. A weak breeze brings up the smell of the sea, that particular sea.

My father begins to rock his shoulders. At first he looks almost funny, as if he's trying to dance. Then the boat lists sharply. He won't even touch me, Richard thinks. His body tells him to check his balance, but his feet can't move, and he stumbles over the side, his cheek striking the surface, the water stinging back. He flaps his arms and claws for the boat. He swallows cold water. His hair is plastered across his eyes. He hears the engine start again as his head dips under. His legs want to kick and his lungs want to breathe, but he can do neither. What a terrible feeling it must be, to want to live.

It's only a guess. My father would have told me everything, I think, if I'd asked, but I said nothing, and he patted my hand and repeated, "That's a good guy." And peeled the tinfoil from his potato and ate.

MY MOTHER RETURNED from Santa Cruz two weeks later. My father had flown down to plead with her, and finally she'd given in. I had to swear to her, he said, that as far as I knew Richard had died in September on the Inside Passage. There would be no more secrets between my father and me, but I was starting to learn that this meant keeping secrets from everyone else.

I cleaned the house and filled the refrigerator, and finally she returned. She looked younger than she had when she'd left. Her hair, dyed a brighter red, hung to the small of her back. She wore a green sundress with white stripes, a dress much too light for a Washington January.

I met her at the front door because my father was at work. She embraced me immediately, holding me tight for minutes. She introduced me to my sister, Em, who had green eyes and white hair. We ate lunch, sandwiches I made because my mother said she was too tired to cook, and then we put Em down in a new crib and watched her sleep from the doorway, saying nothing.

My mother went downstairs to the studio, and I followed. It was the first time I'd been in the basement since December. The mint-green door hung open. They'd cleaned the carpet and put the records back on their shelves, but I could still see the faint black line the chain had drawn along the baseboard. The room still smelled of our cigarettes. My mother brushed her fingers over the record spines and wrinkled her nose.

"Have you been down here?" she asked.

"Yes," I said. The next moment I was crying.

She looked at me strangely. "It's all right," she said. "It's all right. I don't mind at all."

What she suspected, what she knew, was never clear. But she knew enough. A few weeks after she returned we were at the dry cleaner's together, chatting with Mrs. Zhou.

"Your husband," Mrs. Zhou said, "seems to be doing such a hard job. It must have been hard to see that young man die."

My mother just stared, and so I stepped in with some cliché. "It was a difficult time for everybody," something like that. My mother smiled coldly and said nothing until we were back in the car. Then she turned to me and said, "Don't be a liar, Cal. Liars are so boring." I've done my best to prove her wrong ever since.

She never really came back from California, and she left Loyalty Island for good the summer I turned eighteen. She'd only been waiting for me to leave home before she took Em back to Santa Cruz. She'd lost one child to Loyalty Island, I guess, and didn't want to lose another.

How much did she know? Though I still imagine telling her everything, I know I never will. We speak occasionally, but never of Loyalty Island or my father. After the divorce she married a lawyer who has helped raise Em, apparently very well. Over the phone Em has an intelligent voice. Recently she sent me a painting she'd done of Monterey Bay. Last year she won the Latin prize at her school, and she's already a first violin in the high school orchestra, even though she's only fourteen.

ONE NIGHT, toward the end of high school, I was at a party, drunk, yelling at somebody—I don't remember who. I stumbled out, or someone threw me out, the front door onto a wide brick porch. My legs were jelly, and I teetered toward the concrete stairs. I probably would have cracked my head open if Jamie North hadn't been sitting on the ledge, smoking a cigarette.

We hadn't spoken since our winter with Richard, but I'd kept tabs as much as I could. I knew, for example, that he'd stopped haunting the Orpheum, either by choice or by order. I knew that he'd spent the last two summers up north, out for salmon. And I knew that he'd gained a reputation for having a hot temper, that he'd recently broken a friend's nose over a pickup basketball game.

He caught me around the chest and stood me up. I'm not sure if he knew it was me at first, probably he didn't. He was nearly as tall as his father and much stronger than I remembered, much stronger than I was. There was the red shadow of a beard on his jaw.

"You look bad," he said.

I shouldered away and dramatically adjusted my collar. "Hey, I look how I look."

"That's true."

He looked so much like Sam, except his face didn't have Sam's softness. "Hey, man," I said, "listen . . ."

"To what?" he asked. "Listen to what? You better get home."

That was the last time I saw him. Jamie went back to Alaska the next summer, the summer before our senior year, and decided to stay on for king season on the *Cordilleran*.

I had my chance too. The day I graduated high school I heard the words from my father I'd been waiting for as long as I could remember. He had become the head of everything by then, and was lining up the resources to buy the company officially.

He had just come home from work. He'd lost weight, and his hair was a spooky gray at the temples. His hands were spotted with paint, reeking of turpentine, one leg of his jeans completely soaked, the other dry.

"I wanted to catch you," he said.

"You have."

"There's a spot for you on the *Laurentide* if you still want it. Or you can work with Jamie. We can arrange that. He'll be taking over Don's old boat soon."

"You think that's what I want?" I asked. "You really think that?" And I laughed, as if this offer were the funniest thing in the world, as if he couldn't possibly be more wrong about me.

I went on to college. I went as far away as I could. And I told myself that everything that had happened hadn't. I'd learned enough from Richard to know I could never go back to Loyalty Island. But I'd also learned that I might spend a long time, the rest of my life maybe, looking for some way to leave.

One night, years after I'd left home, I walked through falling snow with a girl on my arm. She had thick eyelashes and the snow fell on them and on her hair and on the white fur collar of her coat. I'd shortened my stride some because it was icy and she was wearing yellow high heels. We were on our way to a warm bar filled with friends. I knew that she would be with me that night and the next morning. But, before that, there would be the ritual of arriving at the bar, of shaking the snow off our coats, of hanging the coats on a post by the door and ordering drinks and saying hello with nods and handshakes and taps on the shoulder. Of finding our close friends among the other friends as they leaned and talked at the sanded bar, of saying, "Now that we're all here we should get a booth," of piling into the booth, fitting three or four where only two have room, and lighting cigarettes and talking and laughing. There was nothing else, I realized, to look forward to. There are only two emotions that grant this lack of expectation and disappointment—happiness and fear. And I looked at the girl's face, and I wasn't afraid.

On nights like those, there is almost no memory and almost no past. But other nights I lie in bed awake and the darkness around me becomes the wet light of Loyalty Island. I wait, hoping that the phone will ring with news from my father, or Jamie North. *Come back*, they'll say. *We need you.* I imagine the plane ride to Seattle, the ferry across the Sound, the parking lot in Kingston where Jamie and my father wait in weak sunlight, sipping coffee from paper cups.

But what would I say to them, then? I can't find those words. Not unless I imagine all the miles of cold ocean on earth. Not unless I imagine lying on my back, descending through water shot through with sun, through bands of color, from sky to sea, from green to ink-black. I can't find those words. Not unless I imagine myself drowned.

ACKNOWLEDGMENTS

It seems almost impossible to express the gratitude I owe to so many. Here goes.

Thanks to everyone at Riverhead, especially Becky Saletan for her brilliance, patience, and humor, and Sarah Bowlin for her crucial early support.

Thanks to Julie Barer, whose energy, dedication, and wisdom never cease to amaze.

I relied on many excellent sources for research, especially Spike Walker's outstanding book on Alaskan fishing, *Working on the Edge*.

Thanks to the Michener-Copernicus Society of America, whose generous support made finishing this project a much easier task. Thanks to everyone at the Iowa Writers' Workshop, especially Connie Brothers.

Thanks to Peter Bognanni, Brad Liening, Danny Khalastchi, Sara Houghteling, Jeremy Snodgrass, and John Howard: wonderful friends, invaluable readers. Thanks to Stuart Dybek for reading and rereading over so many years.

Thanks to my family—Caren, Stuart, Anne, and Tim—for more than I could ever say.

And thanks to Madeline McDonnell, without whom I would never have written this book. The only good lines are hers. Grow old with me, please.